W9-BTC-654

THE RAPTOR & THE WREN

ALSO BY CHUCK WENDIG

THE MIRIAM BLACK SERIES
Blackbirds
Mockingbird
The Cormorant
Thunderbird

STAR WARS: THE AFTERMATH TRILOGY
Star Wars: Aftermath
Star Wars: Life Debt
Star Wars: Empire's End

Zerøes
Invasive

ATLANTA BURNS SERIES
Atlanta Burns
The Hunt

THE HEARTLAND TRILOGY
Under the Empyrean Sky
Blightborn
The Harvest

NONFICTION
The Kick-Ass Writer: 1001 Ways to Write Great Fiction, Get Published, and Earn Your Audience
Damn Fine Story

CHUCK WENDIG

THE RAPTOR & THE WREN

MIRIAM BLACK: FIVE

SAGA PRESS

LONDON SYDNEY NEW YORK TORONTO NEW DELHI

1230 AVENUE OF THE AMERICAS, NEW YORK, NEW YORK 10020

Also available in a Saga Press paperback edition + The text for this book was set in New Caledonia. + Manufactured in the United States of America + First Saga Press hardcover edition January 2018 + 10 9 8 7 6 5 4 3 2 1 + CIP date for this book is available from the Library of Congress. + ISBN 978-1-4814-4874-1 (hardcover) + ISBN 978-1-4814-4875-8 (paperback) + ISBN 978-1-4814-4876-5 (eBook)

TO ALL THE FOUL-MOUTHED WOMEN WHO GET SHIT DONE

THE RAPTOR & THE WREN

PART ONE

MAGPIE AND MIMIC

INTERLUDE

AMERICA'S HOT MOIST LAND-WANG

Miriam stands at the door to her mother's house in Florida. The wizard van at her back. She has just arrived. Though it's wet here, so wet the air feels like she can grab a hunk and wring it out, she can still taste the Arizona dust in her mouth, gritty like beach sand. Steam rises from under the hood of the van. It's on its last legs. She says as much into the phone.

Gabby answers: "Every cowboy loses his horse at some point."

"I'm not a cowboy."

"It's just a saying."

"Is it a saying? I've never heard it before."

A pause. Gabby says, "I think I just made it up." Another pause. "You gonna be okay at your mom's?"

Miriam wants to say, *I'm not okay. My brain is literally broken. My heart is broken. My wizard van is broken. Everything is fucking broken and I need you. I need Louis. I need someone. I don't want to be alone.* She says none of those things. Instead, she steels herself with a scowl and says, "I'm good."

"I can come there. I can visit."

"No." That word, too sharply spoken. "Don't. It's fine. I need time alone." That's a lie, but one she's told herself often enough that she has begun to believe it. "I'm going in. I'll talk to you soon."

"I miss you."

I miss you too, she thinks.

Instead, she just hangs up and goes inside the house.

ONE

PURGATORY AND LIMBO

Now.

The game: Egyptian Rat Screw.

The opponent: Rita Shermansky.

The location: Delray Beach, Florida, in the house that once belonged to the late Evelyn Black but now belongs to her daughter, Miriam.

The time: 7:35 PM, late August. Months after the events in Arizona.

It's hot and everything is slippery. The air conditioner in the house is making a sound like a buzz saw trying to chew its way through a coconut.

Miriam's mind is not well connected to her body. It's like there's a three-second delay—she wills her eyes to look left or right, she demands her hand move to the deck of cards on the table, she urges her hips to shift in this uncomfortable dining room chair, and each time she makes the command in her mind, three seconds later, her body wakes up like an old, slow dog before deciding to comply.

That's wine for you.

She hates wine. It's a mom drink. Basically vinegar. She thinks of it as a pickling solution—a bruise-dark brine of grape juice gone awry. But her mother had a lot of it. Miriam's gone through it all, but now she's settled into the same habit: going to the little wine store on Atlantic Avenue, picking out a bottle of something cheap and red, and coming home and drinking it all in one go.

It sucks. She hates it. It's gross.

She does it anyway.

Miriam closes her eyes, lets her nostrils flare, and sucks in wisps of cigarette smoke from the cloud hanging thick about her head. It smells like life. Like death. Like cancer. Like all her synapses firing at once.

"You can fuckin' have one, you know," Rita says.

It's a not-uncommon offer. With it comes the compulsory gesture: Rita jostling the pack of Newports and turning the tips of the coffin nails toward her.

As always, Miriam shakes her head.

"No," she insists, the word sloppy as it gushes out of her mouth. "I'm trying to be *healthy*, I'll have you know."

Rita sniffs. "That explains the wine, then. A real tonic."

"Wine *is* good for you. It's fruit juice. And alcohol is antibacterial. Totally medicinal. Doctors say that—" She thrusts up her finger to make a point, and then she forgets what the point was going to be. "Doctors say you should just shut the fuck up and shuffle the cards, Rita-Rita-Smelly-Feeta."

The old woman lifts her lip in a fishhooked sneer. Rita Shermansky is seventy-two years old and looks like if you took a skeleton, glued little veal cutlet muscles to each of the bones, then wrapped it all in soft orange deerskin leather. She's fit as a fiddle. Taut as an anchor line. Puts the *tan* in *tangerine*. The woman plays tennis, golf, racquetball, some made-up shit called pickleball, and bodyboards. She also smokes like a house fire, drinks like a diabetic bulldog, and curses like the ghost of a pirate who has been wandering the afterlife looking for a treasure chest full of fucks that's long ago been emptied. Her voice is a throaty, mosquito-wing whine. That whine perfectly conveys that shrill New Yawk accent of hers.

Rita dies in eight years.

Her death is ludicrously pleasant. She goes to sleep one night. She dreams of being on top of the Empire State building, the wind making her eyes water. Then death steals her away, gentle as a practiced pickpocket. She never wakes up. Lucky old bitch, that Rita.

"C'mon," Miriam needles her. "Let's play."

"We have time?"

"Pssh. Pfft. We have time. Mervin isn't going anywhere."

Rita raises a drawn-on eyebrow. "Merv's going *somewhere*, honey."

"Just cut the deck."

Egyptian Rat Screw works like this: Everyone gets an equal cut of the deck. Nobody gets to peek at the cards. You flip over cards, flinging them into the middle pile, one after the next, player after player. The goal is to win the stack of cards and to rob the opponent of theirs. If the card is put on another card of the same rank (number or face), you can slap the pile. First hand on the pile gets the stack. Or, if a player puts down a face card, the opponent has a number of tries (three for a king, two for a queen, one for a jack) to put down a face card, too. Failing to drop a face card means the player gets the stack, boom.

None of it has anything to do with Egypt, rodents, or fucking.

This is Rita's game. She's vicious. Fast like a lightning strike with card-dropping and hand-slapping. Worse, she hits like she's trying to kill a wasp.

Miriam puts a four of diamonds down on top of a four of clubs, and in a rare moment of her mind and body pushing past the wall of wine to sync up, she slaps. *Bam!* First on the pile. Rita's slap is close behind: *whap*.

Pain blooms in the back of Miriam's hand. She recoils. "Jesus tits on a banshee," she says, shaking her hand as if to fling the pain away. "You're not killing actual rats here, you old bat."

Rita shrugs it off, like she always does. "Honey, back in the day, if we played this game, I'd put on my old wedding ring and turn it diamond-side down. You get slapped with *that*, it'd pop the skin of your hand like a hole-puncher. Blood right on the playing cards—but we'd keep playing."

Miriam takes another sip of the wine. It tastes like raisins and anger. She winces. "You rolled hard back in that so-called day. You have some kind of competitive Egyptian Rat Screw league? Smoky basements and money changing hands? Italian mob? Chinese tong? Illuminati?"

"Let's just say I had an interesting life once."

"C'mon. Tell me. For fuck's sake, Rita, give up the goods."

Rita's eyes sparkle behind pinched folds of flesh as she takes a hit off her Newport. "You're talking. Which means you're shitting up the flow of the game."

They keep playing. Back and forth. Face cards hitting face cards. Hands hitting hands. Stash goes this way, then back, then the other way once more. Rita's winning. Rita always wins. Miriam's drunk and slow and her hand is starting to throb, but Rita—despite this being her fourth gin and tonic (just a finger-flick of tonic)—doesn't lose a step. And doesn't seem to feel pain.

Finally, Rita takes the stack.

Game over.

"Almost time," Rita says. "Merv's nearly off the clock."

Miriam looks over Rita's shoulder at the clock on the microwave in the kitchen. She has to squint to get the blue LCD numbers to hold still. It's like trying to psychically control ants. *Wouldn't that be a horror show?* she thinks. Ants? Yuck.

Finally, the time stops dancing. It's almost eight. Rita's right. Merv's hour is nearly upon them.

"Lemme ask you something," Rita says.

"No."

"What are you running from?"

“Not running from anything.” Miriam *urps* into her hand. “In fact, I’m sitting right here. I am as stationary as a motherfucking sea cucumber.”

“You drink at night.”

“I drink starting at noon. It’s very precise. If I drank before noon, then I’d be an alcoholic.” This is literally her logic. She tells herself the fact that she can wait to drink is a sign she is not a certifiable boozehound.

“You jog in the mornings.”

“I *run* in the mornings. Jogging is for old people.”

“You don’t have a job.”

Miriam snort-laughs. “Could you imagine.”

“Yet I still see it in those bloodshot eyes of yours. You’re running from something, honey. Maybe you’re running from it in your head, but running is fucking running, you hear me?”

Another puckered-lip drag off that Newport. Another plume of smoke. Miriam feels lost in it for a moment, like a boat in the fog. *What am I running from? I’m not running. I’m just staying real still like a scared little fish, hoping the big bad shark of life swims on by.* There’s so much she doesn’t want to think about, and trying not to think about it just means she’s thinking about it—Louis, his fiancée Samantha, Samantha soon dying by Louis’s hands, Miriam’s dead mother, Miriam’s ex Gabby, the little boy Isaiah, Miriam being out there in the Arizona desert, dead but not dead, birds stitching her wounds with their beaks like she’s some kind of Satanic Disney princess, then the news that she has a traumatic brain injury ready to blow.

“Fuck this,” Miriam says, lurching to a soggy stance. “It’s time.”

“It’s early.”

“*It’s time.* I’m going. You can come or not, I don’t care.”

Rita shrugs. “I’ll come. I still want what’s mine. But I hafta pee first.”

TWO

ATAVISM

It isn't the heat, it's the humidity. That's what they tell you. Miriam never really understood that—heat is heat, hot is hot, and it sucks whether you're roasted over an open fire or sautéed in a pan.

Then she experienced Florida in August.

It's not like being sautéed. It's like being boiled in a saucepot of your own sweat. It's like tucking yourself up under the devil's scrotum. The moistness. The slick sweat and stink. You can't get it off of you. The humidity *clings* like a mummy's swaddling. So, when Miriam steps outside, it washes over her like Hell's hot breath.

She wrinkles her nose against it. Her stomach surges with sudden nausea. Her hair is longer now, the only dye in it is blackbird black, and she runs her fingers through it just to try to cool down. It doesn't work.

For a moment out here, she's alone in this subtropical suburban neighborhood, staring out over the little bungalows and ranchers tucked in amongst the cradling shadows of palm trees and massive crepe myrtle. Insects buzz: a chorus of crickets and katydids.

The noise, the heat, the half-dark, the loneliness. It puts her at the bottom of a funnel, and everything runs toward her. Drowning her. In six months, Louis is going to kill Samantha on their wedding night. In two years, Gabby might commit suicide. Then there's the message that the psychic Mary Stitch left behind for Miriam after the horrific events in Arizona: *You have to reverse what happened. Undo what was done. The thing that made you who you are. You want to get rid of it? Then you, dear Miriam, have to get pregnant.* After all that goddamn time searching for her, combing the country for the one person who was supposed to tell her some way, *any way*, to unravel Miriam's curse and end this god-fucked ability of hers—and this is what she says? *Get pregnant, Miriam?*

More like *get fucked, Mary Stitch, you murderous terroristic whore.*

I can't get pregnant. Did that once. Ruined my insides. And besides, Miriam? A mother? You'd be better off leaving a baby in the care of a pack of starving Chihuahuas.

It takes a village to raise a child, but just a single Miriam to ruin one.

Futility seizes her. It's a crushing fist around her heart. Grief and frustration push through the wave of winedrunk and threaten to drop Miriam to her knees. She can't stop Louis from killing his bride. She can't save Gabby from suicide. She can't save herself from whatever it is that awaits her. She couldn't even save the people in that courthouse in Tucson. Has she made any difference in the world? Any difference for herself or for those trapped in the gale-force winds of the hurricane that is her life? *I've got nothing left,* she thinks. *I'm useless as a pair of tits on a lawnmower. Busted-ass brain and all.* She feels woefully alone. Even the Trespasser has abandoned her. Hasn't been haunted by that imaginary fucker in months.

And then suddenly, Rita is behind her. A steadying hand on Miriam's shoulder—one of those bony slapping rat-screw hands.

"Look like you saw a ghost," Rita says.

"No," Miriam says, failing to keep the tremor of despair out of her voice. "No ghost. Just waiting for you."

"You got *agita*, honey. But we can talk about that later. Right now—"

"Merv."

"Merv it is."

Mervin Delgado lives three houses down. He's got a tan rancher and about a thousand wind chimes. Metal ones, wood ones, chimes made from shells. Even the slightest breeze makes his house tinkly-ting-tingle like it's a fairy wonderland.

The details on Merv are these:

Two kids, three grandkids, all of them living out of state. Wife died five years ago from lung cancer. He's seventy-eight, retired, used to be in the Navy, then worked as a pilot for the airlines. He looks like a couple of old potatoes stacked on top of each other. Has bunions, will tell you about them. Has many conditions, in fact, and will tell you about *all* of them: his hip pain, his osteoporosis, how he had MRSA once on his shin, how his liver numbers are off, how he's thinking of getting one of those cool jazzy chairs you can ride around Walmart. Miriam knows all this because she's spent some time with the little lump. But as soon as they hit on the topic of birds, it was, like, *jackpot*. Now that her powers include the ability to jump into birds, she'd rather know a little something about them. And Merv's got a huge boner for birds. (Bigger than his wind chime boner, even.) He will spend hours talking about them. He likes egrets and bitterns and other Florida birds, but songbirds, too. He told her, "My favorite bird is the mockingbird. Fiercely protective of their babies, but they also make such wonderful, diverse songs." That was the last time she spoke with him, because Miriam may have been a bit drunk and may have gone off the rails a bit, yelling at him about how the mockingbird was a shit bird with no self-respect and no identity or song of its own and fuck that bird and anybody who likes it.

Merv seemed a little stunned as she stormed off.

She feels bad about that.

And now it doesn't matter, because he'll be dead in five minutes.

The way Merv is going to die is this: He'll start by having the worst headache he's ever had in his life. It's probably hitting him right now, in fact. He'll clutch at his head. He won't be able to feel his face or scalp—it will feel less like he's touching his own head and more like he's pawing at a cantaloupe sitting on top of his shoulders. Then the hemorrhagic stroke will punch him in the brain, a little invisible bullet. He will fall down. He will crack his head on the travertine tile of his kitchen. His legs will flop around like those of a puppet in the hands of an epileptic puppeteer. Then he'll be dead.

Fairly fast, all things considered.

Not exactly peaceful, but Miriam knows that—with the exception of Rita and precious few others—death sucks for everybody. There's no nice way to go; there's just gradations of how bad it can get. People use the phrase *pass away*, but nobody just passes away. *Passing away* sounds like a rowboat gently slipping from its dock. It isn't like that. Death is brutal. People throw up blood. They spend minutes, hours, or days in the growing, creeping certainty of what's to come. They piss and shit themselves. They cough so hard, it's like breathing glass. They hallucinate. It's different for everyone and the same for everyone, too. *We're all snowflakes in the same damn blizzard.*

They walk up to Merv's house. Miriam isn't being particularly stealthy and Rita hisses at her to stick to the shadows. Miriam gives her the finger, but fine, the old woman is right, so she escapes the halo of light cast by the streetlamps above. Together, they sidle up alongside a couple ferns so they can slip into Merv's postage-stamp backyard.

"I'll head in, I guess."

"I'll be here, doing my thing," Rita says, lighting a cigarette.

"We could switch places. You could go in this time. I'll stay out here and do the cushy standing-around job."

Rita shrugs. "Nah. I'm too good as a lookout. Have fun, honey."

"Old bitch."

"Young cunt."

Fair enough, Miriam thinks with a shrug.

She staggers across Merv's back patio. Everything is pristine. Merv weeds everything by hand. Not like he's got anything else to do. (*Not like I've got anything else to do,* Miriam thinks, pondering momentarily how her mother's backyard is now sprung up with an infinity of weeds, and how there are bills to pay, and how they already turned off the cable, and, and, and.)

The patio doors are sliding glass. She goes to open one.

Locked. Shit. She tries a few extra times, pulling on the door just in case it's sticky—the humidity around here can do that—but it's a no-go.

The thing about a real good inebriation is this: It sands away any predispositions toward caution. It takes the angel on your right shoulder and drowns it in a glass of whiskey, leaving only the devil on the left. What that devil on Miriam's shoulder says right now is: *Go over there, pick up that cool volcanic landscaping rock at the edge of the patio, then smash it through the glass.*

Which she does, la-dee-da.

The patio door breaks.

It is loud.

Miriam doesn't care, and she totally ignores Rita's hisses of alarm and anger from the far side of the yard. With a surprisingly steady hand, Miriam reaches through the artisanal glass portal she just made and unlocks the door. When her hand returns, blood shines in the moonlight on her palm.

Glass cut me, she thinks. But no. The blood is coming up from dozens of tiny little holes in her hand, like water from sponge pores. The skin is abraded. *The volcanic stone,* she thinks. Sharp like pumice.

Whatever. She wipes that hand on her jeans, then steps inside.

Merv's bird obsession translates to his decor. Above a powder-blue couch hangs a painting of three parakeets in a Roy Lichtensteinian style: heavy cartoon lines and comic book pointillism. The wallpaper clashes: it's all trees and branches and songbirds perched. She's not here for the wallpaper or the painting, though.

Miriam passes by the kitchen. There are Mervin's heels, jutting out from behind a kitchen island. Blood wanders the grooves of the tile. His legs have stopped moving. Which means he's gone on to whatever waits beyond.

(She likes to believe that nothing waits beyond, but given the strangeness of her powers, she holds a great and secret fear that the realms beyond death are myriad and terrible. If there is a Hell, she is bound for it on a fast train. Then again, she's already in Florida, so how bad can it be?)

Miriam kneels by the little potato man. His hair is thin, like strands of thread laid across the liver-spot scalp. His skin in this light looks less tan and more yellow. He doesn't smell like piss or shit, and to that Miriam thinks, *Good for you, Merv, good for you.* She admires someone who preserves dignity even in death.

Gently, she closes his eyes, where the whites have gone the red of crushed raspberries. "I'd sing you a bird song," she tells him, "but it'd be an ugly thing."

She knuckles him gently in the arm. An awkward, go-get-'em gesture.

Now it's time to work.

Turns out, living amongst the elderly is an amazing scam, at least for someone with Miriam's menu of talents. She doesn't know why she didn't think of it before. (*Maybe,* a small voice inside suggests, *you hadn't really hit bottom yet*.) Florida is, as they say, God's waiting room. The people in this neighborhood are old. Many are tap-dancing right on the cliff's edge of life itself. Some live alone. Many in a neighborhood like this also have money. Or things. Or even better: pills. (Doctors give pills to old people like they're giving out candy and every day is Halloween.) All it takes is finding out when they're going to die, and being there not long after it happens.

All it took was going door to door and introducing herself. She stapled a smile onto her face and injected warmth to her voice and walked from one house to the next, saying hi, shaking hands. (And drinking lemonade, and hearing stories about gout, and going through endless photo books. Many amongst the elderly are very lonely and eager to meet people. Most of them have shitty stories, but once in a while, they have something interesting to say: Frank Wornacki down on Blossom Drive said within the first five minutes of meeting her, "I killed a mailman with a slingshot once." Miriam paid attention to that story. Because holy shit, why wouldn't you? Turns out, he was a kid shooting frogs in his backyard and accidentally popped the mailman in the forehead with a rock. Mailman tripped over the lip of a broken curb, fell down, cracked open his skull. Died in the hospital six days later from a resultant brain hemorrhage.)

She pulled this trick the first week she moved into her mother's old place. Six doors down lived a woman—divorced—named Meretta Higgins. Meretta wasn't one of those nice old people—oh, no, she went the other way with it. Rich, nasty little lady. Wrote cookbooks for a living. She wasn't even that old: sixty-eight. Miriam "accidentally" bumped into her on the sidewalk and saw that in two nights, the lady was going to die from an aortic dissection.

The old bitch called her a "little slut" when she bumped into her—because sure, why not call some rando on the sidewalk names—and that sealed the deal. Miriam thought, *I'm going to be there when you die. Then I'm going to take a memento just to spite you.* And she did. She was there the afternoon that Meretta went into the bathroom to take a shower, then died in the tub as her heart ripped like a paper valentine. Once the lady was kaput, Miriam walked whistling into the other room to cherry-pick whatever she wanted. A photo off the wall? Gaudy sapphire earrings off the bedroom dresser? Ooh, ooh! Something from the kitchen. The woman wrote cookbooks, right? Miriam went into a very nice kitchen—granite countertops and white cabinets and everything looking French and provincial—

And when Miriam was face-down in a drawer, looking through melon ballers and juicers and fancy measuring cups, someone cleared her throat.

Enter: Rita Shermansky.

Rita, neighbor to Meretta. Rita, who was coming over to meet Meretta for dinner. Rita, who counted herself a friend to Meretta even though, really, she didn't like her all that much. But company was company, and food was food.

Rita asked Miriam what the hell she thought she was doing.

Miriam answered with the truth, as she was a little bit drunk already.

"The woman who owns this house died in the shower and I'm robbing her." She cleared her throat and added, "Just taking one thing. She was shitty to me earlier, so mostly I just want a souvenir?" As all that spilled out of her mouth, it occurred to her: *I probably should've lied.* "She called me slut, so."

Rita shrugged and said, "I'm going to go get her pill stash, then."

When she saw Miriam's shocked face, she said, "Don't look at me like that, honey. You're already robbing the dead. I'm just following your lead. Besides, when you die, they just take those pills and flush 'em down the crapper, anyway." Rita waved it off like no biggie, then wandered into the bathroom to root around the medicine cabinet.

And so began their scam.

Miriam hasn't explained how she knows about people dying—but she was able to prove it with Geriatric Dead Person Number Two, Bill Nolan, who lived two subdivisions over. (Bill took a nasty fall after tripping on a garden hose, broke his neck in his own backyard.) That convinced Rita well enough.

This is the safer, softer version of what Miriam used to do years ago when she was on the road. (She's a grown-up now, she tells herself. Basically.) They steal cash but no credit cards. They steal jewelry but nothing that looks like a wedding ring or family heirloom, because someone in the estate might miss it.

Rita takes the pills and sells them to the other olds who fell into that Medicare gap and have to pay way too damn much for them otherwise. ("We're providin' a fuckin' service," Rita said, "more or less." Miriam doesn't ask questions. She just takes her fifty-percent cut.)

Merv will be their fifth pillage-and-plunder together.

Miriam decides to go right for the pills. It's where they're getting most of their return, and Merv had so many medical problems, his stash probably looks like it belongs to a pop star.

On the way to his bathroom, though, she sees something in his bedroom.

A bell-shaped shadow hangs from a post.

Miriam enters the dark room, then removes the dark blue cloth draped atop the bell.

Revealed is not a bell but a bird inside a cage. Little and yellow, the bird chirps and trills, hopping about on a wooden dowel running midway through its domicile.

A canary.

For a moment, Miriam's mind slips away. It's like a bar of soap held in a slippery grip—one minute you've got it, the next it's out of your hands. She blinks and there's this faint vacuum sensation . . . then she's looking back at herself from inside the mind of the bird. Miriam's human face shows dark eyes set in a porcelain mask, her midnight hair a chaotic tangle spilling across her shoulders. The Miriam-person's eyes go unfocused, and the mouth opens just a little. She thinks, *What if the bird became me and I became the bird?* (Miriam imagines her bird-possessed body stumbling around town, flapping her human arms uselessly, trilling fruitlessly with dry, puckered lips, *woo, whoo, pfft, pooooft*.) But Miriam's consciousness inside the bird can feel that the bird is in there with her. She can feel its mind. She can feel its stress—trapped here in a cage, trilling not for love or amusement but because it can do nothing else. Every song a plea for escape.

Then it's over. Miriam draws a sharp breath, and once more, she's staring at the bird through human eyes.

She opens the cage. The bird doesn't throw away its shot—it leaps for the exit and in a flutter of lemon-yellow wings it leaves the cage and the room.

Bye-bye, birdie.

Miriam heads for the pill stash.

Merv has all the accouterments of an old person's bathroom: he's got the toilet with the handles, the shower seat for the tub, the extra step to help him get into the tub, the hemorrhoid cream right there on the sink, the stool softener, the arthritis balms. *God,* she thinks, *what a bite it is to get older. Everything slides downward. Your balls, your tits, your heart, your mind. Nothing stays where it's supposed to. Even your asshole turns inside out.*

Enough about mortality, she decides. It's bumming her right the fuck out. She didn't get soggy on cheap Merlot just to sit here and think about old-ass people and their old asses.

The medicine cabinet is a standard affair: a boxy, mirrored affair hanging over the sink. She opens it and therein lurks the standard bounty. Rita told her to look for specifics, though, and ol' Merv, he's got them in spades:

Zoloft, Ativan, Percocet. Rita said that her "clients" really want that holy trinity: something for depression, something for anxiety, something for pain.

Then there's the lesser pantheon: Synthroid for the thyroid, a high-test proton pump inhibitor for the reflux, Boniva for the bone decay. Little gods in tiny packages. Take your pill and pray its favor outweighs the misfortune of side effects.

Miriam whistles a little canary birdsong as she pockets the bottles.

She closes the medicine cabinet. Something has changed.

In the mirror, she sees a face staring over her shoulder. The revelation hits her slow, too slow:

I'm not alone.

There's a brief flash where she sees Merv's face over her shoulder—cheeks striated with dark lines, eyes swimming in bruise-black pools—

Then her head rockets forward into the mirror. *Wham.* The glass craters in a spider-web pattern. *Kssh!* Her brain rocks in her head. Behind her eyes, a fireworks display goes off: *pop pop pop*. Hands, Merv's hands, grip a hank of her hair and wrench her head back—then slam it forward again. And again. As her head rears back once more, she sees the glass is wet with red.

Bits of glistening mirror fall away into the sink, tinkling, clattering.

She gasps. The thought crosses her mind: *The doc back in Tucson told me to protect my head, and this is the furthest thing from protecting my head.* Another hit and her brain could scramble like eggs in a bowl. Miriam holds the sides of the sink for dear life, then stabs back with a hard foot. Merv *oof*s, and his breath is a dead-fish stink pushing over her shoulder, and then his face hovers into view as he presses in behind her.

He leers at her. "You thought you could *steal* from *me*?" he hisses.

Blood fills her mouth as she snarls, whipping her head back. Her skull connects with his nose. It's mushy, like she's head-butting a bowl of raw meat.

"Those are *my* pills." He grunts nasally but doesn't let go, jamming her head forward—

She resists—

Her neck tendons pull like taffy—

He cups the underside of her jaw, pulling down—

Her arm muscles strain like a hangman's rope—

Merv urges her forward so her open mouth is forced around the sink faucet. She tries to close her mouth, but he's strong, too strong, and the metal slips past her lips and presses past her teeth, cold and insistent. Her tongue bunches up to stop it. It scrapes the roof of her mouth. More blood on her tongue. Tears press against her eyes. She does everything in her power not to gag.

His soft carcass hands reach past her, going for the faucet handle.

He's going to turn it on.

He's going to drown me.

Miriam does her own grabbing then—her hand sliding along the inside of the sink. It's there she finds a shard of broken mirror.

She stabs backward, in the space over her right shoulder.

The glass buries in his face. Merv howls—a gargling, banshee roar. He's off her now, arms pinwheeling. The dead man's heel catches on one of the toilet railings and he topples backward into the tub, the back of his head whacking the subway tile there and sending a lightning-bolt crack up through the porcelain. Blood oozes down his scalp and neck as he slumps into the tub.

"You thought you could leave me," he says, his voice warping and distorting until it's not Merv's voice at all. It's not one voice she knows but all of them: it's Louis, it's Ashley, it's Ethan Key.

Mushy and garbled. Something like black tar runs over his lower lip, feathers caught in that sticky mess. He says it again, louder, this time a question: *"You thought you could leave me?"*

It's him. The Trespasser.

Her imaginary friend has returned.

"Fuck you," she says.

"Miss me?" the Trespasser asks. Underneath the skin of his face, the bones shift and crackle like a string of firecrackers going off. She sees Louis's soft, sandy beard. She sees Ashley's smug sneer. She sees Ethan Key's eyes staring back at her. The face keeps shifting. Bulging. Deflating. Skin rippling.

"I'm done with you."

"Haaaardly," he moans. "You know how you get rid of me, and you just can't do it." His face puffs up and sinks in once more, like a cake collapsing in the oven. Now it's Mary Stitch staring at her, stringy hair in her eyes, lips charred like fire-kissed charcoals. When she talks, smoke drifts from her mouth. "Your babymaker is a broken vase, bitch. Can't glue it back together. Can't stitch up that wound. You're the breaker of rivers. You're fate's foe. You're buckled in, baby. And the river, boy howdy, it's rising, it's surging, it's hungry like a dragon."

Miriam spits blood at him. Her. It. The Trespasser doesn't even flinch as the red splatter hits its cheek.

"Even with this power, I don't have to do what you want," she says.

"Good luck with that, Miriam."

"I don't want you anymore."

"And yet here we are."

"I'm out. Suck a dick."

She storms to the bathroom door. It's closed. The knob won't budge. The Trespasser chuckles: a rheumy, damp sound. Like trying to pull a stuck boot from greasy mud. It's the sound of sickness and swamp.

Miriam hammers at the door with her shoulder. Then she kicks it. Still nothing. She cries out, wrenching the knob with both hands.

"See? You can't leave me if I don't want you to."

She turns toward the Trespasser with her fist raised—

The hallucination, or ghost, or demon, or whatever the fuck it is, it sits there in the tub, swelling up. Skin stretching and tearing. Eyes bulging like apples in a pig's mouth. The belly is the worst, gassily inflating. The belly ripples and rumbles, like it's digesting something—or failing to digest something.

One of the eyes pops out and rolls into the tub. *Plonk.*

From the socket, a canary emerges. Its feathers are frothy and slick. It chirps a discordant song. Miriam cries out as the Trespasser in its entirety ruptures, filling the bathroom with a hundred canaries, a thousand—everything gone yellow, feathers everywhere, beaks sticking her in the skin, little claws scratching her like rose thorns, and—

THREE
ONE BROKEN COOKIE

Gasp.

Awake.

Miriam lurches up in her bed. (*My mother's bed,* she thinks.) Instantly, her hands move to her face. Though her skull throbs from where her head slammed into Merv's mirror, there's nothing broken, no cuts or abrasions. She still tastes blood, but as she tongues the roof of her mouth, she finds no scrapes there, either.

Jesus. Did any of that happen? She knows the visions are dubious at best, mired in the worst kind of unreality. But was she ever over there at all? Did Merv die? Is any of this real? She remembers being back in Tucson, the doc there told her she had a TBI: traumatic brain injury. Born of repeated concussions. He told her, *You're one broken cookie!* and then laughed.

Is her gourd finally and truly cracked?

She stands up. It's still night outside—the black bleeds past the blinds. Her toe nudges a wine bottle. It rolls away.

Miriam staggers out into the living room.

"You're awake."

The voice damn near gives her cause to pee.

It's not Rita.

"Grosky?" she asks, genuinely surprised.

The big man fills a recliner. He rocks forward on it, leaning so that he can put his hands on his knees. Next to the chair is a leather briefcase. No—a computer case. *Like for a laptop,* she thinks.

"You had a little adventure tonight, huh?"

She says, "Why, Special Agent Thomas Richard Grosky, I don't know what you mean."

"Few doors down. Mervin Delgado." He thumbs toward the window. Through the curtains, Miriam spies the strobe of red and blue police lights.

"I didn't kill him."

"Okay."

"You're here for him? For that? How long was I asleep?"

"I'm not here for that," he says, grunting as he stands up. "That happened a few hours ago, best as I can tell. I was parked in a rental car outside the house when an old woman came up with you. You were on your way to being passed-out drunk by the look of it—she was helping you walk. I asked her where you were coming from and the lady told me to go fuck myself with a plastic flamingo."

Sounds like Rita.

"I, ummm." Miriam winces, scratching at her head, messing her hair up further. "What the hell are you doing here?"

"Saving your ass, for one."

"I doubt that very much."

"Ye of little faith," he says with a chuckle. "I went and talked to the cops real quick over there at Mr. Delgado's house. Did you know the patio door was smashed with a rock? Volcanic rock. Had a little blood on it. Funny, too, because when you take a look at your hand, looks like you got a little boo-boo." He shrugs those beefy shoulders. "But I'm sure that's just a coinkydink, hm?"

She looks down. The palm is scabbed over in a pattern roughly consistent with running your hand over a cheese grater. "Yeah. That."

"So, you don't want me to, say, discourage them from running a test on that blood? Because I could do that. I got pull down here. I used some of it the last time you and I tangoed down here in Florida. You didn't kill Merv?"

Her jaw sets a hard line. "I didn't kill Merv."

"He die naturally?"

"Hemorrhagic stroke. Natural as spring water."

"Let's have a conversation. I'll make a deal with you."

"I don't do deals."

"Not even for keeping your bacon out of the fire with Delray PD?"

Miriam grouses, then pulls out one of the breakfast nook chairs with the toe of her foot before sitting down. In a monotone robot voice she says, "No, please, let us talk. I am very excited to hear your proposal, especially at—" She glances at the microwave clock. "At three thirty in the hell-fucked morning."

Grosky sits. He's out of his suit. He wears a pastel polo that might be described as "seafoam" in color, as if seafoam is ever so pretty. In Florida, seafoam is often a grotty, muddy, jizz-colored froth.

"I'm writing a book," he says.

"Bully for you. Lemme guess: self-help? Weight loss?"

"Sure, go ahead, needle me about my weight. My doc says it doesn't matter how big you are. Just how healthy you are."

"Who is your doctor? Ronald McDonald?"

"I'm fit. Okay? All my numbers are good. I'm healthier than you."

She winces. "Nnnyeah, okay, that's probably true."

"The book," he continues, "is about fringe-case serial killers. Not the big cases everyone knows. But ones that fell off the books. Plus some cold cases and other mysteries." As he talks, he gets out a notebook computer from his leather satchel. He pops the screen open. His face is icy from the blue glow of the monitor. "You see that *Making a Murderer*? True crime is big now."

"Great. More power to you. Hope you get a TV deal. But watch out: Hollywood can be pretty fickle."

"I want you in the book."

"Pressed like a butterfly?"

"As a topic. Maybe an interview. Maybe a whole chapter or more."

"No."

"Hear me out—"

"I'm *not* a serial killer."

Grosky hesitates. The smile on his face strikes her as eerily predatory. Less like he wants to kill her and eat her and more like *I know something you don't.* "By some metrics, you are."

"Carl Keener was the serial killer."

"And you?"

She swallows. *Just a regular killer,* she thinks but does not say. Instead, she answers with "I don't want to be in your book."

"So, you can tell me about Carl Keener, then. Or whatever was going on here in Florida the last time. Or whatever happened with that fella, Weldon Stitch, in Colorado. We focus the book more on them, less on you."

"Oh, it's a whole book now? Go pound sand, Grosky. I'm not public. I'm not a known quantity. I'm a nobody and I like it that way."

"Then I got bad news for you, Miriam."

She gives him a quizzical stare.

He spins his laptop computer toward her and shows her something.

FOUR

UH-OH SPAGHETTIOS

"You know what a subreddit is?" he asks.

Miriam arches an eyebrow. "It's a sex thing?"

"It's not a sex thing. Look, there's a site called Reddit and people create forums, message boards, public spaces centered around different topics. These forums are called subreddits."

"And that has fuckall to do with me."

He clucks his tongue. "Don't be so hasty. Look at this one."

Still blinking sleep and wine haze from her eyes, Miriam squints and leans in toward the screen. She sees a word that makes no sense at all.

"'Creepypasta'?"

"Yeah. That's the forum."

"Okay, I'm still thinking that maybe I'm stroking out here and none of this is real, because pasta is not, and never will be, creepy. Further, that has nothing to do with me except that I like to eat pasta occasionally. Not even that creepily."

"No. Creepypasta—it's like, some kinda Internet thing. Spooky stories that started on the Internet and get copy-pasted around social media. Like Slenderman or Ben Drowned. Folklore for the modern age."

"Whatever. I don't care. The Internet is dumb."

"You should care, because you're in here."

Grosky taps the screen. Underneath the pad of his index finger is a header: ANGEL OF DEATH VIDEO – TUSCON CREEPY AF.

"They misspelled *Tucson*."

"I know. That's not the point. Click it."

"I don't wanna click it. I wanna go back to bed."

"Miriam, *you're* the Angel of Death they're talking about."

Dubious, Miriam clicks the mouse. At the top is another link to a video and a forum full of comments beneath it. She goes to the video first.

It's portrait view. Filmed on a cell phone, she guesses. The whole thing is just twenty seconds long. It's blurry and pixelated. It's filmed from someone looking down from a vantage point—a second- or third-story window, maybe. It takes her a second to even realize what she's looking at: a man with a shock of ginger hair standing there, his gun pointed. A woman enters the view of the camera: a haggard, ragged slip of a woman that Miriam suddenly realizes is *her*. There's a flash of something black, a flutter of wings, and it whips across the area underneath the man's chin. Red sprays. He drops his gun and Miriam watches herself go pick it up as the air fills with birds.

The video ends.

Her hand shakes.

Her heart hammers against her breastbone like it's trying to escape.

She wants to say something—but what? Her jaw works but no words come out. Instead she pulls the laptop closer and starts reading the comments.

> **killervamp**: looks fake to me—has anyone run this by an expert?
>
> **Jackhole99:** This is not fake. This is real. And it ties into a government conspiracy too—Google THE COMING STORM. Fringe militia, taken out behind the

scenes by government agents not wanting this to turn into a Waco Ruby Ridge shitstorm. But someone there took video and this emerged. Which, in case you're not paying attention, could mean our Angel of Death is working for the US Government. Any hackers out there? Chinese, Russian, domestic? Could try to hack gov servers, see if we can find proof of this. This is MK-Ultra stuff upgraded. Nazi, KGB shit.

scamspikes: STUPID VIRAL VIDEO FOR SOME DUMB UPCOMING FOUND FOOTAGE HORROR MOVIE PROBLY

scarlet-tanager99: the angel of death will save us all and I know who she is

UncaFester: can't be her—ANGEL OF DEATH sighting at the same time in Lock Haven, PA

FentanylFrank: Newer sighting in Falls Creek, PA. Last week.

pyroclast: hey what is this—is there more to it or what

Jizzwailer42: yeah, start here, got an archive going

A new link. Which Miriam clicks.

It opens a text page. White background. Basic black font.

Her heart feels like it stops beating altogether—held fast in her chest like a bird caught in a closing, crushing fist. She sees names and places that walk backward through her own life: Tucson. Collbran. Miami. Peter Lake. An ATM camera from

Philadelphia. The Caldecott School. Interspersed are just as many—or even more—misses among the hits. One post reads: ANGEL OF DEATH—ALASKA? Another says, SANDMAN AND ANGEL TOGETHER: LOS ANGELES? Below that: ANGEL SIGHTING AT THE EL MAR.

Time slips through Miriam's fingers as she hunkers down over the laptop, the world narrowing to just her and the glow from the screen. The archive is an endless parade of bullshit and speculation mixed in with actual facts. She's left a trail. That much is clear now. It's not a trail that's easy to find, but for a gaggle of amateur sleuths on the Internet, it's a trail of ants leading to a forgotten, forbidden picnic. The archive takes her back to Reddit, where she digests theory after theory about who she is: Is she merciful or malevolent? Some of them think she's human. A serial killer. Maybe a government assassin or spy. A genetic experiment gone wrong. Or like one of those nurses who ushers the sick and dying to a quiet death. There are other, fringier theories: omg she's a vampire, holy shit she's a real angel, or a demon, or a goddess, or a ghost, or a "glitch in the Matrix" manifesting itself in the code of our "VR reality." They talk too about how her hair changes color—one poster says that's a sign she's trying to hide her identity, and like a half-dozen other ding-dongs chime in to call that crazy, instead offering the more "plausible" theory that it's proof she's a series of clones like in some show called *Orphan Black*. "Clones? *Clones?* I'm an A-1 original, bitch," Miriam mutters.

All the while, Grosky comes and goes—he heads out, checks in with the Delray PD, sends them on their way, pokes through her fridge. All of it is background noise to her as she falls down the rabbit hole.

Through the blinds is the searing magma line of the coming sun. Miriam leans back in the chair. She's shaking. Trying not to cry.

She feels suddenly, grotesquely exposed. All that she is and has done—it's always felt precious and illicit. The subreddit makes her feel like a blood diamond: all her work, all the blood spilled, all the lives lost, are now just something for other people to enjoy.

She's become conspiracy wank-fodder for a gaggle of amateur-hour Internet detectives.

Worse, it used to be hers and hers alone. Something grotesque, yes. But precious, too, in its way. All this was something she fought for. *Killed* for. It belonged to her, and only a few others ever even witnessed it: Louis, Gabby, Agent Grosky. In a way, she *did* feel like a ghost, passing through this life and affecting it in ways unseen and unrealized—nudging fate this way and that, cutting a thread here and letting another unspool far longer than destiny had decided to allow. But her passing was invisible. Or so she thought.

They don't know who she is. And they don't know all that she's done—or what it all means. But given enough time, they'll be able to tie these ropes together into a clumsy knot. Then again, maybe she doesn't know who she is, either. Maybe this is all one big delusion. Maybe she *is* a government assassin. Maybe Grosky's been her handler this whole time and it's why he keeps showing up.

One broken cookie.

With a grunt of rage and a sniffle, she shoves the computer away.

Grosky snorts awake in the recliner. "Huh? You, uh—you done over there?"

"I'm done. You snore."

"I got sleep apnea."

"The pinnacle of health, you are."

He ignores her barb and comes to sit at the table. "You okay?"

"Just zippity-doo-dah dandy," she lies, wetting her lips with her tongue and blinking back tears.

"You didn't know."

"No."

"It's gotta be upsetting."

"I feel fucking . . ." She bats at the laptop like a bear taking one last angry swat at a wasp's nest. "I feel pissed. I don't like being . . . ripped open and shown to the world. I don't like it one little goddamn bit. They don't know who I am. This isn't for them. I'm not for their *fun*."

"There's more."

"Do I want to know?"

"No. But yeah."

She closes her eyes: rising in her is the feeling of slowly clicka-clacking to the top of the first rollercoaster hill, everything clenching and cinching in her guts as she knows full well that going up slow means coming down fast. Part of her wants to just hold on to the chair and grit her teeth and go silent and still until all this is over. Leave it alone. Get in a car or a plane or on a boat and hightail it the hell out of here. Find an island somewhere. A mountain. A cave.

Instead, she says: "Show me."

So he does.

FIVE
FALLS CREEK

Grosky goes back to the subreddit and shows her the comment about a sighting in Falls Creek, PA. Just last week.

Then he closes his browser window and pulls up a file folder on his notebook. Inside Miriam sees photos and documents.

He pulls up one of the photos.

It is an image of a dead man slumped against an interior wall. The wall is wood paneling—old, water-stained, dinged up. The man's blue denim shirt is soaked through with so much blood, it looks like he spilled a gallon of grape juice on himself. The shirt is vented with little slash marks, each a couple inches wide.

"Stab wounds," she says.

Grosky nods. "Yeah."

She leans in. Something's written on his forehead. Wait. No. Something has been *carved* into the skin there. Grosky taps the mouse and goes to the next photo.

It's a close-up.

Four words, though the first is half-buried under a mat of sweat-stuck hair:

THE RIVER IS RISING.

Miriam fails to stifle an animal-like sound—a moan of shock and bewilderment. "Jesus. Shit."

"That familiar to you?"

She blinks. "Yeah. Yes. This was last week?"

"Yup. You wanna go get a coffee?"

"Fuck, yes. Let's get some coffee."

SIX

BLACK COFFEE

"Not hungry?"

"No," she says. Steam frames her face above the cup of black coffee held in her hand below.

Grosky shrugs. "Your loss; this is good."

He cuts into his veggie omelet like a connoisseur. Miriam is a glutton. Usually, if you put breakfast in front of her, she'll have to restrain herself from faceplanting into the meal and eating it the way Pac-Man eats a line of glowing dots. Grosky, though, is delicate in how he eats: a knife urges food to the fork, the fork carries it to his mouth with an airiness of movement, and then when he sucks it off the tines, he closes his eyes just for a moment, gently rocking his head side to side. Little sounds emerge: *mm*, *ahh*, *oh*. A savoring act. Every bite.

So annoying.

She watches him eat with the intensity of an irritated mantis. All around, the diner is a clamor of noise: forks scraping plates, coffeepots clinking against mug rims, the murmur of many voices gone mushy together. The diner itself is pretty standard for Florida. The décor is a cobbled-together monstrosity, like if you took a pink flamingo and a powder-blue lawn chair and then melted them together under a hot flame.

Finally, she can't take it anymore.

"Stop face-fucking your food," she snaps.

He pauses, midbite, then gently swallows before setting his fork down. He dabs at his face with his napkin, giving her the side-eye. "Fine. You recognized something. Something in that photo."

"Yeah."

"What was it?"

She hesitates. She doesn't know Grosky's game. Why he's here all of a damn sudden. Miriam wants to trust him, but she is afraid to trust anybody anymore. Even herself.

Finally, she commits to it. She says: "The phrase. I recognized the phrase."

"'The river is rising,'" he says.

"Yeah."

"What's it mean?"

She eyes him up. "This for your book?"

"No. Not unless you want it to be."

"Isn't the FBI pissed you're writing books about current cases?"

He laughs it off. "I'm not with the Bureau anymore."

"What?"

"I quit. Retired. Whatever. They've been refocusing for a long time on different threat management profiles. Putting more men on terrorism—domestic, if you believe it. Like those whacknuts in Arizona you tangled with." He leans back, possessing a level of comfort she finds surprising—and troubling. As if he's let a heavy burden slide from his shoulders and the freedom from it has buoyed him. He's not as bothered by this as she is. He's too easy about it. "They still got me here and there doing consultant work. After all, there's still serial killers to catch, just less focus on catching them."

"Same question: they don't mind you writing a book?"

"It's not classified information. I'm not talking Russian spies. This is law enforcement. Everybody's good with it. I still have friends there and they know I'm not going to make the Bureau look like a buncha dummies."

She licks her lips. "This doesn't go in the book, what I'm about to tell you."

"Fine." He holds up both hands, showing he has no pen, no recorder, no nothing. "What's the deal?"

"You know what I can do."

"Supposedly."

"*Supposedly?* Remember Vills? Remember Tap-Tap? Arizona? It's like shaking Santa's hand and asking him if he's real as you do it."

"I'm just saying."

"Whatever. This *thing* of mine, it's more than just the touch, more than just the vision. I have a visitor. I have the Trespasser. It's a— You know, I still don't know what it is. Maybe it's a hallucination, but I don't think so. It knows things I don't or can't know. I've come around to thinking it's something else, something separate from me—like a ghost, or a demon. Not that I think those things exist, but . . . *shit.*" She presses the heels of her hands into her eyes hard enough that she sees fireworks. This fucking sucks. Miriam has gone over this in her own head hundreds, even thousands of times, and none of it makes any sense. Out loud, it sounds bugfuck batshit cray-cray.

"What's this thing want?"

"I don't know. I mean, I think I do know. It wants me to do my job."

"Your job?"

"Yeah. I see how things are supposed to be—people dying according to some invisible destiny. Then I come along and I fuck it all up. I spit in destiny's eye. The river's going one way, then I'm the boulder that drops into it, breaks the current in two. I'm meant to be this fate-breaker."

"River. As in, *the river is rising.*"

"That's something the Trespasser told me. Before I got involved with the Caldecott School and the Mockingbird killers, the Trespasser appeared to me in a motel room. It looked like me and, ah, it puked up some nasty water and then whispered that to me. *The river is rising, Miriam.* And that's exactly what happened. A storm came in. With the rains, the river rose. And then I found Eleanor Caldecott trying to drown a girl named Lauren Martin—Wren. I went into the river after them, and me and the girl almost died." *But my friend Louis pulled us out. Louis, who will in six months murder his own bride. Something I have not yet told him.* And why is that, exactly? Why hasn't she told him? That is a rock she is unwilling to overturn. Instead, she keeps talking: "Caldecott died. Which I'm sure you know."

Grosky nods. "Yeah. The Bureau's still after whoever did all that. Left behind quite a mess there. Eleanor Caldecott. Carl Keener. Earl, Beck, Edwin. That whole family tree cut down. Not that it wasn't rotten from the inside. The evidence stacked up against them—we knew they were a whole clan doing nasty work. But the Bureau never did figure out who killed the killers."

"Did you?"

"Not then. Only later. After meeting you."

"But you didn't tell."

He smiles. "In the Behavioral Unit, we always had pet theories that, ah, governed how we did things. But psychic shit, no. I had no proof. Only thing I had was meeting up with you. And I'd already written you out of the Vills narrative. Couldn't easily write you back in."

"Thanks."

"Don't thank me. I didn't do it out of the goodness of my heart. I did it because I couldn't explain it. I couldn't fit you to any of it without all of this nonsense. The death visions. The birds. I'd have tanked my career."

She shrugs, and sips the coffee. "So, what now?"

"Here's the thing. That dead guy in the cabin up in Falls Creek, he's not the only one. We have more bodies. Bodies I don't think link to you. But they *do* pair up with other sightings of the Angel of Death."

"The myth of me."

"Right."

"So, someone's out there killing in my name."

"Or at least in your style."

"Whoever is doing it, they know about the Trespasser." *Or they are the Trespasser.* An icicle sticks her right through the heart with that thought. Is that even possible? What if the Trespasser isn't a vision at all?

What if he's someone else?

Another psychic? Someone who can get in her head.

Her hand shakes. She quick-gulps the coffee to burn out the cold feeling that's started to nest in the shallows of her chest. "I want to go there."

"Go where?"

"Falls Creek."

"Why?"

"I don't know. I just do. It just happened, didn't it? If someone's pretending to be me"—*someone who may have tapped a line to the Trespasser too. Or who may* be *the Trespasser*—"Maybe whoever did this left something behind. Or is still there. Plus, if those fuckwhistles online are starting to put it together, it won't be long before one of your law enforcement buddies starts putting pieces together, too. This'll wash up on my shore, and I don't want it to. Whoever is doing this . . . they need to stop."

"And you're going to stop them?"

She finishes her coffee. "Yes."

"Let's go to Falls Creek. I'll book us a flight."

"No," she says, the word so abrupt she almost gags on the last drops of coffee. She wipes her mouth. "God, Jesus, no. No planes."

"Bad experience on one?"

"You could say that. We drive."

He nods. "Get your stuff together. We leave on your word."

SEVEN

A FEATHER, MISSING

Miriam has not yet colonized her mother's bedroom. She sleeps there, yes. But the bed is the only acreage of the room she can call her own—the rest remains firmly her mother's, regardless of the woman's unliving status. She's never really had the interest (*never had the guts*, a small voice chides her) in going through her mother's remnants. The dresser still has her mother's clothes in it, and now Miriam has the less-than-envious task of looking through those drawers. Tearing through them, actually, as she looks for something that has gone missing.

In the drawers she finds beachy T-shirts, old lady capri pants, giant granny panties that you could use as a parasail, huge underwire bras the color of wet sand and sadness. None of these things are the things Miriam is looking for.

What she is looking for is this:

Back in the hospital, in Tucson, the doc pulled something out of her body—from within one of her wounds, he excised a long black feather. (Even just thinking about it—the flock of birds stuffing her wounds with grass and stones and stitching her up out there in the desert when she was supposed to die—the memory hits her like a Mac truck going eighty. She has to regain her footing lest she drop to the floor.) That doctor took that feather and put it in a narrow jar with a cork in the top of it.

She took that jar with the feather in it and brought it here.

She put it somewhere, and now she can't find it.

It's with her stuff. Her stuff sits in a heap by the dresser, and she went through it like a biologist fishing for the keys he lost in a pile of steaming elephant dung. Now she wonders, did she put it in one of her mother's drawers? Could it be in there? In a drunken fit, did Miriam hide the feather jar amidst her mother's things?

So far, no. One drawer, then the next, then the next, and then—

Miriam's hand flies to her mouth.

"No," she whispers.

Her gorge rises when she sees what waits for her in the bottom drawer:

A vibrator. And a bottle of lube.

She gasps and steps back. "Aw, c'mon," Miriam says, making the face of someone who just ate a bug. It probably smells like cigarettes and Febreze. With a toe, Miriam gingerly eases the drawer back in, wincing until the demon is once more contained in its eternal prison.

Outside the room, she hears a door open and close.

"It's Rita," comes a voice.

"In here." *Finding my mother's diddle-rod.*

Rita pokes her head in wearing one of those tinted visors that poker players wear. "You lose the suit?" she asks.

"He wasn't wearing a suit."

"Not on the outside, but on the *inside.*" She taps her chest, over her heart. Rita sneers, then lights a cigarette. "He was a cop, wasn't he?"

"A Fed."

"Even worse." Her puckered wrinkle-slit lips drag on the cancer stick and loose a plume of smoke into the room. "I can smell 'em. I always had a gift. I can spot a cop a mile away. They're like a tiny little shitstain in an otherwise clean pair of undies. Fuck that pig. He onto us?"

"Rita-Rita-Eat-a-Pita, you're a hardcore motherfucker. And

cool as a cucumber." Just the same, she feels the woman's stare poking holes in her—like a pin lancing blisters. "No, he's not onto us."

"Good." She sniffs. "Whatcha doing?"

"Looking for something. You see a jar around here? With a long black feather in it?"

"Sorry, hon."

"Shit."

Rita's gaze drifts from Miriam and the dresser to the bag there on the floor. "So, you leavin' me?" Rita asks.

"I am."

"Gotta run from the law, huh."

"No." *Not yet, anyway.* "I've got business to take care of up north. Some things to do with my mother's estate. My friend—"

"The pig."

"Yeah, the pig, he and I are taking a road trip."

Rita narrows her gaze. "This isn't about me and you stealing meds?"

"No."

"Good. But I guess this means our little operation is dried up already."

Miriam turns and leans against the dresser. "I have one more name on the list. Someone I know is gonna bite it, if you want the gig."

"I'm listening."

"A little quid pro quo first."

"Go on."

"I want to know who the hell you are. Or were."

Rita plays it coy. "I don't follow. I'm just an old New York broad put out to the Florida pasture, is all."

"Bullshit. You're something else. You play cards like a hit man. Then all this talk of *pigs* and whatever? C'mon. There's a story there."

"Not a big one."

"I'll take whatever it is."

Rita shrugs. "Back in the day, I ran with Ari Monk and Sticky Goldstein—you know? Kosher Nostra? Sticky ran cons on Orthodox men who were unfaithful, got them to pay him to keep their secrets. Ari ran diamonds. I was Ari's girl for a while, until he got plugged in the Heights by what they say was the Jamaicans but I know was the Italians. So, I took over his business for a little while. Made some money. Had a good time. Now I'm retired."

"You used to run illicit diamonds for the Jewish mob?"

"Maybe."

"Rita-Rita-Packin'-Heat-A."

"More like Rita-Rita-Let's-Keep-It-Discreet-A. Or Rita-Rita-Turn-You-to-Dead-Meat-A, huh?"

"Hey, fair enough."

"Quid pro quo. So. Spill it. Who's gonna suck a shoe?"

Miriam lowers her voice—why, she doesn't know, but it feels more respectful, as if not to taunt death or the soon-to-be-dead. "You know that creepy scarecrow-looking guy down on Mangrove? The one with the picket-fence teeth? Always wears the tan jacket with the red pocket square?"

"Malcolm, ennnh, Barnes? Burns?"

"Burnside."

"Uh-huh. Right, right. One creepy fuckin' weirdo right there. He's like a mummy, that one. Always walking around with his arms out a little bit, a tiny moan coming out of his mouth like he's happy but also sad, and definitely gassy." Rita does a fast, spot-on impression of him: her eyes wide, arms stiff, a dead smile on her face as she goes, "Eyyynnnhhh."

"That's the one. He's got bone cancer."

Rita blinks. "Oh. Well, aren't I a real shithead."

"Everybody dies, Rita. The guy's eighty-seven. He had a good run."

“You’re right. Fuck him. That mummy asshole. I bet he’s got good pills.”

“I leave it to you to find out.”

Miriam sighs, then starts stuffing clothes into a duffel bag in big, unruly handfuls. Rita hovers still. “Lemme ask you something.”

“What’s that?”

“This trip you’re taking. Is it you running away from something, or running toward it?”

“I don’t know yet.” She stiffens as a strange fear twists inside her. “If I had to lay money on it, I’d say a bit of both.”

“Can I give you a bit of advice?”

“Can I stop you?”

“Not without me putting up a fight.”

“Then please, by all means.”

Rita takes a last drag off her cigarette before licking her thumb and forefinger and pinching the smoldering cherry to a quick extinction. She licks her lips when she says, “They say life is short, but it ain’t. Life is long. It’s minutes stacked on hours stacked on days, and all that ends up in years that chain together, on and on, and you always think, *Here it comes, here’s the end. I can’t live past thirty, or forty, or fifty, sixty, seventy.* And yet you do. But all we do is keep kicking the can down the road, hoping one day we can kick it past the point where we kick the can for good, but it doesn’t work out like that. So, you got things to deal with? You got problems to fix? Don’t sit on your hands. Deal with all the shit you gotta deal with, honey, and not because life is short but because life is too damn long and those problems won’t go away. They just get bigger and meaner, and they’ll hunt you like a starving dog. You get me?”

“I get you, Rita.”

“Take care, Miriam.”

“I’ll be back.”

"Don't make promises you can't keep." Then she tosses something to Miriam: a pack of cigarettes. "Just in case you decide to stop being a quitter."

"Fuck you, Rita."

"Fuck you, too, honey."

They smile at each other, and then Rita leaves.

PART TWO

NORTHERN MIGRATION OF THE PENNSYLVANIA SHITBIRD

EIGHT

THE RIVER THAT IS THE ROAD

Delray Beach, Florida, to Falls Creek, Pennsylvania. Eighteen hours, bare minimum. And with traffic and construction and general highway bullshit, probably more than that. Grosky says they can stop overnight in North Carolina, and Miriam tells him no, hell with that, drive straight through.

Most of the trip, she stays silent. Her head lies pressed against the passenger-side glass in Grosky's four-door Ford sedan. She watches the world blur on past, smearing like wet paint. Occasionally, she plants a hand on the dashboard and lifts up her arm at the elbow so to get the air conditioning blasting right up her shirt, into her pits, to cool her down.

Grosky chuckles when she does it and she gives him a stabbing glance. He asks, "You okay?"

"Ding-dong-ducky," she says, her voice black as her last name.

"You don't seem okay."

"It's just that this feels like—" *It feels like driving around with Louis. Me in the passenger seat. Him driving. The highways and back roads racing underneath us like rivers of dark, churning asphalt.* Or her and Gabby, out there in the desert, just driving. To somewhere. To nowhere. The urge arises in her to call one or both of them. "Nothing. It feels like nothing."

That unsettles him, it seems. Grosky quiets down and drives the car, hands on the wheel, ten and two.

But she, too, is unsettled. She feels a great pressure coming up from behind. Something is chasing her, something riding that same asphalt river, hungry for her, eager to tear into her and rip all of who she is apart. An ill wind, a demon racer, the Trespasser riding a bicycle in the night—going as slow or as fast as it wants to, because no matter how slow or fast she goes, it will always catch up.

It's not just the Trespasser. It's all the shit she's not dealing with, too. Louis being the worst of her unacknowledged problems. Once again, the clock is ticking for him. Death has found him anew, and this time, he won't be the victim.

He'll be the killer.

He'll take his fiancée.

He'll drown her in a tub.

She will struggle. She will fail. And she will die by his hand.

Now, the rules on this are pretty clear as far as Miriam's understanding of her curse goes—if she wants to save Samantha, that means she has to kill Louis.

And that ain't happening.

She can't do it. She *won't* do it. Hell, why would she want to? Maybe Samantha deserves it.

Miriam's middle tightens. The woman was in obvious pain and fear. Louis was brimming with rage, red in the face like a bag of blood squeezed in an ever-tightening grip. Her first thought is *Fuck her, she gets what's coming to her.* The next thought in line is *If you just let her die, then you helped kill her.* Other thoughts struggle to be heard: if Louis kills her, will he be caught? Will he go to jail? What if it's not Louis that kills her, but someone with a mask or disguise? Is that even possible? The Mockingbird killers certainly knew how to mimic someone's voice. She thinks of someone mimicking her out there, killing with her look, carving the Trespasser's words into the skull of one of the corpses.

She wants to call Louis. That's the smart play. Call him, get ahead of this. Wouldn't take much right now to ring him up, get him out here, tell him what she knows. And yet she doesn't. She could call Gabby, too, see how she's doing with Isaiah, maybe get her opinion or her help or another traveling companion.

Nope. Miriam doesn't do that, either.

She tells herself it's nobler to leave them alone. That old refrain: *They're better off without me.* Maybe they are. But the decision is also selfish. Staying away means Miriam can pretend she didn't change everything for them. She can exist under the delusion that she didn't leave scars across both. A man without an eye who will one day soon kill his wife-to-be. A young woman with a cut-up face, now in charge of a boy who can kill you just by touching you. Miriam crashed through their lives like a freight train through an orphanage.

It's easier to look away from the carnage. Easier to stay away, too.

They keep driving.

A hundred miles go past, then two. Day into night. Miriam lets her mind drift—not just inside her head but outside it, too. The world is alive with birds: geese and egrets and orioles. Endless vultures. Infinite crows. She can reach out to them, find them, ride them for a few moments. She's getting better at it. But that worries her too. Like in Merv's place—her just slipping out of her own head and into that canary's? She's never done that before. It wasn't something she controlled. Even though most of her life is about ceding control to everything else, Miriam lies and tells herself she enjoys control. That she's a control freak.

After dark, Grosky stops for coffee at McDonald's, brings her a burger and fries even though she tells him she's not hungry. She insists she's not hungry even as she devours them with the viciousness of a bear eating a goat. He sips his coffee and gets back on the road without saying much.

Finally, she says, "Tell me about the dead guy."

"Hnnh?"

"The dead guy," she says around a cheekful of food. She taps her forehead. "With the words carved in his noggin. Who"—she swallows a wad of burger—"Who was he?"

"Oh. Mark Daley. Security guard at the DuBois Mall. Divorced, two kids. Split custody. He died in a cabin back behind the lake up there."

"His cabin?"

"Uh-huh. He owned it, plus he rents a small duplex north of here."

"Any history of naughty business? Crimes committed? Skeletons hanging in the back of his closet?"

"I seem to recall a domestic report. Neighbors said a fight between him and his wife got out of hand. No charges. Divorce came soon after. Why?"

She licks salt from her fingertips. It tastes so good, she considers just eating her fingertips. "Just curious. Whoever this dude is, he died for a reason."

"When you kill, it's for a reason, isn't it?" His eyes flash in the half-dark of the car like headlights passing over puddles.

"Don't push me, Grosky."

"Everyone needs a little push now and again, Miriam."

NINE

A CABIN IN THE WOODS

The short drive through the geographical hiccup that is Falls Creek shows Miriam what she's seen in so many other towns in Pennsylvania—and across the whole damn country. It's mostly white. It's not exactly poor, but the middle class is a boat leaving the shore and the people in this town aren't on it. In a span of three minutes, they pass three churches of different denominations. The people here need something to count on, and that something is an Imaginary Sky God. Because the Imaginary Sky God is way more reliable than their jobs, their families, their futures, and probably the water that comes out of their taps.

They pass an old hardware store. A strip mall. A rotting Victorian, condemned. A rancher with a ratty yard and a chain link fence and a Rottweiler chained up outside. An empty lot with scrubby bushes and pebbled gravel.

The town absorbs them, then shits them back out the other side. They're a bullet passing through a dead man's heart. Behind them, the town is swallowed up by patchy pine trees. "Nice town," Grosky says.

Miriam doesn't take the bait. She just stares out the window as the dark evergreens fill her gaze.

Soon, the trees give away to the murky, mucky waters of a huge lake. A rotten, cockeyed dock juts out into the algae-slick surface. On the other side, the cabins start to appear as the road winds around the bank and back into the trees.

When they find Mark Daley's cabin, it is appropriately rustic—run-down but not a termite-infested tower of sawdust. Dark logs comprise its walls. Grosky pulls the car up into a gravel lot, cuts the engine. Somewhere, wind chimes *tink-tink-tink*, and Miriam has the odd thought that somewhere in Heaven, freshly dead Mervin Delgado just got his wings. Or came in his pants.

They get out. The air is humid. The ground, spongy and mulchy. The smells of damp wood and fishy lake compete inside Miriam's nose. She follows Grosky up to the cabin, passing planters and pots full of dry dirt but empty of flowers.

The wraparound porch is screened in, and tied off with a clumsy swaddling of police tape. Above it on the door hangs a NO ENTRY, CRIME SCENE notice. Grosky lifts a ratty welcome mat with the toe of his shoe. "Staties told me they put a key there." He lifts the tape as she takes the key and opens the door.

The smell of death does not take long to find her. It's not overpowering, but it's there. It'll never not be there. Death is like cat piss and cigarette smoke: it gets into everything, and that smell will never come out (out, out, damn spot). Here it manifests as a sour stink, like a truck-struck deer on the highway a half-mile off.

The cabin isn't much to look at. One room, mostly. Bed in the corner. Kitchenette on the other side. Only separate room looks like a bathroom.

Miriam steps over a ratty red rug, past a pellet stove, and it's then she sees it: it's like one of those Magic Eye paintings where the image emerges from the chaos. The bloodstains are hard to see against the wood, but they're there just the same. The stain is sloppy, uneven, a Rorschach blot where the wood of the cabin wall is darker, redder. It's there in the floor, too, shaping out around the legs of where the dead man once sat.

"No struggle," she says.

"Hm? No."

"That means it didn't happen here. The murder."

Grosky gives a small, polite clap. "Nicely done. You should've been a detective."

"I'm more used to solving murders before they happen, not after."

"There's a first for everything."

"They didn't find the murder weapon?"

Grosky is watching her carefully now. "Actually, they did."

"Well?"

"A knife."

"No shit, a knife. I didn't think those holes in his chest were from a spork."

"Near the body they found a spring-loaded knife. Cheap, Chinese knock-off."

Her blood goes to ice water, and she knows what he's about to tell her next.

"Funny thing. Some of the injuries related to the Mockingbird killers were consistent with that same kind of knife. Coincidence?"

I used to have a knife like that.

She no longer has it. Lost it when she stuck it into Carl Keener's leg. Keener—the one she thought was the singular Mockingbird killer. But it was the whole family, wasn't it? And then Beck, that prick, showed up with her knife and slashed the throat of one of the security guards at the Caldecott School.

Security guard. Just like Mark Daley was a security guard. *Shit!*

This feels like a trap. It was a trap then—Beck wanted to blame the murder on her. But there was no way to really pin it on her, and with the way everything went down, nobody ever turned an eye in her direction because obvious killers were, well, obvious. Now, though, it feels like a noose is tightening gently around her neck.

Something's going on.

She understands none of it.

And yet it's connected. Somehow.

She needs a moment away from the stain, the smell, the shadow of the dead. Miriam storms out of the cabin with Grosky calling after her. She ignores him. Beneath her feet, a carpet of pine needles crunches—they're slippery, and she almost loses her footing as she stomps off into the trees. As she walks, she tries to suss it all out, tries untangling this constricting knot as the wind kicks up around her, stirring the leaves and the needles.

Someone killed Mark Daley. Daley was a security guard at a mall. Divorced. Maybe an abuser. Is that why he's dead? Or is it something else? Whoever killed him knows the words of the Trespasser. And used her knife—or at least a knife just like it, which can't be a coincidence. Can it? And all this is happening—what? How far from the Caldecott School? About two hours east? Another coincidence? And also not far from her home.

An old urge hits her like a brick to the head. Next thing she knows, she's pulling out the pack of Newports that Rita gave her. With hungry hands and trembling fingers, she opens the top and fishes out a cancer stick, plugging in between her lips and then—

She has no lighter.

Goddamnit, she has *no lighter*.

Miriam tries to stifle her cry of frustration and in doing so crushes the end of the cigarette with mashing lips. That just pisses her off even more, and she throws both the cancer stick and the pack into the trees. "Shit! Dick! God! *Fuck.*" She kicks pine needles. She kicks a rock. Her arms pinwheel as she punches the air. Then, panting, she plants her hand on a tree.

And her hand comes away sticky with pinesap.

She turns to look at her palm—it's the same hand she used to throw a rock through ol' Merv's sliding glass doors, the one abraded by the angry volcano rock. And it's scabbed over good.

And now tacky with pine jizz. She growls and tries to wipe the sap off, but it just gets the fingers on her other hand sticky, too, and then she finds a scabby nub, and before she knows it, she's gone and broken that off, and now fresh blood flows—a red balloon blood-bead blowing up, up, up—and something pokes out of the hole, something that must be more scab.

Miriam picks at it, but it's blood-slick and hard to pinch. She uses her nail to scrape at it—

And it's hard, too hard. Not a scab at all. It's sharp. Like bone but softer, like keratin, and she picks, picks, picks at it—each time sending a vibration of pain through her hand. But it's now an obsession, she *has* to get this out, and suddenly she's digging at the skin around it, pushing her finger in around the margins until more blood wells up—

There. She has it. *Pinch, pinch, pinch.* She begins to pull—

She can feel something deep in her hand move. Like the bones are shifting. Pain flashes. Her fingers curl inward like the legs of a dead spider—

From the wound she pulls out something long and slick, fringed on the side. A feather. Not black. Rotten brown and wet with red. It comes, but it keeps coming, and with it come more, clumped together, bundled in a visceral knot. By now the pain is white-hot. It runs to her elbow. She can feel it in her shoulders. Her heart flutters like a caged canary. She keeps pulling.

The wound stretches as something yearns to be born. Miriam grits her teeth and draws it out, out (damn spot!), and soon the whole of her palm is filled with the thing that is working free from inside her hand, and she knows this isn't possible, but that doesn't matter—

A whole bird begins to emerge. Smaller than a crow, bigger than a chickadee. First come the tail feathers. Then the scraping dead claws. Then the fat of its swollen belly and all the way down to its narrow head, until the whole thing is free from her hand. Black blood runs like a waterfall over the side of her palm. It spatters against the mat of needles.

She's holding a dead robin. Orange belly. Brown feathers. Its head has a hole in it. Clean all the way through so you can peek into his skull and out the other side. Its beak hangs open.

Someone whispers over her shoulder:

"Nicely done, killer."

Miriam wheels and throws a fist—

Wham. Grosky's head snaps back and he grunts, staggering back. His hand flies to cup his nose. "Jethus!" he cries, his fingers red with blood. "Whath the fuck."

Miriam looks down at her hand.

No hole. Just the old scabs and a little bit of pinesap.

No dead robin. No feather. No anything.

I'm losing my fucking mind.

"Damn right you are," Grosky says, and she realizes the thing she thinks she thought is actually a thing she said out loud. "Why'd you hit me?"

"I don't know," she lies.

"God*damn*it. Can we just go back into the cabin?"

The cabin. With the death stains. A dead man. Stabbed with a knife like mine . . . That's when she realizes it.

"You," she says. "You're not telling me everything."

"What?"

"Don't *what* me. You know more about what's happening than you're letting on, motherfucker. Back there in the cabin? You weren't surprised it was a knife like the one I used to have. You knew it already! You had that little fact stored up and ready to spring on me like the blade of that knife. Like you're staging the scene for a reality show, like the cameras needed to catch my—"

Surprise.

No. Not cameras.

Suddenly, she's on him like a cloud of mosquitoes. She pats

him down, fishing in his pockets, ignoring the blood still coming out of his bopped nose. He's objecting, trying to get her away, but she knees him hard in the crotch. Grosky *oofs* and doubles over, and that's when she finds it.

It's in the back pocket of his khakis.

"A digital recorder?" she asks, holding it up. It's on right now. Green light, go. He grabs for it uselessly—she juggles it out of his grip as she steps back. "You were recording me."

"Miriam, it's not like that—"

"It's not like what? What is this? A sting? You trying to get me to confess on tape so you can bring the heat down on me?"

"No, I—"

"Fuck that. Fuck this. Fuck *you*." She marches back out of the trees, toward the cabin, toward the lake. Grosky is slow but soon he's behind her, pleading.

"Please, hey, no—that's a good recorder. I spent good money on it."

"I hope you spent enough to get a waterproof model." She gives it a hard throw. The recorder spirals through the air, then *kerploonks* into the lake.

"Shit," he says, hands on his knees, wincing.

"Guess it wasn't waterproof."

"No. It wasn't."

"Give me the keys."

"What?"

"The keys. To your car. I'm going to steal it and then drive away, leaving you here by this smelly lake to think about what you've done."

"No. I'm not gonna—"

"I will beat you so bad you sneeze, piss, and shit blood for a week. The keys. Give them to me."

"Can I explain?"

"No. *Keys*."

"It was for the book, okay! The book. I was never going to name you. I just—I didn't quit the Bureau. I didn't quit. They, they, they fucking fired me."

"Fired you?"

"You remember how I said everybody has their pet theory, but I would never tell the Bureau about all this psychic voodoo horseshit?" He groans. "Yeah, no, I told them. I became obsessed with it. They thought I went off my rocker."

"Maybe you did."

"Maybe I did. But this stuff is real. I can see that. You're the real deal."

"No duh, dumbass." She says it, but in the back of her mind is a growing uncertainty. She's starting to lean into the *It's all just a hallucination from a head injury* theory. A gloriously scary hypothesis that binds all this horror together. And yet, it all feels real, doesn't it? "But I'm not your book. I'm a real person caught up in something I don't understand. You were recording me without my say-so. Ever hear of enthusiastic consent, motherfucker? Never mind the fact you know way more than you're telling me, don't you?"

He swallows hard and nods. "I do."

"You're going to tell me everything."

"Okay."

"But first I need to—" She looks down at her sap-tacky hand. "I need to wash my hands."

She storms back into the cabin.

TEN

THE SECRET LANGUAGE OF MIRRORS

Miriam strides past the stain that once was Mark Daley's inner fluids and heads into the bathroom. It's mostly a closet. The toilet looks like a composting toilet. The sink is a metal bin. She needs to get her damn hands clean, so she spins the faucet.

Blasting hot water comes out. She yelps, pulling her hand back. The knob on the faucet rolls off when she tries to turn it off. Because of course it does.

Steam fills the room.

And then the water gutters and sputters and stops. Whatever tank was supplying it just ran out. *The river ain't rising no more.*

Miriam grumbles and awkwardly wipes her hand on the inside of the sink bowl, trying to get the sap off her palm. Slowly, the steam begins to recede.

When it does, it reveals a message in the mirror. A message written once upon a time with a fingertip, a message lingering in the steamed-up glass.

Two words, all caps:

HEY, PSYCHO.

Miriam throws up in the composting toilet. When she looks up again, the message is still there. Then the steam leaves the room, the mirror un-fogs, and those two words fade away.

She knows her mimic.

INTERLUDE

THE STABBED MAN

Mark Daley is dying. The girl drugged him at the bar, and now here he is, propped up against the wall of his own cabin, bleeding out. He can't move. The drugs, whatever they were, are still in him. All he can do is look down and watch fluids leak out of him like he's a wet sponge being slowly squished.

It's that or watch her. She's still here. Pacing back and forth. Dark hair framing a pale face—the hair dyed in red streaks through the black. White T-shirt. Ragged, blood-spattered jeans. She marches back and forth, back and forth, mumbling, clutching fistfuls of her hair so hard, he thinks she might pull them out. He tries to say something, tries to ask her why, but all that comes out is "Guh." Then something wet splashes down his chin.

She's arguing with somebody, but nobody else is here.

Finally, she gets fed up and storms into the bathroom and washes her hands. Steam wraiths flee through the open door. He hears her writing something on the mirror glass, *squeak, streak, squeak*. Then Mark Daley is staring down into the abyss of his own death. *I probably deserve this,* he thinks, before falling in.

ELEVEN

MURDER BALLADS

Closest place to set up camp is a shitty B&B five miles from the lake, and it's one of those classic B&Bs—the old Victorian house, the Victorian furniture, the named suites (the Gardenia, the Rose Garden, the Mildew and Sadness Special), the one cat for every three steps you take, and of course, the vegan old lady proprietor who will make you a kale omelet for breakfast. They get inside and Miriam tells her that she doesn't want breakfast, Grosky and she are not a couple, and if any one of these four hundred cats touches her, she will throw it out a window. The woman doesn't like any of that and sends them packing.

It's another ten miles down the road to a Best Western straight out of 1976. She makes Grosky get them two rooms. "You snore."

"Fine."

Then she leaves her room and goes to his, and she demands that he tell her everything or she'll cut him up and eat him for breakfast.

He sighs and spills it.

"Mark Daley was drugged. That's why there wasn't a struggle."

Miriam twitches. "Let me guess: ketamine."

"Yeah. How'd you know?"

Because some cuckoo hooker in Colorado dosed me with it. Back when she was on the trail looking for Mary Stitch, she met a woman in the west end of the state who had, well, something of a *fan crush* on Miriam. Melora was her name. Pretended to be Miriam's sister—not in blood but in a strange, cosmic way. Just as Miriam was down under the water in a rushing river, Melora was being drowned in a bathtub by her boyfriend. And there again, all of what's happening now seems a shadow cast by her past: Melora was a fan too. Dressed up in one of those plague doctor bird masks just like the Mockingbird killer.

Boyfriend tried to drown her in a tub.

Louis drowning Samantha in a tub on their wedding night.

Plague doctor mask.

Ketamine.

Cheap-ass spring-loaded knife.

It's like an old, bad song with rhymes and repeated lines. A cruel murder ballad of which she is the subject.

"What else?" she asks him.

"We think this killer's been operating for about three months. And we've already got five people dead."

"Is there any kind of pattern? Who are the victims?"

Grosky sighs. "Mostly men. Mostly white. Wide range of ages. Within a 150-mile radius. Not a lot of traits shared between them beyond that."

"They all die by knife?"

"A couple." He goes through his pack, pulls out some files. "Bob Bender, 44. Trucker. Stabbed through the eye with a fishing knife—"

Like Louis would've died.

Next page. "Danny Stinson, 60, had his throat opened with a pair of—well, they originally said scissors, but Berks County medical examiner said he thought it was a pair of wire cutters."

That's how I killed Carl Keener. The original Mockingbird.

"Then we've got Harley June Jacobs. She's the only lady in the pack. Thirty-seven, shot with a small caliber pistol—.22

by the look of it—right in the ear. Bullet never left her head. Just rattled around in there like dice in a cup, scrambling her brains."

Harriet Adams died when I shot her in the ear. She was a venomous one. Ingersoll's most valued killer. Thought herself cold and clinical, but her cruelty betrayed that, didn't it? Nothing cold about cruelty. Cruelty runs hot.

"Then?" Miriam asks.

"Sims. Wayland Sims, 18. Definitely the most interesting death of the pack, I think. Another neck injury—"

"Let me guess," she says, her stomach churning. "Barbecue fork."

Grosky gives her a look that mirrors the feeling in her guts. "Yeah. And you knew that how?"

"I, ah." Her mouth is dry and she tries to find words. "Story for another time."

I killed a man inside a Long Beach Island store with a barbecue fork to the neck. Man in dark glasses, in all black. A shooter. He was going to take out half the store—and worst of all, he was going to kill Walt the cart-boy, who never said a bad word to anybody. Before he died, that gunman said things to her. *Did the voices send you, too?* he asked. *You're the one always messing with things.*

More rhymes and echoes.

"After that, Mark Daley," he says. "And we're caught up."

She swallows a hard knot, which she's pretty sure is just a bezoar stone of anxiety and calcified fear-barf. "There's something in common. These five died for some reason. It isn't random."

"Serial killings, by their nature, usually aren't."

"But this isn't—" She realizes it's hopeless. Grosky has his world where everything has to fit a certain way: every circle hole gets a square peg, nuance be damned. "Wren isn't a serial killer."

He looks confused, like a bear staring at its own reflection in a mirror. "Wren? Wren who? That girl you told me about, Lauren, uh—"

"Martin. Lauren Martin. Wren. She's the one doing this."

"And you know this how?"

"I don't know it, but I *know* it." She taps her chest. "It's the way things add up. The river is rising? Hey, psycho?"

"What's that? 'Hey, psycho'?"

"It had been written on the mirror. At Daley's cabin."

"And that matters why?"

"It's something she used to say to me."

He leans in. "So, this is a message. To you. You're at the heart of this."

She shrugs. "Seems I'm at the heart of everything, big fella."

"What's next, then? You're the boss. We'll play it how you want to play it. Where do we go? How do we find her?"

"First, we need to figure out how the victims are connected. The cops didn't do it right. They missed something. We start with Daley."

"Okay."

"He had property elsewhere, didn't he? A duplex or something."

"Rents, not owns, but yeah."

She stands up. "Then let's go."

"Can we get a bite to eat first?"

"Really? The fat guy wants to eat?"

"Miriam, people need to actually eat food. It's how we survive. Keeps our metabolism going, our blood sugar even, it fuels our brain—"

"We eat after."

"Fine."

"Fine."

TWELVE

DUPED AT THE DUPLEX

The house is rotting from the bottom up, like the earth is trying to reclaim its materials. The porch at the bottom is crumbling. The powder blue siding is water-damaged and sagging. The flowerbeds are overmulched and shot through with mushrooms. But if you let your gaze tick upward, the house looks okay—it's got a wooden porch split by a wooden rail, with a door on each side indicating that this is, indeed, a duplex: a house split Solomonically in twain, with each half given over to a different owner or renter.

The house sits down a little side avenue stuffed with houses that all look similar: most are one story, on little postage-stamp properties. These aren't poor houses, but these aren't rich houses, either. These are people, Miriam figures, who pay their bills but just barely. A vacation means a fishing day at the lake. A new car means somebody else's old car.

Still, better than how a lot of people live, she figures.

Miriam and Grosky step out of the car and head up to the porch. A centipede dances ahead of her, its feathery legs carrying it swiftly away.

She steps right up, knocks on the screen door. It rattle-bangs in its ill-fitted frame. Grosky gives her a look. "Told you, nobody was here. Guy lived alone."

"Right, I'm just making sure."

"Making sure why?"

"Because we go around back and—" She's about to say *throw a brick through a window*, but the door to the neighboring apartment opens suddenly. Miriam nearly pees herself. "Jesus."

A woman peeks her head out. Older, but not old. Maybe late forties. Her hair looks like a helmet made from broom straw and planted indelicately atop a moonish, freckle-specked face. Her eyes narrow to slits, and her mouth purses.

"Whaddya want," the woman asks.

"Ma'am," Grosky says, but Miriam interrupts him.

"We're cops."

The lady's eyes shut even tighter, like the pinch of a thumb against a forefinger. "You don't look like cops." Pause. "Well, he does. And the cops were already here. I gave them what they wanted."

"What did they want?" Miriam asks.

"Whaddya think they wanted? To look around. Ask a couple questions."

"We're not cop-cops," Miriam says as Grosky gives her a *don't do this* look, a look she returns with her own *I am totally doing this* look. "We're Feds. Like, the Bureau? Grosky and Black. He's Grosky, obviously. I mean, could you imagine me with that name? Ugh, no, thank you. Grosky is the real Fed, and I'm, like, a consultant?"

"Consultant." The woman repeats the word like it's gibberish, like it's a foreign word she doesn't understand.

"Right."

"All right. Fine. You want in his apartment?"

Grosky says, "Ma'am, I don't know that it'll be—"

"Yes," Miriam says. "We want in his apartment."

"I'll get the keys; hold on."

The lady disappears. Grosky hisses, "You're going to get me in trouble."

"You already got fired. There's no trouble deeper than fired."

"There's sued. There's arrested."

"Eh. We'll be fine. I do stupid shit like this all the time."

"Yeah, and it's catching up to—"

The woman is back, coming out of her house like a turtle poking out of its shell. She's got a hunch to her back and a shuffle to her feet even as she pulls a ratty sweatshirt over her shoulders despite the waning summer heat.

The woman takes a painstakingly slow journey down her own steps and around the railing and back up the steps of the neighboring unit. Miriam is tempted to reach out and brush that strawmop hair away from her ear just to get a glimpse of her death. She imagines it's about the dullest death imaginable—a slow, creeping death to match her slothful shuffle—but the desire to see death paraded out in front of her, tawdry and exposed, makes her skin itch with the formicative tingle of insects crawling. Miriam restrains herself. *Now is not the time.* She clears her throat.

"You're the landlord, that right?"

"Uh-huh," the lady says, except with her accent it's more *ehheh*. "Yeah, I rented to Mark," and she goes on and on in this non-story story about who she rented to before that, how there was Pete (no, *Paul*), and before that there was a nice Guatemalan couple, and before that there was this guy and that gal and oh she decided to take her house and turn it into two units because her son said it would be good extra income for her since she lost her job at the Giant Eagle and it's not like she used the whole house anyway since he went away but then he died in Afghanistan and she didn't have nobody anyway since her son's father left her six months after Billy (the son) was born.

By the time she's done with the story, she's fidgeted with the keys and opened the door. Miriam hates this woman and feels bad for her in equal measure. Maybe she hates her because she feels bad for her. She doesn't know. All she knows is that she's pretty sure it makes her a crappy person. Which is not exactly national fucking news, is it? "I'm Debbie," the woman says, the name sounding like the bleat of a hurt animal.

They go inside.

Mark's side of the apartment is spare, like the cabin. IKEA furniture throughout. *Ikea furniture,* Miriam thinks, *for college students and divorced assholes.*

"Shame what happened to Mark," Debbie says, sucking her teeth. "Just a real shame that somebody would do that to him."

"Cops look around much?" Grosky asks.

"Nah," Debbie says, waving it off. "They were in and out pretty quick. Asked me some questions, then done. Mark was quiet. Nice enough. I know he had some trouble, but that's not my business, and I don't know who did what in that story. Sometimes, people deserve what they get."

Irony of ironies, Miriam thinks. Mark hits his wife but maybe she deserved what she got, is what Debbie is saying. Mark then goes and gets stabbed to death, and it's a real shame what happened to him. She wants to go off on this woman. She wants to tell her, *Well, maybe Mark fucking deserved what he fucking got, and maybe he shouldn't hit women*, but she restrains herself.

She mentally marks that as a note of personal growth. *Go me.*

Grosky asks if they can look around, and Debbie says sure, sure. So, they do. They poke and they peek. But there's not much here. The pantry is spare, with a few perishables. The fridge is mostly empty. ("I cleaned it out, didn't want a smell for the next tenant," Debbie explains.) It's a two-bedroom unit. One of the bedrooms is indeed a bedroom. Nothing exceptional here. Nothing under the bed. Naught but clothes in the drawers. The other bedroom is an office with a small glass-top desk, a laptop, and right next to that setup, a treadmill (which is used in the traditional way: to hang clothes).

Miriam opens the laptop screen gingerly and with grave distaste, like she's handling old underpants filled with medical waste. She's had to use computers more and more in this life of hers, and it's irritating every time. They're so obtuse and belligerent, computers. She's happy that the technology is advancing to the point where you can just push a button and yell your desires into a microphone hole so the computer just does whatever the fuck you ask it to do.

Screen ticks on.

Windows Vista.

Password line, empty. Cursor blinking.

Password: *stabbed.*

No.

Password: *deadguy.*

No.

Password: *markdaley123.*

No.

Password: *eatshitanddieyoufuckingmachine23452.*

Also no.

Grosky sidles up next to her. "Lemme get this," he says in a low voice. She shies away from his bulk as he leans in, fingers *ticka-tack*ing across the keyboard so fast, she's pretty sure he might be half-robot.

He narrates what he's doing as he does it. "This is an old piece-of-shit Windows Vista install. Load into safe mode, then just pop open a command line from the start, pull up the username records, then—" Across the screen he types *USERNAME markdaley NEWPASSWORD markdaley*. "Voila."

It logs her in.

Now she's looking at a field full of icons and boxes and blinky things, and she holds up her hands like a poker playing tapping out. "Eeeeeeh."

"You are a real Luddite," Grosky says.

"*You're* a real Luddite."

"You don't know what a Luddite is, do you?"

"Yes." Blink, blink. "No."

"Move over. I'll do this. You keep looking around."

"Fine," she says. "You big *Luddite*."

Debbie seems to regard this exchange with little interest. Miriam strolls up. "This the whole house?"

"'S'also the basement."

"Can I see?"

"Sure, c'mon." She brings Miriam to a door across from the bathroom, which opens to a set of uneven wooden stairs that complain with every step. Debbie flips a switch before they head down, illuminating the basement in the light of a single bare bulb that swings every time she takes a step. Like the rest of the house, not much to look at down here. In the corner is a stack mount of a washer and dryer. Next to that is a set of metal shelves, home only to a few scattered tools. On the other wall is a chest freezer. Miriam scoots over to that.

She flips it open.

Empty. Pink stains in the bottom.

"I threw out what was in there," Debbie says.

"What was in there?"

"Deer meat. Mark was a hunter."

"Bambi," Miriam says. "It's what's for dinner, huh?"

"Yeah." But now Debbie's beady eyes are stuck to her like pins in a voodoo doll. "Yanno, you don't look like a cop."

"Fed. Like I said, a Fed."

Debbie makes a nasal *hmm*. "You don't look like a Fed, neither."

"Fine. Like I said, a *consultant* for the Feds." She does a Vanna White demonstration of her clothing: the classic white T-shirt and knife-slash jeans. "We're, like, the rock stars of the law enforcement world. Creative punks, get to dress how we like, come to work whenever. I'm a rebel, Debbie. A loner."

“Oh. Okay.” Debbie says it not like she’s blowing her off but like that was legitimately enough to pop the flurry of doubt-bubbles in her brain.

Past Debbie, Miriam sees a wooden door in the concrete-block wall. A latch is fixed with a padlock. “What’s that?”

“That’s a door.”

“Yes, Debbie, I gathered that it was a door. I didn’t think it was art.”

“That’d be neat art, though. Clever.”

“Very,” Miriam says, smiling in a feral, overwrought way that says, *I am not smiling but I have to make this face in order not to bite your head clean off your slumpy shoulders.* “What lies *beyond* that door, Debbie?”

“My basement.”

“Ah. Okay. So, Mark didn’t have access to that.”

“Oh, sure he did.”

“He did? But it’s your basement.”

“Sure, sure, but you know, it’s, ah, it’s fine. It’s no big thing.”

There. Debbie’s eyes flash like moonlight on pond water. That’s fear. Miriam likes fear. Fear is an injury. It’s like a bullet hole—you find it, you can stick your thumb in there and press until you get a reaction.

“Debbie, did the officers look in there?”

“I . . . I don’t recall.” She’s no longer meeting Miriam’s eyes. She’s watching her own feet. Her fingers pluck at other fingers like she’s a spider tending to a damaged web.

“They didn’t.”

“I don’t remember. Maybe they did.”

“Debbie. Between you and me, I’m just a consultant. I don’t have any real authority. So, you let me in on whatever you’re hiding, and I can’t do anything about it, and I won’t tell anyone. But if I have to drag my Fed friend down here, and he has to drag the cops back out here—probably at a late hour—it’s gonna get messy. You don't want to end up in prison. Nobody would rent this place." Now for the final press of the thumb: "What would your son think?"

Debbie looks up. New fear glints in her eye, electric and alive—she's now more afraid of the consequences of not speaking up. Good. *Spill it, Deb.*

"I . . . I know it's not right, what I did."

"Go on."

"The arrangement Mark and I had—it's off the books, okay?"

"Yep, waaaaaay off the books. What arrangement?"

Debbie sighs. Tears glint in her eyes. "C'mon, I'll show you."

Out comes the key ring and she finds the one that corresponds to the padlock. She pops the lock and it drops against the cement, *thud*. The door swings open and what awaits is a basement that is nearly the mirror image of this one, with one chief difference—

"It's the HVAC system," Debbie says, pointing to a monstrous furnace sitting against the back wall.

Miriam's guts clench. Mark was burning stuff in here. Evidence. Bodies. Debbie helped.

This is why Mark died, isn't it? With the somberness of a confessional priest she says, "Debbie, tell me about the furnace."

"Mark maintained it."

"Okay."

"I know that's not right."

"Okay."

"It's an oil furnace—I know, I know, global warming." Her voice almost breaks. "He said he knew a little bit about these things, about how to change the filter and do the dampers and I . . . I don't even understand it, but he did the maintenance on it, and I only have the one system in here for two houses." Her eyes shine now and she blinks back tears. "It's not up to code, I know."

"Oh . . . o . . . kay."

"Am I in trouble?"

"For what?"

"For just having one system. In two houses. For the code."

"What fucking code?"

"The building code."

"Debbie," Miriam hisses, "I don't give a dildo about building codes! Is this what you were hiding?"

"Yes," Debbie says, somehow both penitent and reverent, as if this confession has cleared the baggage of sin from her wayward soul. "Of course."

"Jesus tits," Miriam says with her jaw so tight, she's afraid it might freeze that way. "Debbie, nobody, and I mean nobody in the whole wide stupid world, cares about building codes or, or, or your HVAC bullshit. Did Mark do anything with the furnace? Anything untoward?"

"Like, sex?"

"What? Sex? Nobody has sex with furnaces. That's not even a thing. I mean did he have bodies down here or ever a strange smell or—"

Hold up.

What's that?

"What's that?"

Debbie follows Miriam's finger. There, on a set of metal shelves—similar to the ones in the other side—sits a lock box.

"It's a box."

It's a door. It's a box. "I see that. What's in it?"

"I don't know; it's Mark's."

"Open it."

"I said it's Mark's. I don't have the key."

Miriam growls, "Fine, I'll open it." She storms over, finds another padlock on it—this one is tiny, like a padlock an elf might use to hide his stash of precious tree cookies—and she takes the flimsy metal box and slams it again and again padlock-side first against the metal shelf.

With each hit, Debbie cries out, startled.

Takes ten tries, but the padlock pops off like a broken tooth from a ruined jaw. When it does, the box opens in Miriam's hand.

Photographs spill out.

Miriam doesn't have to pick them up to see the faces of girls, teenagers, staring up at her. They're not nude. They're not sexual. Some look like yearbook shots cut out. Others look like photographs taken from between hedgerows or behind trees—they contain that green blur of intruding foliage.

"I don't know what those are," Debbie says. Way she says it tells Miriam it's true—she isn't nervous about it. Bewildered, maybe.

Just in case, she sets down the box and reaches out and touches her. Debbie isn't paying attention and fails to flinch away. Miriam brushes her fingers against Debbie's cheek and then—

THIRTEEN

DEBBIE DOES DEADTOWN

*The clot of store-brand mac and cheese lodges inside Debbie's throat like a golf ball in a pool filter, and she shudders and makes four sounds—*Hkk! Hkkaaa! Rrrk! Urrr!*—before her lips go purple and she sees her son sitting across from her at the kitchen table, his skull blown open but a warm smile on his face as he opens his arms to welcome her, and then Debbie faceplants, dead.*

FOURTEEN

YOU'RE ALL I WANT, MY FANTASY

Debbie looks at Miriam's hand like it's a moth, and she bats at it.

"Sorry," Miriam says. Her sadness for Debbie finally outweighs her disdain. Debbie dies choking on a glob of mac and cheese. It happens in six years. Right before Thanksgiving. Sad and alone and seeing her dead son as she goes. But at least there are no secrets there. Death exposes secrets, she finds. Whatever you thought would stay hidden somehow comes out in those moments—either in how you go or in what you say when you do. Debbie had none. Debbie had—and has, by the looks of it—nothing. Poor fucking Debbie.

Miriam clears the image out of her mind and looks down again at the photos. Here comes Grosky now, hurrying down the steps and calling out her name before seeing them through the secondary doorway connecting the two basements.

"What's going on?" he asks, and because she's a judgmental shitbird, Miriam expects him to be out of breath but he's totally not. "I heard banging and . . ." His eyes drift downward to the photos. "Whoa."

"Mark had access to the whole basement," Miriam explains. "This was a box of his." She begins to scoop up the photos. The ones she turns over are more of the same: teen girls. Dozens of them. All different. No duplicates. "Some boys collect baseball cards. Mark had a different collection."

Debbie says, "I didn't know nothing about any of this. I swear."

"We know," Miriam says. To Grosky: "Find anything?"

"Yeah. Maybe. We'll see."

They leave Debbie behind, telling her someone will be in touch, even though nobody will.

FIFTEEN

FUTURE DEAD GIRLS

They spend the next day at the Best Western, going over a list Grosky found on Mark Daley's laptop. No printer was connected, so Grosky snapped a pic with his phone.

It's a list of addresses. No names.

Miriam watches shitty nighttime—and then daytime—TV as Grosky runs background checks on all the addresses. She asks him if this is some kind of FBI privilege he should have had revoked, and he just laughs, tells her, "No, anybody can do background checks on other people, long as you know the right websites and pay the money."

By noon the next day, she's asleep again. He wakes her.

"The addresses match," he says.

"Wuzza? Huh?" Her mouth is tacky with night-spit.

"The addresses. They belong to the girls." He sits down on the edge on the bed, which irritates her. "Each of the addresses belongs to people who are parents, who have kids in school. A good number of them I was able to pull up through Instagram or Facebook because kids post selfies all the time, and they leave a pretty wide digital trail. Wasn't hard to match up a good number of these addresses to these girls."

She sits up against the pillow, blinking sleep from her eyes. "They dead?"

"Not a one of them. All alive. Three of them go to school with his daughter, Patty, and his son, Jason. And one of them—" He pulls a photo of a young girl who looks like a millennial version of Marcia from the Brady Bunch. "One of them *is* his daughter. This is Patty."

"He had a photo of his own daughter in a locked box with other photos of similarly aged girls."

"Uh-huh. Some of the photos looked like they were taken at the DuBois Mall, from behind planters or pillars."

"He took some of the photos himself."

"Seems to be, though no way to confirm."

She blinks. "He was going to hurt those girls. Maybe kill them."

"We don't know that, but a guy takes photos of girls like this, in this way, with a repeated pattern, it's a good bet he was at least thinking about doing something nasty."

"Wren killed him to stop him."

"You don't know that."

"I know me. And I know that all this feels like me."

"It's a stretch."

"Only if you don't understand what it's like. And I understand."

He shrugs it off. "What's next?"

"We wait. We watch. We find her."

PART THREE

TRESPASSERS

SIXTEEN

HOME IS WHERE THE HEART IS, PROBABLY IN A BOX OR MAYBE A JAR

Miriam goes home.

Home-home. The house on Dark Hollow Road. She tells Grosky no reason to spend money on crap-ass dick-suck hotels when they can just install themselves in a house that she owns. One of two houses, in fact. This one, the Pennsylvania house.

The house of her youth.

(The house where everything went to shit.)

This house, Evelyn had been leasing to her wayward brother, Jack, until Miriam had him kicked out. Now she's got the house opened anew. This house of odd angles. Of cobwebs clinging to the corners like recalcitrant ghosts. Of that smell of mildew and wood dust and the faint perfume of her mother still lingering in the air like an improbable memory. She finds a dead mouse in the kitchen. A pile of dead carpenter ants in the sink. A dead bird outside, near the living room window, the glass cracked where the bird must have flown into it, aggressively chasing its own dumb reflection. *Nicely done, killer.*

They set up shop there for a month.

Grosky stays in her mother's old room, pecking away at his book, keeping an eye on police scanners for Wren. Miriam stays downstairs, on the couch, swaddled in dusty old crocheted afghans like a colorful mummy.

Nothing worth a good goddamn happens.

Miriam haunts the house at night and sleeps during the day. She sometimes takes Grosky's car and trolls the highways, expecting . . . what, exactly? That she'll pass by some old bus stop or driveway and see Wren standing there, waving?

Sometimes, the Trespasser is there. Just as she haunts the house, the Trespasser haunts her head. But not like he usually does. The motherfucker never shows up right in her face—no twisted set pieces, no drawn-out roleplaying dioramas of nightmare fuel where her snatch is sewn up or her eyes are plucked out so blackbirds can be stuffed in the holes. The Trespasser is only there in glimpses now. Pass by a painting in the hallway and she can see his reflection—sometimes he's Louis, sometimes he's Ben Hodge. She's seen him standing outside on the lawn as she walks past a window. He's been in the woods. He's been in the rearview mirror of the car. Never says a word.

Often, though, he's smiling.

Like he knows something she doesn't.

That curdles her blood, like vinegar in milk.

She stops drinking. No wine, no booze. Just to be sure what's real and what's not. Her body rejects her rejection, and for days she feels headachy and shaky, so she switches to coffee, and it works. Coffee is the blunderbuss that blasts away the fog of withdrawal. It also wires her. Eyes wide. Fingers vibrating such that it feels like she could reach into the walls and pull apart the very molecules of reality. It keeps her alert. Hypervigilant. Persistently in a fight-or-flight-but-really-probably-fight mode. Good. She needs it.

It helps her, too, find birds out there in the woods, beyond the house. Sparrows and turtledoves and catbirds with their mocking mewls. Titmice (teehee) and nuthatches (ha-ha) and woodpeckers (okay who the fuck decided to name all these birds it's getting embarrassing). She finds vultures wheeling in the sky. Hawks perched on the hunt. Owls silently stalking the dark.

It feels like progress but it isn't progress. It's just killing time. A hobby. All while nothing happens.

Nothing until the first Tuesday in October.

Then everything goes to shit.

SEVENTEEN

THAT TUESDAY

On that Tuesday, a dead body turns up in Schuylkill County. A white supremacist biker who goes by the inauspicious name of Tuggy Bear is found with a gunshot through his heart and a nasty bite from a chainsaw running across his face, starting at the lower left jaw and ending above his right eye. Grosky says it doesn't sound like something a young girl could manage, but Miriam says, "Fuck you, dude, you have no idea what we 'girls' can do. We wanna kill a man with a chainsaw, we kill a man with a chainsaw." She doesn't tell him that on the chase to find Mary Stitch, she ended the life of a wild-eyed meth-cook by the name of Johnny Tratez by knocking him into his own spinning chainsaw blade.

Together, she and Grosky—who's now sporting a patchy writer beard, which she figures is the result of him being a lazy-ass more than a literary up-and-comer—look at the map they've got taped to the living room wall. He's got red Sharpie dots where the last five were killed, and it shows a clear progression across the state from east to west—Easton, PA, to Wilkes-Barre, to Williamsport, to Lock Haven, to Falls Creek where they found potential future rapist or killer Mark Daley punctured like a pincushion.

But this newest death breaks the pattern. If Wren—and Miriam thinks that it is Wren—continued with the pattern, she should hew closer west, maybe near Pittsburgh. The death of Tuggy Bear (aka Donald Tuggins) is in Pottsville, which is back east. Closer to where it all began.

Grosky says, "Isn't her."

Miriam says, "I think it is."

"Tuggins was a career criminal. The other five weren't, outside a few misdemeanors."

"What'd Tuggins do?"

"What didn't he do? Guy's got a rap sheet with more pages than the King James Bible, and almost as nasty. He ran with a biker gang, the Devil Kings, and they sold both meth and that new synthetic heroin that's going around. He's a driver, a legbreaker, an all-around poison pill. And likely one who got got by one of his own—that's how these things usually go."

"When people like me are involved, how things 'usually go' ain't how they end up actually happening."

Grosky scratched his beard. "People like you?"

She taps her head. "Uh-huh. Mind-readers. Fate-breakers." *Head cases.*

"You think Wren is like you now."

"Maybe. It makes sense."

Anybody who manifests some cursed power or another gets there through trauma. Mary Stitch told her that. Even Eleanor Caldecott said it: *Power and wisdom are born of trauma.* And Miriam tends to have a ripple effect. First Ashley. And now Wren. Lauren Martin dragged to her own drowning by the wretched witch Eleanor Caldecott—that would tweak anybody's gourd.

Miriam's left to wonder, what's driving Wren? What cursed power is bleeding from her broken brain? Can she see death, like Miriam can?

She feels grotesquely responsible. *I entered her life and ripped her apart like a Kleenex.* Sure, Miriam also saved her life. But to what end? She saved her just to damn her. Just as Miriam was herself saved, in a way. *Maybe better to die than to be this.* Her heartbeat spikes and she quickly has to shove these dark thoughts away, lest that old specter rise again: the one that sings songs of ending it all to be spared the curse. A curse she hates.

Or maybe a curse she hates to love.

"This is her work," Miriam says, throwing on a hoodie over her T-shirt and grabbing Grosky's keys off the counter. "She's nearby."

"Where are you going?"

"Out" is all she says. Grosky would want to come. She can't have him along. This is her cross to bear, she decides.

She feels energized. Wren is close, she can feel it: a gossamer spider thread undulating in the wind. If only she could reach out and grab it. But she's guideless—she drives the hour to Pottsville, then has no idea what to do next. Pottsville has the earmarks of an old coal town that got too big for its britches. All the white brick, red brick, brown brick. Rust on metal. Cracks in sidewalks.

All around, too, she spies graffiti: FUCK THE COPS. The number 88. A swastika. The anarchist's brutal A. Most of it has been painted over with white, then painted over with new graffiti, the ongoing war of the artist versus the authority, the vandal versus the censor.

She drives around and around, not knowing what she's looking for. The crime scene was at a biker bar on the north side of town, and she drives there but there's still a cop car in the lot, and she figures if Wren's on camera and Wren looks like Miriam, maybe it's not the hottest idea to go waltzing in. Her normal pluck would have her doing exactly that, but things feel more fragile, more precious, like there's somehow more at stake that she fails to truly understand. That deserves the thing she's very bad at:

Caution.

So, instead, she parks the car a few miles away in the lot of some old defunct strip mall, and she screams and punches the steering wheel and cries.

(And eventually asks herself, *Am I drinking too much coffee?* It feels like all her particles will soon dissociate and she'll turn into vapor.)

(So, yeah, maybe she's drinking too much coffee.)

Her phone rings and she jumps. Her thumb is faster than her eyeballs. She answers it, thinking it's Grosky.

But across the caller ID screen she sees one name:

Louis.

Shit shit shit shit.

She gets it together, then brings the phone to her ear. Way too chirpily she says, "Hey, you." *Stupid.* She immediately injects a darker attitude: "What?" *Damnit that's not right, either.* "Uh."

"Miriam," Louis says, the softness of his voice betrayed by the urgency of its tone. "We need to talk."

"Cutting right to the chase," she says. "I admire that."

"I'm nearby," he says.

Wait, what? Her heartbeat spikes as adrenaline and cortisol throttle her with separate hands. She's fighting just how badly she wants to take flight straight into Louis's big cannon-sized arms. It makes her feel small and stupid and yet, the heart wants what the heart wants, and right now her heart wants to kung-fu kick its way out of her breastbone and leap toward him.

"How are you nearby? Are you stalking me, weirdo?"

"No—I just—I know where you live? Remember? I thought we could catch up at that same diner we met last time, the one where you met Samantha."

"That's in Florida."

He hesitates. "Yeah, I know. Aren't you . . . Oh."

"I'm not there, Louis. I'm sorry. I'm in Pennsylvania."

"Oh. Hell. I just figured—"

"With me, never figure anything. Always assume you're wrong

about whatever it is you think when it regards my narrow ass."

He laughs, even though she means it as genuinely serious advice. "I can be up there in a couple days."

"You on the road again?"

"I am, but this is on vacation."

"Samantha with you?" *Samantha, who you will strangle and drown in, oh, about five months?* "I don't know if I want to—"

"No. She's not here. It's not that kind of vacation. I needed time off. I need to see you. It's . . . it's about her."

"What does that mean?"

"I need to show you something."

She presses the phone to her chest and cranes her head back. She whispers a scream to the roof of the car. Then, back into the phone: "Fine. Be up here in a couple days. I'm dealing with stuff up here, so—"

"From your mother's estate?"

"Sure." *We can go with that.*

"I can help."

"You can't help with this." And she doesn't want to drag him in, either. Though a venomous part of her bites back: *You're culpable, Louie, given that you were the one who dove into that river to save Wren and me.* And then her middle tightens with sudden, renewed desire, and under her neck and at her wrists she feels blooms of heat. She wants him here. No—she wants him. Period. She wants him on top of her, around her, behind her, inside of her. "Just be here."

She hangs up.

And screams in her car. Then laughs. Then cries. Then wonders just what the hell is happening, and what she thinks she's doing.

EIGHTEEN
HEADLIGHTS IN THE DARK

Night and the lonely road.

She doesn't find Wren because she has no way to find Wren. It was a delusion to think differently. Miriam feels wired and tired in equal measure. Feels like a body without its skin—raw, cold, bleeding. Every thud of her heart felt keenly across every inch of her. She starts to think, *Just let it all go. You don't owe anybody any part of this.* But she does. She's responsible. Is this what being an adult feels like? It's gross. She wants to drink and smoke and fuck some rando and eat a whole bag of Skittles before hitchhiking on to the next place. That was her life once, and she hated it. But she misses it, too.

Because in its own way, it was easy.

But this? This isn't easy.

Caring. Feeling obligated. Having a heart that isn't a wicker basket full of dead birds. Ugh. *So* not worth it.

Darkness settles into the trees all around her. Oaks and pines. Thoughts of Louis stalk her like prey, and she has to keep ducking and running away from her own brain lest those thoughts catch her, pin her, consume her.

She pulls onto Dark Hollow Road—

And a car pulls in behind her.

Headlights like monster eyes. A new predator in pursuit. This one real.

It's silly. It's paranoid. Cars can drive on public roads. And Dark Hollow has other houses on it. The road doesn't end in a wall—it goes on to other roads, as roads are wont to do. It's only 9 PM. If it were 3 AM and some car were tailing her onto her road, she should be worried. This? Not so much.

And yet she's worried.

It's the coffee. And the lack of sleep. And Wren, and Louis and, and, and—she feels like she's tiptoeing across a tightrope, and on one side is spiders and on the other side is sharks. And it's windy. And the rope is on fire at both ends.

She pulls ahead to the house. Her mother's house—a tall, dark sentinel standing vigil against the forest.

The car behind her slows.

It strikes her: *I don't have a weapon.* She always has a weapon. A knife. A gun. A brick. Something. What does she have now? Miriam's been so confuzzled over everything, she's missing things. Bits are slipping through her fingers like earthworms struggling to escape a handful of dirt. She quick-searches around Grosky's sedan but finds nothing—no gun under the seat, no knife in the cup-holder, no grenade belt in the glove compartment. *Fucking Grosky.*

The car drives up, and she thinks: *Keep going, keep going, keep going.*

The car turns into the driveway behind her.

Miriam kicks open the sedan door and launches herself out of it, striding toward the boxy-looking Buick pulling in behind her. Her eyes flit to the side of the driveway, where she spots a rock, palm-sized but jagged, like something one caveman could use to open the head of a second caveman. She lopes to the side, snatches it up, and marches toward her new enemy with grim purpose. She raises it high, ready to smash a windshield, ready to crush a skull—

Both doors to the Buick pop open. Shadows step out—because

with the headlights staring her down, that's all she can see. Dark shapes. Demons.

Then a voice comes out of the night. One she recognizes. One she hates that she recognizes.

"Hey, killer."

Uncle.

Fucking.

Goddamn.

Lanky-strip-of-turd-jerky.

Jack.

NINETEEN

CRACKS IN THE GLASS

They sit in the living room. Her, Jack, and Jack's lawyer.

Uncle Jack has tried to clean himself up a little for this meeting, it seems, which is a bit like a chimpanzee putting on a suit and pretending he's not a chimpanzee. He's stuffed his long length-of-rope body into an overstarched white button-down with tobacco spit stains on the collar and sleeve. The tie that hangs from his neck is an ugly maroon thing. A lumpy knot keeps the thing too short, and the accessory lies across his belly like the lazy, panting tongue of a Labrador with heat stroke.

It's the lawyer she's watching. Stumpy prick in a corduroy suit, his head so round he deserves to be in the Peanuts gang with Charlie Brown and Linus. He's got a thin pencil sketch of a mustache and eyebrows that look so thick and so rough, you might want to use them to clean shit off your boot. Pale, too. The pale of a grub that has lived its entire life so far in the bark of a rotting tree.

"Young lady," Jack says, all fakey-fakey proper-like. "As I said, this is my lawyer, Mr. Diamond—"

"Diamond," Miriam repeats, failing to repress a snort-laugh. "Oh, damn. That's rich. You guys are aware that irony is alive and well, right. I mean, this is textbook irony. You could teach it in English class."

Jack looks confused. The lawyer adjusts his tie and tries to sit up straight. "I do not understand your point," he says all too crisply, and Miriam imagines them as children standing on one another's shoulders while stuffed in Daddy's overcoat. This isn't the kind of lawyer you find at an office. This is the kind of lawyer you find advertised on a bus. Or you find peeing in the parking lot of a local bar.

"I mean that the word *diamond* evokes something pristine, something clean and precious," she says, sneering. "You, on the other hand, look like the opposite of that. You look like a goblin who just bathed in a toilet. You look less like a gem and more like a squirrel's afterbirth. Hence: irony."

The lawyer shrivels at that, but ignores it when he says, "My client—"

"Jack is not a client. And you're not a lawyer. This is a sham."

"My *client* informs me you're the executor of the Evelyn Black estate."

"That is correct," she saws, jaw tight. "Executor and executioner."

"My client—"

"Uncle Dick-turd."

"—*Jackson Black* feels that he is owed a portion of the estate, as Evelyn's brother. And as her loyal and loving brother—"

"You mean as a sucking leech stuck to her side, milking her blood like the human parasite that he always was?"

"He feels that he is owed at least twenty-five percent of the estate—"

"I'd counter that he is owed twenty-five percent of my dick," Miriam says.

"*And failing that*, he will gladly take possession of this house as recompense. Given the hostility here, we feel we have no recourse but to sue."

Jack's face fails to hide his delight at this. A greasy smirk on his face lifts and separates the hairs of his knotty, grotty goatee.

"What's all this?" says Grosky coming up from behind.

"Grosky," Miriam says. "This is my mother's brother, my dear Uncle Jack. And this is the poop he pooped out this morning, a poop he has hired as his legal representation on this Earth, a 'lawyer'"—here she does dramatic air quotes—"whose last name is, I kid you not, *Diamond*."

"You need help down here?" the once-agent asks her.

"Aw, Grosky, that's sweet you think I need help handling my business."

He shrugs in response.

Jack leans in and says, "Well, young lady, did you find yourself a man? He's a bit older than you, little out of shape, but it's nice to see."

She curls her lip, stands up with her chin out and her fists back. Miriam hisses: "Jack, Grosky could run a hundred laps around you before you manage to get your bony ass out of that chair. His asshole literally contains more brain cells than your actual brain." Once again, she feels like she's vibrating, like the mitochondria in all her cells are singing a single humming, thrumming hymn to her exasperation. In the noise of her mind, something else pings it—a sensation scratching at the top of her awareness.

"We will take you to court to resolve this—" the so-called lawyer starts to say, but she clacks her teeth at him and holds up a finger.

"Don't interrupt me. Here's how this is going to go. You're going to sit there thinking you have some way to pry coins out of my mother's dead hand, and I'm going to tell you a secret. Are you ready for my secret, Uncle Jack?"

"You're a lezzie? Always kinda wondered—"

"I control birds with my mind."

Pause for effect.

The reaction is predictable. Jack looks shocked. Diamond gives her a look like she's cuckoo canary crazy. Then the both of them laugh, unsure if it's a joke or some special brand of lunacy.

“Miss,” Diamond says, trying to compose himself. “This mockery of our request will not distract from—”

She silences him by holding up three fingers.

Then she takes one away: two fingers.

Her eyes look to the living room window—the one with the cracked glass where a small bird hit it. Then her eyes roll back in her head.

She finds what touched her mind out there in the black.

Two fingers become one, and then none.

Jack starts to say something—

The living room window shatters inward. Jack shrieks. Diamond cries out and hunkers down like he's on a crashing airliner, head between his knees, hands over his head. Even Grosky startles.

Miriam doesn't. Because she's riding the owl when it hits the glass. Her mind is inside its mind. She is with it in the trees. She is with it as it takes flight. She wills it to find the glinting, flashing rectangle of light that is the glass window. The owl is a great horned owl, bigger than a red-tailed hawk, aggressive, angry, a female bigger than her male counterparts, and, to boot, a mighty hunter of the night who swoops on silent wing—

Now she's inside. The bird wants to freak out, going through the glass like that, but she fills it with sinister calm and determined rage. Miriam splits her consciousness between herself and the bird (*hey, I can do that?*) as it lands atop the lawyer's head, talons clawing their way across his slimy comb-over. Then it leaps to Jack, wings beating him about the head and neck, *whumpf whumpf whumpf*. He bats at it, but the owl doesn't give a shit. The owl scrapes and scrabbles, fluttering her wings—

And then Miriam lets her go, sending her back out the open, broken window. She glides effortlessly away, making nary a sound.

The chaos in its wake is glorious. The lawyer paws at his head, his hands coming away red with blood. Jack's still swatting at his own hair as if the owl remains upon him. And Grosky just stands there with eyes as big as his open mouth, staring out after the owl. Glass everywhere. Blood spattered.

She snaps her fingers. Diamond looks up, shell-shocked, blood streaking down his face in ruddy red rivulets.

"Get out," she barks. "And you ever contact me again with any of this horseshit, I will have your eyes pecked out by hummingbirds."

They hurry out of the house.

Her house.

Miriam feels like a god.

TWENTY
CHASING SHADOWS

The high doesn't last. Sending Jack and his lawyer on their way fuels her only for so long, and then it's time to settle into the realization that she doesn't know what she's doing or where to go next. Even finding Mary Stitch seemed easier, somehow—there she had leads. But finding Wren isn't just a needle-in-a-haystack scenario: it's trying to find a sewing needle in a pile of hypodermics. One will help her tie the thread. The rest will just stick her.

She spends two days barely sleeping. She and Grosky are on full alert, listening to local police scanners, and him getting tips from back in the Bureau. Into the second day, they send along a traffic cam photo from a stoplight about a quarter-mile from the bar where Donald "Tuggy Bear" Tuggins got chainsawed.

Grosky turns his laptop toward her.

Her guts go into her throat.

It's like looking in a mirror. An alternate-reality mirror.

It's her from five, ten years ago. Walking on the shoulder of the road as cars pass her by. Got that rangy, coyote walk that she used to have (maybe still has)—a young Miriam Black, stalking the highways, stealing from the dead. Even with the heavily pixelated image, she can see the same hungry glare. But this glare is not of a scavenger but of a hunter. This Miriam is already weaponized. This Miriam isn't opportunistic. This version of her is already a killer—one who has preconfigured her grim purpose.

She holds her hand over her mouth. "That's her."

That's me.

Grosky stares at her as she stares at the image. "She looks like you."

"I know. She used to have red hair." Now it's all dyed black except for a few streaks of red. "The hell happened to her, Grosky?"

He looks to his laptop, starts summing up what he sees there. "Lauren Martin. Now age fifteen. Father on record hasn't been a part of her life since she was born. Mother was a heroin addict, left her in an apartment. State eventually assumed custody, and the Caldecott School became her home at age ten."

"Yeah, and Eleanor Caldecott, alongside her brood of murder-maggots, was using the school to weed out 'bad girls' like Annie Valentine and Wren, killing them before they could be inflicted upon the world."

Eleanor Caldecott could see things too. The gift, she called it. It was her ability to see not how a person died but the consequences of how they lived. Annie Valentine was a girl who would leave a swath of human wreckage in her wake, and so through the Mockingbird, Eleanor had her killed—an agent of the goddess Atropos, snipping threads of fate so that destiny was changed, changing the future by murdering the present. Even now, Miriam tries to avoid the discomfort of thinking herself somehow like the Caldecott witch. What Eleanor did was active. She hunted girls, "bad" girls, to kill them. Miriam is passive: she sees when someone is going to die, and then she tries to save them—and sometimes, *sometimes* that means killing a killer. She tells herself that what she does is purer somehow. Smaller. Cleaner.

Sometimes, though, she's not so sure. Eleanor thought what she was doing was the right thing, too. Caldecott talked of cancer inside the body and how, to save the body, sometimes you had to remove an organ or cut off a limb. A grander, greater, colder view of the universe.

What is Wren's view of the universe? She's fifteen. How does she justify what she's doing? What is her so-called gift?

Then, out of the dark, more words of Eleanor rise up.

Of Wren, Eleanor said to Miriam: *You are a part of her life. You are just one more piece of her wreckage. Because of Lauren Martin, a piece of you will one day go missing.*

Another proclamation. Ripples from a rock thrown in water.

Grosky keeps talking, shaking Miriam from her morose reverie. "Thing is, after you came through the place like a wrecking ball, the Caldecott School—and its three sister schools, Woodwine, Bell Athyn, Breckworth—all shut down."

"You say that like it's my fault."

"It is. Strictly speaking."

"Grosky, I saw a greenhouse full of jars. And in those jars were tongues. Tongues taken from girls that Eleanor Caldecott deemed too poisonous to live. Had to be fifty, sixty jars there. Tell me, the cops ever find that?"

"They did."

"It ever hit the news?"

"Nope. The Caldecott family proper was wiped out, but they still had a legacy to protect, and family from overseas made sure that legacy was preserved. It's why I'm writing this book. Because it's frustrating. Power, money, legacy. All that protects the worst people."

"So, fine, whatever, the Caldecott legacy is preserved even as the schools are shuttered. Where'd the girls go? The ones who went there."

"The ones who could pay went on to other fancy schools."

"And the ones who couldn't?"

"Whisked away to foster care."

Her nostrils flare as the insomniac edge of sleeplessness threatens to drag her down. "And let me guess: Wren did not go to foster care."

"She was assigned a family, and a bus picked her up. But when they stopped to get gas, she hotfooted it out the back."

"And that's the last we see of her."

He nods. "Bingo."

"And all we have now is this photo of her on the side of the road."

"Also true."

"Shit."

"Yeah."

She leans back, grinding her teeth. "How do we find her?"

"Let's talk it through."

"I'd rather use magic."

"Do you have that kind of magic?"

"No."

"Then let's talk it through. She's a fifteen-year-old girl, Miriam. How's a girl like that survive on the street?"

Miriam sighs. "Same way I did, probably. She's picking from the dead."

"Okay, good. Could she be using the vics' credit cards?"

"I did sometimes. Small purchases, so as not to draw any attention."

"All right. I'll flag those. And she's gotta be staying somewhere. Right?"

"Unless she dissipates into a vampiric mist every night, yeah. I stayed at dogfuck motels when I could afford it. Sometimes, I spent nights under overpasses or in abandoned cars—you'd be amazed at how many abandoned cars are out there. Sometimes, I'd sleep in the woods. And other times . . ." Her voice dies in her throat.

"Other times what?"

"I'd shack up with randos."

"At that age?"

"I hit the road at sixteen but didn't start fucking strangers until . . . maybe seventeen, eighteen years old. But yeah."

"You think Wren is doing the same?"

"I have no idea what she's doing. But if she's somehow inadvertently or purposefully echoing what I did, then yeah."

Grosky nods. "That's another angle, then. Look, she's on foot—"

"I hitchhiked my ass up and down the highway, too."

"Even still, she doesn't have a car of her own. She's not going far. We'll look for reports of her. We'll ping the system, see if those cards are getting used. See if we can get a look at anybody she might be with or have been with."

"Jesus."

"We're closing in."

"If you say so."

"Hey, I want to say thanks."

She arches an eyebrow so high, she's pretty sure it must be floating above her head. "Listen, I think it's great you wanna live a life of gratitude, but I'm not sure I deserve any of it."

"The other day with your Uncle Jack? You said something nice about me."

She *ennhs* at him. "I said some things that were not explicitly cruel."

"For you, that's pretty nice."

"Fair point."

"So, thanks."

"Don't tell anybody, Grosky, but I think you're all right."

"Can you say that again? I'd like to broadcast it across Twitter."

"I don't know what that means."

"Never mind. Get some sleep."

She nods, tells him okay.

But she doesn't really sleep. She just rolls and tumbles around her mother's bed, sweating, freezing, feeling her heart beating in her neck, her wrists, her teeth, her toes. When sleep finds her in fits and starts, it drags her down into deep, dark water, where hands of wet weeds slide around her neck, and her mouth opens and water fills her throat as she gags on mud, blood and a dead girl's hair.

TWENTY-ONE

ONE BLACK FEATHER

It's nearly evening. She waits for him at a little coffee joint: not some fancy micro-roaster, not some hipster pour-over cafe, but a shack off the highway that's just a counter and a brutish bulldog lady who pours you coffee, maybe serves you up a slice of pie from local Amish bakers. In this case, it's Miriam with a cup of black coffee and the remnants of half a shoo-fly pie. Not half a slice. Half a pie.

The doorway out has a window, and a shape darkens it—a big shape, tall and broad and with the bulk of Frankenstein's monster.

It feels like she's falling through the floor. Everything rushes up around her even as it stays still. The blood in her ears is a river as Louis steps in.

He's the same. And he's different. Hair a little longer now. Stubble gone to a soft, short beard. Like he's some kind of lumberjack. Her jaw tightens as saliva wets her mouth.

Only other person in the six-table joint is an old man whose entire body looks like a sand castle half-eroded by the sea. So, it doesn't take Louis long to zero in on her and pull up a chair. She thinks to stand and hug him, but mostly, she's paralyzed by her awkwardness. *How do I react?* Her first urge is to climb him like a ladder, drop him to the ground, and fuck him till he's dry. Her second urge is to revisit the not-yet-happened image of him choking the life out of his bride. And then the next thought to go through her head is *You can choke me any time you like, big fella*, which squicks her out and turns her on in equal measure, thus proving what the doc said about her:

One. Broken. Cookie.

Though all this, all she does is sit and stare.

"Hey," he says.

"Yo," she says, puckering and popping her lips, puffing out her cheeks, sighing loudly. "Ah. Uh. How's life?"

Louis frowns a little. "Complicated."

"You and me both. I still miss the sexy pirate eyepatch—"

"I need to show you something."

"Is it a growth? A skin tag or asymmetrical blotch? I'm not a doctor."

He puts something on the table. It nearly steals her breath.

"That's mine," she says in a low growl.

Sitting there is a glass vial. In that glass vial is a long black vulture feather.

"You had it," she says.

"No, I didn't."

"Then where the fuck did you get it?" Anger, inexplicable and uncontrollable, winds through her like a spitting serpent.

He sighs. "I don't . . . I don't want you to judge her too harshly."

Oh. *Oh*.

"Samantha took it," Miriam says.

"Yeah. I found it in her drawer."

"Why?"

"I was looking for her phone charger—"

"No, I mean, why does she have it?"

"I don't know."

"Did you ask her?"

"Yeah. She got real . . . She got upset. Said I shouldn't have been going through her things like that, even though she was the one asked me to find her phone charger. She stormed out.

Went to stay with her mother. She won't answer my calls, but she texted me a few times to tell me she's okay, that she just needs time. I don't know why she has this." He takes the vial, rattles it. Inside, the nub end of the feather *tink*s against the glass.

She snatches it out of his hand. "She must've taken it from me. In Florida, when you guys came. That's the only time she could've taken it. That means she was in my stuff, Louis. Why would she want to be in my stuff?"

On that, he's quiet. At first, she thinks it's because he doesn't know.

But then she realizes: it's because he does know. "Louis. Look at me. What aren't you telling me?"

"She, ah. She talks about you. A lot."

"Does she, now."

"Lots of questions about you and me, our time together. She said it was just jealousy, and she wanted to understand our relationship, but I'm not so sure."

Click, click, click, like pins and tumblers in a lock. None of this explains why Louis decides to kill his bride on the night of their wedding, but it sure feels like a few puzzle pieces have just dropped into place. Samantha isn't some sweet angel composed of pure niceness. Something's going on there.

Something to do with Miriam.

Tell him, she thinks. *Tell him about your vision.*

And yet her mouth hangs open. Nothing comes out.

Worse, any thoughts she had of telling him anything evaporate the moment her phone rings. It startles her bad enough she almost knocks over her coffee.

It's Grosky.

"Yeah?" she says.

"We got a lead. It's Wren. I know where she is."

INTERLUDE

UNCLE JACK

The bar's got bottle caps on the wood, and a lacquer over top of them. Beer has sloshed out of the pint glass. Jack sits, eyeing up the Yuengling lager that has foamed up over the glass and down the back of his hand. He forms his lips into a vacuum O and sucks it up. The world shifts and dips. It's his fourth—no, wait, shit, his fifth—beer. And he doesn't mean for it to be his last.

The bartender is a scruffy sheep-faced dude, name of Rick. Rick's no prick, that's what everyone says. Rick's no prick, he always serves me. Rick's no prick, he always has a bowl of peanuts. Rick's no prick, he let me talk his ear off and then he let me crash on the couch in the back. Sometimes, Rick will even sell you weed. Good weed, too, like, medical-grade stuff. Everyone likes Rick. Sucks now, though, because Rick only works three days a week, and the rest of the time it's that fucking cooze-y bitch, Valerie. Dog-faced Valerie. She's a bite in the pants, that one. No fun at all. Doesn't like drunks. Doesn't want to hear anybody's problems. Won't let anyone crash on the back couch. Staggs says she lets him fuck her in the ass on that couch sometimes for fifty bucks, but everyone knows Staggs lies about just about everything, and Staggs wouldn't have fifty bucks on him, anyway. Valerie's too cold for that kind of warm-up.

Needless to say, Jack's glad that it's Rick on duty tonight, because Valerie wouldn't let him drown himself in beer like this. Jack plans on planting himself here all night long and taking the couch when it's time to lock up.

Rick gives him a wink from behind the bar, says, "What's up, Jack? You look like a hound dog haunted by the smell of his own ass."

"My fucking niece," Jack says, his voice mushy like mashed potatoes.

"That's a new one. Didn't know you had a niece."

"Yeah. Miriam." He says her name like a playground taunt. Mir-ee-yuuuum. Sticks out his tongue after. "Get this. She—" He burps into his hand. Vurp. Vomit burp. Beer fumes come through his nose too, and he has to shake it off before continuing. "So, her God-loving mother dies and leaves her everything. This ungrateful little shit girl that she is and boom, leaves it all to her. Including the house here, the house I'd been staying at! Staying in. Whatever. You believe that shit? That house. My house, basically. I had to move out my, my, my fuckin' recliner and all my shit, move it into a storage unit."

Sheep-faced Rick nods and whistles real low. "That's no small misery."

"Right. Right. Then I hire a lawyer and . . ." He thinks to not tell this part but the last four beers have done a pretty good job of washing away any sense of self-examination that Jack might have, so he lets the freak flag fly. "We go up there because the lawyer is confident that we can get the property back because, you know, I may not have a real good claim to it but Diamond said that with an estate anybody can contest anything and lotta times if you keep pushin' they'll throw you a bone just to shut you up. It's, like, dealing with an estate is hard enough already because it's this thing that happened because someone you loved died, so people's defenses are down and it's a good time to get what's yours."

Somewhere like a stray, wandering dog in the back of his mind is the thought that he must sound like a real asshole. But then he reminds himself, *You deserve good things, Jack. This is about justice.* He's comforted by the thought of being righteous in this, so he keeps talking.

"But the lawyer, after we went and talked to her, he's done. He's off the case. Doesn't want to talk to me, doesn't want to see her again."

Rick *hmms* and shakes his head like a good bartender. "Why is that?"

"You won't believe it, but—" Urp. "I'monna tell you anyway. We go up there. I dress up a little. Diamond looks like a real—a real professional." Except that word comes out *fropessional*, but fuck it, Rick knows what he means. "And then I swear to Christ, the girl she like, does this snapping her fingers or this countdown or something, and then an owl comes in through the window. Like, breaking the glass and shit! And she's laughing like a devil and there's this fat fuck there too, this FBI agent, and the owl is scratching at us and biting us and its fucking wings are flapping. She tells us, You go on, you get the hell out of here and you don't come back or I'll kill you with birds."

Rick seems to have lost the thread now. He's not doing that nice nod-and-smile commiseration. No, he's got this look on his face like he's watching something he can't believe, like a pig fucking a goat or something.

But Jack doesn't care, he just keeps on keeping on, sipping at his beer and using his bottom lip to grab the foam off his upper lip. "Here's the real kicker, Rick. Miriam, you know, I didn't know her that well when she was a little girl. But one time, I remember helping her shoot—helping her learn to shoot a goddamn BB gun, right? And she shot a robin. You know, the bird. Right through the head—" He turns his finger into a gun and drops the hammer, boom. "And I called her killer and thought it was funny, but she was real upset. Cried and cried and cried. I always remember that. That fucking bird."

"Good story, Jack," Rick says, and Jack can tell that Rick doesn't believe him. *Fuck you, Rick. Rick the prick.*

He sits there, staring into his beer.

Then a hand falls onto his shoulder. A small hand. And with it comes a woman's voice in his ear:

"Did you say your niece is named Miriam?"

TWENTY-TWO

WHO'S ON FIRST

Night. With it, the last few crickets of the year and a late start to October's chill—a crispness to the air like cold silverware.

"What are we doing here?" Louis asks. The two of them are parked in his pickup outside a campground. A yellow sign nearby says KOA.

"Looking for somebody."

"Who?"

Miriam hesitates. Part of her wants to keep him in the dark and send him on his way. But the other part likes that he's here. The grim, mad nostalgia of just like old times surges inside her like a vomit burp. "Remember Wren?"

That name lands like a slap to his face. Louis seems literally taken aback. "Of course. I think about her sometimes."

"I didn't think about her enough, as it turns out," Miriam says. She's still not sure how much to tell him, but then it occurs to her that keeping secrets is not her strong suit. Like a bulimic, she purges, tells him the whole thing. How someone who looks like Miriam has been killing. How she's been working with an FBI agent—sorry, ex-agent of the Bureau—to find out that the person has been Wren all along. She tells him about the victims. About what they found in Mark Daley's little box. About Tuggins.

All the while, he listens intently, as is his way. He's taking it all in and she watches the wave of it rise up and crash down on his shores. When she's done, he slumps back against the seat, almost like he's exhausted. Eroded.

"And you think she's here," Louis says.

"There was a credit card hit. Not from Daley or Tuggins but from one of the earlier victims—Harley June Jacobs." Which makes sense, when she thinks about it. It's a woman's card, and Wren is a girl, so people might be less inclined to ask questions. If the card said Mark Daley on it, that might raise flags. "Someone's been using that card to pay for one-night stays at KOA campgrounds around the state." She wrinkles her nose. "What's KOA stand for? Isn't that, like, *killed on arrival* or something?"

"DOA is *dead on arrival*. KIA is *killed in action*."

"I thought Kia was a car company."

"It is."

"So, what's KOA?"

"Kampgrounds of America."

"Campgrounds starts with *C*."

He looks frustrated. "Miriam, I don't know, and this isn't important. What's the plan? Why aren't the cops here?"

"Grosky said on the phone he can buy us some time. The site she procured is in the back—site 454. He said it's a tent site, no hookup for water or power."

Louis nods, leaning forward in his seat. "I used to camp. Some spots are reserved for people with campers; others are cabins. Then there are those for tents, but you get a water hookup so you can wash your hands or whatever, and electricity so you can run a hot plate or a lantern or so on, so forth. The real cheap spots are the ones boondockers use—it's a space set up just for a tent. It's a square of dirt and grass, pretty much, for those who want to rough it."

"She's out there."

"She might be dangerous."

"She almost certainly is dangerous. But we have to help her."

"Maybe we let the cops take this one."

"No. *No.* You and me? We made this girl who she is."

He laughs, but it isn't a happy sound. "No, the Caldecotts made her who she is, Miriam, not us."

"We saved her from them. We changed her story. That's on us."

Louis sighs. He rubs his hands across his cheeks—the rasp of calluses against his stubble gets her hot, and that's dumb, but she can't help it.

Finally, he says, "You're right. We owe her that. We ran away from her when she needed someone. Like a superhero who kills the villain but doesn't do anything about the wreckage of the city he left behind."

She pops the door and as she gets out feels compelled to remind him: "Yeah, but just remember, we're not superheroes."

"On that point, I suppose you're right," he says, stepping outside.

"I figure we barely even qualify as heroes."

"Just a couple of jerks?"

"Just a couple of jerks."

He meets her around the front of the truck. Above, the moon is pregnant with light and shining bold through the intertwined fingers of red and yellow leaves. "We go in, find Wren. Then what do we do?"

She winces. "Would it surprise you to learn I haven't thought that far?"

"It would not."

"Then let's go get our girl."

TWENTY-THREE
BLACK DOG

The two of them creep through the dark of the campground. In the distance, lanterns glow through trees as they hear the dull fuzz of Led Zeppelin coming from the other direction—it's "Black Dog," *eyes that shine, burning red*, the song grinding up and winding back down on itself. Someone hoots. A woman laughs. Then comes the sound of cans clanking against other cans in a trash bin.

Louis turns toward her as they walk through the trees, and says, "The black dog is a portent of death."

She turns to give him a look, and he keeps walking and talking. "The Dartmoor Dog. The Barghest. Cerberus. The black dog guards the gates of Hell, Miriam. The Hateful Thing warns us that death is coming, always coming, and if we keep moving forward, as we are doing now, we are entering *his* realm, the realm of death, the realm of Hell." And now the words are coming faster and faster, and Louis's eyes are glowing red, and behind his words grow a thrumming growl and an insectile hum. "You hunt the dog, but the dog hunts you. Death is ahead of you and behind you. Keep stepping, Miriam, but the slope is slippery ahead, slippery with blood and wishes, death and fishes." And now he's laughing and she feels all the forest closing in around her, branches pinning her down as Louis stands over her, his jaw cracking and his mouth widening—

And then it's like a vacu-seal *pop* in her ears. The sensation is over as fast as it came. Her skin shudders with goosebumps.

"Did you just say something?" she asks.

"Not really, I was just muttering under my breath about those RV assholes." She gives him a look, which he interprets as confusion and not as what it really is: fear because for half a second, Louis and the Trespasser were one. Or that's what the Trespasser wanted her to think. "The music is coming from a buncha yokels who bring their fifth-wheels or their RVs and it's just party time for them. I used to camp with my dad and those guys would always try to ruin it. Keep you up late with music and cigarette smoke."

She shakes off the bad vibes from the vision, forcing a laugh. "You sound like an old man shaking his cane at the clouds."

But Miriam can't ignore the feeling: *We're being pursued. Hunted by something, even as we hunt in turn.* The black dog. Death in front and behind . . .

They cut toward a red gravel path. Trees have old wooden signs hung to them with fading numbers painted on. They're in the 200s, then the 300s, and that means they're getting close to Wren. They creep along like specters, and Louis points to a tree ahead that has the magic number on it.

454.

The lot is small. Just a postage stamp of dirt and grass, like Louis said it would be. A single tent sits in the center of it. The tent glows with lantern light, and that glow shows them the faint shape of a person in there.

It's her.

She jerks her finger, indicating he come closer, and when he does, she tells him in a low whisper, "I'll go up to the tent. You stay out here. If she bolts, you . . . I dunno, catch her."

"Catch her?"

"Yeah, catch her. Use those big beef-sticks you call arms and scoop her up. We can't let her get away. This is our one shot."

He sighs. "All right. Be careful. You don't know what she's capable of. If you're right, this girl has killed people."

"Don't forget who you're talking to."

Nicely done, killer.

He just backs away and fades into the shadows. Miriam turns toward the tent.

Every part of her tightens up like a hangman's rope.

She skulks up to the tent, and then—she's not sure what to do. She can't knock. There's not a door. And the flap is zipped shut. The tent itself is grimy, years old, its margins stained with dirt and rain-spatter. It's staked into ground gone dry since it hasn't rained in a while. Does she kick over the tent-stakes, trapping Wren inside? Does she crawl under like a fucking snake?

Hell with it. She reaches down, grabs the external zipper, and—

Vvvvvviiiip.

She opens the portal to hell.

And there sits Lauren Martin. Wren. Nearly a mirror image of Miriam. Hair almost the same length. Red streaks that Miriam had in her own 'do once upon a time. The girl sits hunched over, a book in her lap, hair framing her face like the curtains on a stage.

Her head turns. She looks at Miriam, utterly unfazed. Her nose wrinkles a little like she's detecting a bad smell. Her gaze narrows moments before she rolls her eyes.

"Hey, psycho," she says. Droll, dull, like she's irritated. Exasperated. *Bored.* "You're early."

"Early."

"Yeah, so like, fuck off for a while. I'm not taking requests right now."

"Requests."

Wren's voice spikes. "Yes. I'm reading. Can't you see?" She waves a paperback book that flops about like a dead bird, making strange shadows on the wall by the light of the Coleman lantern behind her. It's Stephen King's *Doctor Sleep*. "I'm not taking appointments. So, shoo, fuck off, you're free to go."

Miriam's jaw hangs slack. She doesn't understand.

Until suddenly she does.

"You don't think I'm real," she says.

"You're real fucking annoying, is what you are."

Miriam flicks her gaze around the small two-person tent. Across from Wren's feet is a sleeping bag. Near that is a blue steel, small-caliber revolver.

The girl rolls her eyes so aggressively, Miriam's pretty sure they're both going to roll out her ear. Then she scoots closer, reaching for the zipper to close the tent.

Miriam catches her wrist.

And that's the moment.

There's no vision—Miriam can't see how the girl is going to die because she saw it once: Lauren Martin was fated to die on the Mockingbird's table as the killer sung his condemning song and then chopped off her head with a fire ax. A second shot at life yields no such second shot for Miriam's visions. Once it's done, it's done. But while Miriam is afforded no such revelation . . .

Wren's eyes go wide as she looks to Miriam's hand on her wrist. She doesn't even try to pull away. She just stares. Gaping.

"You," Wren says, breathless.

"It's me, Wren."

The girl regards her with wide, fearful eyes. Her gaze settles on the center of Miriam's chest. "The black mark."

"What?"

"You're dead."

A threat? Or something else?

Miriam's about to protest—

But the words never make it past her lips. Wren karate-chops Miriam right in the throat. Pain and panic explode like firecrackers inside her as she staggers back, gasping, clutching at her trachea. The tent shakes as Wren launches herself free, gun glinting in her hand. With a clumsy, swiping paw, Miriam grabs for her—but it's no use. The girl easily evades her grip and dashes toward the trees.

Stupid, stupid, stupid, Miriam thinks. She forgot—when she met Wren a few years ago, what was the girl practicing under the tutelage of one of the Mockingbird killers? Self-defense. Go for the eyes, the crotch, and of course, the throat. Finally, she pulls in some air and the white bleeding around the darkness of her vision recedes. She calls out for Louis. But her voice is small and squeaky, the protest of a mouse in the claws of a hawk.

Voices reach her. Louis, yelling. Wren, screaming. Then a gunshot pierces the dark. Miriam's heart rate is a tent spike in her chest, and she pumps her legs fast as they'll take her toward the sound—

Louis is there. On the ground. He's clutching his head.

Shit, no, shit—

She drops to her knees, skidding toward him, and she's got his head in her hands and she's looking for the hole, the blood, something, anything. But all he's doing is clutching his ear, and that's not bleeding either. Louis says loud, too loud, "She fired the gun. Can't hear anything. Goddamnit!"

She's in the wind. I have to find her.

Miriam kisses him on the cheek—a dumb, foolish, instinctual reaction that feels miserably, painfully right—and then launches herself back to her feet.

Lights cut through the dark. Red and blue strobe. Then comes the *woop-woop* of a warning siren. Police. No, no, no. They're going to ruin everything. This is too soon. She needed a chance. If they catch Wren, they'll take her away. And if they don't catch her, they'll spook her into running far and fast. Down at the end of the gravel path is a small road, and a cruiser cuts off the path. A shadowy shape darts in front of the car. *Wren.* Miriam bolts toward it—

A massive arm catches her around the middle. She *oof*s as the air blasts from her. It's Louis. He shakes his head. "Cops."

"I know; let me go!" She punches at him.

"She looks like you. They catch you, it's all over."

His voice is calm. His voice does what it often does—and it achieves what so few can achieve. It calms her. His reason infects her like a disease.

Damnit, damnit, damnit.

He points toward a small deer trail. "Come on. This way."

She curses under her breath and then follows after.

They make a mad dash through the campground. They dart out in front of one path only to end up in the headlights of a cop car. Louis pulls her into the brush, and they hear the pop and slam of a car door. Ahead, flashlight beams spear the dark, sweeping across it. Louis pulls her close, pressing down on the center of her back to keep her low. And then they're free. Ahead is his truck.

The jangle of keys, the growl of an engine, the spitting-animal snarl of tires kicking up loose stone—and then they're gone as Louis guns it out of the campground lot. No headlights in pursuit. No red and blue. Just the dark road ahead. *And death,* Miriam thinks. *Always death ahead.*

TWENTY-FOUR

HUNGRY LIKE A WOLF

They eat. They have to. It all adds up—Wren, the gunshot, the cops, the escape, it tunes the both of them up so bad that it's like a fire consuming all their fuel. That leaves them only one recourse: hamburgers.

The pickup sits parked under the crooked red roof of an old drive-up twenty-four-hour burger stand called JJ's. It's right off the highway, and from here they can see the late-night traffic whisking past in the distance. Tractor-trailers barrel forward. Sometimes their Jake brakes stutter and judder as traffic changes.

Louis sits on the dropped gate of the pickup bed. Miriam paces the asphalt, slaloming through potholes and fissures as she downs one hamburger after the next. Presently, she's eating her third, and it's like she can't get enough. Like she just wants to unhinge her jaw and swallow the whole burger stand whole. It's times like these she thinks, *I could eat a guy.* Like, the Donner Party? She wouldn't have held out that long. A half-hour into hungertown and she'd be picking up a rock and bludgeoning the fattest, slowest one.

"Fuck!" she says around a mouthful of food. "We had her."

"I know."

"Now the cops might have her. Or she's in the wind."

"I don't know which would be better."

"Her being on her own is better. Trust me."

Louis leans forward, crumpling up his burger wrapper into a waxy boulder. "I dunno, you said she was killing people. Better she be off the streets, then."

"All the more reason why she shouldn't be with the police. They're going to want to punish her for this."

"She's killed people. That's usually how it works."

Miriam stops, cheek bulging with barely-chewed burger. "Oh, really? Should I be locked away? How about you? Don't pretend like we both haven't done some nasty business. I bristle at self-righteousness."

He sighs. "You're right. But what we did was different."

"Maybe. Maybe not." This isn't helping. She switches tracks, her mind furious to walk another road. "Wren recognized me, but at the same time, she didn't."

"I don't follow."

"I think she thinks I wasn't real. She said I was dead."

He fishes into a carton, pulling out a wad of fries. "You said you have a Trespasser. Maybe she has one too." He brushes salt from his hands. "Your Trespasser sometimes looks like me. Maybe her Trespasser looks like you."

That hits her like a howitzer round to her middle.

"That's fucking scary," she says. She remembers what Sugar, another psychic like her, said to her down in the Keys.

Miriam: I have work to do.

Sugar: Is that what the trespassing specter in your head tells you?

Miriam: . . . The Trespasser.

Sugar: That's what you call it?

Miriam: Yeah. You have one too?

Sugar: I do.

Miriam: What do you call yours?

Sugar: The Ghost.

It's real. It's in her. It was in Sugar. And now it's in Wren. Maybe they each have their own demon. Or maybe there's just one—and it's unshakably upon each of them, fast and fixed as a shadow.

Suddenly, everything feels like it hinges on that: the Trespasser. She wants to see him now. Miriam is half-tempted to hold her fists to the sky and try to summon her diabolical companion. Her shadow has been scant of late, and now she thinks even that is the demon playing with her. Plucking her strings. Negging her like a fucking pickup artist. Somewhere in the ether, the Trespasser is flitting about, taunting her: *If you don't want me, then I don't want you. And that in turn will only make you want me more, you stupid little bitch. . . .*

She can almost hear the monster breathing down her neck.

Louis says, "I know it's not my place, but I want to say, I'm proud of you."

"Hnnh?" she asks, genuinely incredulous. "Dear god, why?"

He laughs. "You haven't had a cigarette. You haven't had a drink. I mean, sure, you ate, like, fifty hamburgers, but even still, you look like you're in shape. I just—" He stutters, then stops. "It's nice, is all."

Part of her wants to scream, *Fuck you, dude, I don't need your approval*.

Part of her wants to hiss, *Fuck me, fuck me, fuck me right now, because I will gladly take your approval all hot-and-sweaty-like in the back of your truck*.

She settles on the middle path: "Thanks."

He reaches out a hand. She takes it. His grip is firm and yet soft. His hand is so big around hers. They sit there like that for a while. It's nice.

TWENTY-FIVE

WELL, IT *WAS* NICE

Eventually, Miriam says, "If I touched your dick right now, would that ruin the moment?"

Louis clears his throat. "I think so."

They keep holding hands, but now his grip is stiff, and he's staring out at the highway like he's trying not to acknowledge her.

"I ruined the moment," she says.

"Yeah, pretty much."

TWENTY-SIX
INCHES AWAY

Back to her house. (Though that still seems strange to think. Her house. *Whose house?* My *house.*) The truck idles outside the driveway. It's a diesel, so it chug-chug-chugs as it sits there. The low engine vibrates up through her feet, her legs, into her hips. Deeper still.

Their hands are palm-down on the seat. Her left hand is three inches from his right hand. *I borked that all up,* she thinks.

"We still need to talk about Samantha," she says, rattling the feather in its glass vial.

"I know. But not tonight. I'm tired."

"You could come in. I'm a homeowner now. Hell, I own two houses. It doesn't get much more respectable than that. I'm basically two adults."

He laughs. "Don't you have a houseguest?"

"I do, but I'm pretty sure he's asleep." She tried calling Grosky on the way over, and no answer. She's pretty sure she's going to go right in there and wake his ass up, though, because she needs to know what he knows about what happened tonight. But if Louis comes in, that can wait till morning. . . . "Come on. Whaddya say? It's either that or some chump-change motel."

"I *am* used to having my tractor trailer to sleep in."

"So, my casa is your casa."

"I shouldn't. If I do . . ."

His voice crawls back down his throat before he finishes that sentence, but she knows where the sentiment is going. *If I do, who knows where we'll end up?* She knows what will happen. She wants it to happen. She can see in his eyes that he wants it too, unless she's imagining things. And with that done, they can both put Samantha the Fiancée in her proper place: as a shared enemy suitable for castigation and maybe destruction. But as long as he hangs on to her, Miriam's not sure what happens next. *I need you with me, big guy.*

"I'll see you in the morning?" she asks, suddenly fearful that when the sun comes up, he'll turn to vapor once more, gone from her life anew.

He nods. "Have a good night, Miriam."

"Nighty-night, Frankenstein."

TWENTY-SEVEN

THE HOUSE OF BLOOD

As she walks up to the house, the fatigue falls on her like a lead blanket. The caffeine that powered her, the adrenaline that pushed her, the hamburgers that fueled her furnace—it's all over, and the tiredness that results is the kind that winds around her bones like climbing vines, ever tightening, threatening to pull her down to the ground, pull her apart, make her one with the earth in a great big old dirtnap.

She thinks to go and wake Grosky up, but what's the point? It's after midnight and she's exhausted.

It's time to sleep.

She flings Grosky's keys down on the table. *I totally left his car at the coffee counter, didn't I? Shit.* All the more reason not to wake him up.

Eyelids heavy, she pokes her way up the dark stairs. Creaky wood complains underfoot. Thoughts of Louis and Wren flit through her head like night birds. And Gabby, too. *I should really call her.*

Down the hall. To the end of the hall. To her mother's old room. She's not going to stay downstairs. Not tonight. Tonight, she wants a proper bed, damnit.

Her hand falls to the doorknob, a brass Victorian affair with a square-petaled flower on it.

But as the door drifts open into darkness, the smell hits her.

It is a smell with which Miriam is woefully, intimately acquainted. There, on the air, is the coppery spice of blood. And with it, an odorous sublayer of human leavings: shit, piss, sweat. Then comes the sound—

The binaural buzz of fly wings.

Miriam paws at the light switch.

Light bathes her mother's bedroom.

But blood has bathed the room first.

Grosky's body is splayed across the top of the comforter, arms out in cruciform, one leg tucked awkwardly under the bulk of the body. Blood spatters the pale walls, specks the ceiling, and is lost against the dark cherry wood of the nightstand and the bedposts. The pillows have been plumped up and set to the side, and sitting atop them is his head.

His head is not attached to his body.

His mouth is wrenched open in a silent, permanent howl. The eyes are already disappearing beneath eyelids so swollen they look like puffy-lipped mouths. A pair of flies lands on his forehead and dances across his dead skin.

(Don't tell anybody, Grosky, but I think you're all right.)

The fatigue is gone from her, sandblasted away in a scouring, abrading wave. It reduces her down to powder. She wants to collapse here into fragments, like dust escaping through the gaps in the floorboards.

Questions chase questions. *Who did this? Why? Could it have been Wren? Did I judge her poorly? What monster is she? Is this just a dream?* She tries to say the words *Stop fucking with me*, hoping the Trespasser will hear her and end this display, but the words come out as a popping, incomprehensible whisper.

Behind her, the wood groans under the weight of a footstep.

Miriam slowly turns to meet whoever it is.

No.

"You're dead," she says.

(You're dead, Wren says.)

"And yet here I stand," says Harriet Adams.

Harriet Adams: one of the two murderous goons that worked for Ingersoll, the Eurotrash drug baron meant to kill Louis until Miriam shot him. Harriet Adams, who thought she was so smart, who believed herself such a master of cruelty that she left a gun in Miriam's hand in the unshakable belief Miriam would use it to end her own life instead of firing through the door and putting a bullet in Harriet's ear. Harriet, whose brains got scrambled by a lead bumblebee ricocheting around the inside of her skull, and so the last thing she muttered was the nonsense phrase *carpet noodle*. She is dead. Miriam killed her. Miriam stood over her body as her blood and brains leaked out of her ears and onto the floor of that Pine Barrens house.

And yet here I stand.

She is a brutish plug of a woman. Dark hair like a helmet, chopped at hard knife-slash angles. Face so pale, it's the porcelain of an urn meant for human remains. Harriet stands stuffed in a pair of dark dungarees and a maroon sweater, wearing a dead look on her face: implacable and distant.

In her hand is a machete.

Its blade is thick with congealing blood.

Miriam trembles, feeling suddenly cold.

"You're not real," Miriam says.

"I am as real as anything you've faced."

Her voice shakes when she says, "I shot you. In the head."

Harriet tilts her head sideways—showing that her left ear is a ruined, crumpled mess, like a rotten Brussels sprout mashed against the side of her skull. "I remember." She shrugs. "I earned it. I don't blame you. I was overconfident, and that blinded me to what was to come."

A clot of blood slides off the machete and plops against the floor.

Miriam realizes: Harriet is blocking her way to the stairs. If she's even real. She's still waiting for Harriet's face to shift, for her skull to split like an axe-cloven pumpkin and for the Trespasser to emerge, singing and dancing: *Hello my honey, hello my baby, hello my ragtime gal.*

"I've been looking for you," Harriet says. "And now I found you."

Fuck this. Miriam runs.

She knows better than to go through the dead woman with the machete, so she goes the other way instead—her toes plant and she twists around, bolting back through the doorway and into her mother's bedroom, where Grosky's body and head wait separately on the bed like jilted lovers. As she powers through the open space, she palms the door and slams it hard behind her, *wham*.

The bedroom has no other door.

But there's a window. And beyond it, a roof.

She sprints across the room—

It happens so fast, it takes her a few seconds after she face-plants onto the floorboards to figure out what happened. *I slipped,* she thinks. *In the blood.*

The door to the bedroom flies open, bashing against the wall. Harriet Adams, unliving monster, stalks forward as Miriam scrabbles to her feet. She's slow, too slow, and she realizes much too late that if she wants to survive, she's going to have to fight.

Miriam stabs out with a foot, catching Harriet in her chest. It's like kicking a tree stump. The woman barely budges—she doesn't even make a sound. All she does is raise the machete, and Miriam sees a glimpse of the future where the blade cuts down clean through her leg, her foot flopping onto the floor like a fish off a line, and suddenly her mind goes to Ashley Gaynes. Ashley, one foot gone after Harriet cut it off in a speeding SUV.

Ashley, eaten on a boat by greedy gannets. Ashley, one more monster in Miriam's life who came to hunt her.

(Miriam Black: fate-taker, river-breaker, monster-maker.)

Harriet brings the machete down, slicing through open air. *Swish.* Miriam's already somersaulting backward—a clumsy maneuver that has her slamming back into her mother's old walnut dresser. The mirror atop it rattles and bangs. Miriam uses the dresser to get to her feet—

Harriet lurches in, swinging—

Miriam cries out, pressing herself against the corner as the machete blade drops hard against the top of the dresser. It *thunks* into the wood.

And there it remains, stuck.

Harriet growls like a trapped animal as she gives the blade three futile tugs. Miriam doesn't waste the opportunity. She kicks out hard against the side of Harriet's knee. The leg bends inward, in a way legs are not supposed to bend. Something snaps as the limb kinks.

Bitch, I'll break you into sticks, Miriam thinks. *For Grosky.*

But the other woman seems to register no pain at all even as her hip dips from her injured leg. And the hard motion is enough to jar the machete free.

Harriet clubs Miriam in the face with the back of her fist. A white nuclear flash goes off behind Miriam's eyes. Her legs carry her backward as her hands instinctively fly up. The machete blade grazes the side of her left forearm, peeling off a flap of skin and sending up a spray of blood. Miriam, half-blind and dazed, throws a punch. It whiffs through open air.

One of Harriet's stubby hands grabs the back of Miriam's neck like she's a whelped, whooped puppy—

Next thing she knows, she's flung forward into one of the bedposts. Her shoulder cracks hard against it. Her foot hits the slick of blood and slips out from underneath her. She goes down.

Ears ringing like sirens. Everything pounding like war drums. Even as she grabs the bed and tries to pull herself up, a boot presses against her back, pushing her to the floor.

Harriet clambers atop her, mouth up against Miriam's ear.

This is what Harriet tells her.

INTERLUDE
HARRIET'S STORY

I have been looking for you for a very long time, Miriam.

Hold still. No, no, don't struggle. I want you to know this. I want you to know my torment. I want you to be aware of what I went through to be here with you, right now, my knee in your back, a machete against your throat.

Once, I thought myself the paragon of the natural world. Mankind, as I saw it, had gotten too far away from its animal nature. Do you know why we have canine teeth? Because we are predators, Miriam. Hunters red in tooth and nail. We are driven by our genes to hunt and to conquer, to kill and to eat what we kill. Our genes are expressed in our ideas—memetics to mirror our genetics. But we have convinced ourselves that our ideas are of a higher mind. That we are somehow better than our crass, predatory nature. And yet, our ideas drive us to be more like the predators we hope we are not. This cognitive dissonance weakens us, I once believed. We struggled against our nature in the way of one struggling against the sucking force of quicksand. The more we fight, the deeper we sink.

I thought I had it all figured out.

I thought I was better than you. I truly did. I found that diary of yours. Your countdown to suicide. I saw a way to prove that I was the alpha and you were the omega. I would not have to kill you—I would let you kill yourself.

And then you shot me.

You put a bullet through a door and into my head.

You proved me wrong. I died there on the floor.

Or so I thought.

From darkness, light bloomed behind my eyes. Something pushed and pulled at my wound, like a finger probing. A shadow came to me. A shadow shaped like Ingersoll, long and lean, lithe and hairless. It slid atop me. It filled me up through that hole in my head. Breath plumped my lungs once more. And again my heart began to beat.

I sat up.

My mouth tasted like pennies and rot.

By the time I walked back to the world, I found that I had been gone from it for six months. My body never decayed. Nobody ever found me there in the Pine Barrens. I lay there for those months, beetles colonizing my bowels, worms filling my spaces. I had to vomit them up. I had to defecate them out. I spent days purging what was in me: emptying what had laid claim to my void.

By the time I came back, the world had moved on without me. Frankie was alive and had found new work. Ingersoll was dead—another casualty of you.

My memory was alive and well. I did not forget.

And in me now was something new: that shadow. A second being inside me. It's what I imagine it's like to be with child. I feel it in my spaces. A parasite, but a beneficent one. I give to it. And it gives me life.

It told me to bide my time and I did. I returned to what I knew to do: I went back and slowly, surely began rebuilding Ingersoll's empire. I reconstructed relationships. I resurrected supply lines. Just as I had been reborn, so too would the work. I never forgot you, though. I lost you, yes, but I knew one day I would find you. I knew we would meet again and I would kill you. The shadow assured me that this was my intersection. That it was my destiny.

That is a thing I believe in that I did not before. Destiny. I should have seen it all along. I hadn't really been listening to Ingersoll. He believed in a greater, stranger universe: a universe of fate and mystery, where one could portend the future and direct the outcome by rolling knucklebones or by sorting through a pile of hot entrails. I believed in nature over everything.

But I believe in something else now:

Supernature.

That is why you defeated me the first time. I was nature. You were supernature. You had power. You had a gift. Ingersoll knew this but I was blind to that. Now his shadow has filled me, and now I have power too.

I looked for you for a long time. I almost found you. When a competitor of mine—the Haitian, Tap-Tap—found himself unseated from his throne, it did not take long to discover that Miriam Black had been present, once more toying with fate and, in this case, changing my world for the better. Tap-Tap's end helped my business flourish. More recently, in Tucson, the cartels reported that someone had intervened—they had planned to kill a man named Ethan Key, but they found that someone had already done that job for them.

And again, my job got easier.

I should thank you, I suppose. You made me who I am now.

Thank you. Thank you for teaching me how weak I was. Thank you for aiding my work. I mean it. *Thank you.* But make no mistake: my gratitude does not come part and parcel with forgiveness. Our nature is not to forgive, is it? You do not forgive. You act. You change fate. You move the world, one degree at a time. One life saved, another taken. Forgiveness is passive—it is taking your hands off the wheel and letting go. But you never take your hands off the wheel.

And that's how I found you. Because here you are, doing what you do. Meddling in my business once more. You left a string of bodies across this state, and the latest was one of mine. Donald Tuggins. He is dead by your hand, and so I am conjured. I am conjured and fate has pushed me to you. This time, fate worked in the hands of one of your own:

Your uncle, Jack.

He was very glad to tell me where I could find you, Miriam.

And so here I am. And here you are. It is time to end our dance.

Here is what's going to happen:

I'm going to cut off your head.

And then I'm going to take our your heart.

Your head I will leave behind to watch as I eat your heart. That is how I take your power. That is how I conquer.

TWENTY-EIGHT

DEUTERONOMY 19:21

As Harriet goes on and on, mashing Miriam's face to the floor, it comes up out of her like the howling wind of a coming hurricane: one moment, Harriet is ending her tale with *That is how I conquer*, and in the next, Miriam's chest is tightening and a white giddy bloom is filling her mind. She laughs. No, she guffaws, breathless and constant and without restraint. Her eyes are wet with tears. The blood is sticky underneath her forehead. Miriam laughs and laughs and laughs, braying like a happy cow in defiance of the slaughter to come.

"Shut up," Harriet seethes, tightening the blade underneath Miriam's throat. But Miriam can't stop. She keeps on cackling, even as the blade nicks the skin around her neck, her blood joining with that of Grosky's.

"Can't . . . ," Miriam gasps. "Can't stop. Too funny."

"Why? Why are you laughing?" Harriet demands.

"Laughing because . . ." Miriam swallows hard, and the knot in her throat has to pass the cold steel of the machete pressed there. "Because for being so smart, you're such a dumb, dumb cunt."

"What?"

"You've been looking for me all this time and—" Miriam laughs harder. "I haven't been hiding! My name is on police reports. I own *two* houses. You could've just Googled me, you stupid fucking bitch." She laughs so hard she's crying now, barely gulping air.

"Shut up," Harriet says. But when Miriam won't quit, she bellows it: "Shut. Up!" She pounds her fist against the baseboard of the bed, *wham*.

Across the room, a new sound—

A thump.

It's enough to distract her. Harriet lifts her head over the bed to look in that direction, toward the window—

Miriam grabs the bedpost and pulls, dragging herself out from beneath Harriet and under her mother's old bed. Into cobwebs and lint, into dust bunnies stuck to the floor in coagulating blood. Harriet grabs at her ankle, but Miriam twists and wrenches away, sliding completely under the bed. Thus begins a game that would be cartoonish were it not for the stakes—Miriam slides to one side of the bed, and when Harriet goes to that side to reach under, Miriam slides to the other side. Back and forth, back and forth, careful to keep all her parts away from Harriet's grabbing hand and slicing machete. *(Keep all limbs inside the vehicle at all times.)* Finally, Harriet has had enough.

She picks a side and begins to crawl under, pawing and slashing.

Miriam goes out the other side—

And as she draws herself up and back toward her mother's walnut dresser, she sees what caused the distracting thump in the first place:

Grosky's head. It fell off the pillow when Harriet hit the baseboard.

Here she comes.

The venomous bulldog woman is back up over the far side of the bed, crawling across it with her normally dead-eyed face alive with hate. She's like a rabid animal, driven by the singular urge to kill, kill, kill.

I need a weapon. I need something—

And then she has it. Miriam reaches down, grabs a hank of Grosky's hair, and just as the woman gets close, she smashes the dead man's severed head into the side of Harriet's face. The woman grunts, rolling off the end of the bed and hitting the floor so hard, the whole room judders. Miriam whispers a hasty apology to the head, then flings it in that direction—it bounces off the wall, knocking a painting of Jesus off its anchor. Both the head and the painting land on Harriet as she struggles to stand. Glass shatters. Harriet rages.

Time bleeds like arterial spray. Miriam cannot waste any of it. She pushes herself up against the window, continuing her original plan—two flips of her thumb disengage the lock, and she gets under the window and forces it open. A blast of October air hits her in the face and robs her breath. She reaches out, grabs the outer ledge of the exterior window, and hauls herself out.

Hands grab her ankles. Firm, crushing hands. Gone is the machete—Harriet must have dropped it. The tendons and muscles in Miriam's arms burn as she struggles to keep pulling herself out. She thrashes about, kicking her legs. She looks back over her shoulder, sees Harriet's eyes are bright and cruel as knives, and the grin on her face is a maniac's half-moon smile. As if to confirm, she opens that maw of hers wide, wider—

She bites down on Miriam's calf. Teeth sink into muscle. Miriam screams. Blood bubbles around Harriet's lips and across her pale, puffed-up cheeks.

The air stirs with movement. The wind is suddenly fierce, riffling through Miriam's hair like a pair of fingers. And with that, a shape swoops in past her, a shadow pulling away from the night.

The great horned owl dives silently though the window, claws up and out, pointed right at Harriet's face. The woman has no time to react. The bird's talons go right for her eyes, and suddenly, the teeth embedded in Miriam's calf are gone as Harriet juggles her own feet backward, an owl attached to her face.

Miriam pulls herself free, and then she can't help it:

She looks back in through the window.

The owl's wings beat furiously, keeping her aloft as its talons anchor into the meat around Harriet's eyes. The woman lets out a sound like a teakettle going off full-blast: it's a high-pitched whine, not of pain but of something greater, something deeper, some ancient frustration.

Miriam puts herself into the owl's mind. For just a moment. She feels the satisfying urgency of talons easing through human meat. She detects the pleasant plumpness of those claws closing in around two round orbs. And then the owl pulls free, Harriet's eyeballs clutched in her talons like precious wet pearls. The owl utters a triumphant squawk and returns to the night, taking Harriet's eyes with her. Miriam blinks and she's back in her own mind.

She kneels outside the window, breath punching in and out of her lungs. Inside the room, Harriet pirouettes blindly, making wordless, rage-fueled noises. She swings at the open air.

And then she stops.

She focuses.

Her head spins and she orients toward the window. Toward Miriam. She bares her teeth, red with Miriam's gore, somehow still staring with those great bleeding holes in her skull, the skin around them claw-fringed into red ribbons.

Harriet charges toward the window.

Holy shit.

Miriam turns and drops her ass onto the shingles and slides down, bump, bump, bump. Though she's never gone out this window, she made a habit in her teenage years of knowing how to get down to the ground. It's not hard as long as you're careful, but caution has, like Miriam, gone way the fuck out the window.

She bounces down to the gutter, clumsily tries to catch it, misses, and falls. Miriam tumbles down from the end of the roof and into the old flowerbeds around the side of the house. Flowers haven't grown here in years, and she hits a berm of hard, desiccated mulch. The air blasts out of her. Her hands work furiously through patches of weeds to get her back to standing.

As she does she thinks, *This is it, this is over.*

But it's not. Not at all. Above her head, the roof bangs and shakes. Harriet comes hurrying down toward the roof's edge face first, on all fours, loping more like a dog than a human being. She calls out Miriam's name in a groaning, grinding, inhuman voice: *"Miiiiiiriaaaaaam."*

Harriet doesn't stop. She leaps off the edge of the roof. Miriam backpedals, nearly stumbling into the trees as Harriet lands hard, her arm snapping—*kkkt!*—the bone spearing through the skin. And even that does not stop her. She gets back up, the one arm dangling around the ejected bone, and she fixes those dead sockets right on Miriam. She again roars Miriam's name—*Miiiiiiriaaaaaam!*

That's all it takes.

Miriam bolts through the trees.

TWENTY-NINE

JESUS FUCK WHAT THE FUCKING FUCK JUST HAPPENED

Time passes. She has no idea how much, and an absurd part of her fears that this night is forever and the sun will never rise.

Miriam is in the woods, and then she's walking across an open field, behind someone's barn. And then she's back in the woods before reaching a crooked gravel road. She's lost. No idea at all where she is.

This is what she knows.

First, she is being followed. For once, maybe for the first time ever, this gives her comfort. Because what's following her is an owl.

Miriam can't see the bird. But she can sense her in the trees. The beast is up there, gliding soundlessly from branch to branch, staying just out of sight a hundred feet back. Once in a while, the owl leaves her, returning minutes later, her beak wet with mouse blood. Miriam blinks sometimes and can taste it: a dead mouse aftertaste clinging to her tongue like a film. She can taste its fur, its fear, can feel its tail whipping about her throat. Her bird mind is hungry and excited, and her human stomach churns with pure quease.

She concentrates on the creature. Sharing space with the owl lets her know the owl. The knowledge she obtains is both general and intimate. She knows about this owl and, by proxy, about all the owls of its kind.

This is the same bird who she called to attack Jack and his "lawyer." The owl is a great horned owl. This bird is two feet tall, and has a wingspan over twice that. And yet it only weighs as much as the average Chihuahua. She glides silently because she weighs so little, because her bones are hollow. Her feet are zygodactyl—two claws in the front, two in the back. Good for perching on branches. Good for holding food.

Good for plucking out eyeballs.

My, what big eyes you have.

The owl will digest its mouse and regurgitate the parts it did not use—a thick, globby wad of pelt and bones and other biological detritus. Then it will hunt again. The owl is always on the hunt.

This owl had a mate once. A mate struck by a car. A mate gone.

But she is strong and she perseveres. She is large and one day will find another mate. For now, the owl hunts alone.

No . . .

For now, she hunts with me.

Miriam blinks as gravel grinds underneath her boots.

I think I have an owl.

It should comfort her. And it does, in a small way—in the way that it is a fraying rope, a fucking *shoelace* to which she clings, allowing her to dangle over a very wide and very deep abyss. Grosky is dead. Harriet—somehow!—is not. Images flash in her mind like lightning strikes: *Harriet, leg snapped inward. Eyes robbed from her head. Bone sticking out of her arm.* And still she kept coming.

Maybe she's not alive after all.

Maybe she's dead and her body just doesn't know it yet.

Or maybe that shadow she spoke of just won't let her go.

What unholy, unearthly power has resurrected someone like Harriet Adams?

Harriet has a shadow in her, but Miriam has a Trespasser

outside of herself, just as Sugar had the Ghost, and just as Wren may have some strange vision of her. Is it the same thing? Ashley Gaynes never spoke much about an external presence—but he did talk about voices.

So did that shooter in the Ship Bottom shop on Long Beach Island. The one Miriam dispatched with a barbecue fork to the neck. He spoke of voices too.

What drove Eleanor Caldecott? Or Karen Key? Were they fate-breakers like her? Or were they on the other side of it? Are there even sides, or are they all products of the same trauma-fucked system? The questions haunt her as she staggers forward, exhaustion dogging her every step. Something larger is going on here, and she has no idea what it is. She can't get her hands around it. Can't see the big picture.

Her mind loops and whorls. A snake slurping its own tail like a spaghetti noodle.

Carpet noodle.

The fucked thing is, it seems that these forces are conspiring to get Miriam to stop doing what she's doing. But she doesn't *want* to do it anymore. She wants to stop! That's why she went after Mary Stitch. The only one who wants her to keep riding this hell-train is her passenger, her plague: the Trespasser. That demon, that ghost, that stain on her wall ever-spreading. The Trespasser is herding her toward something, some outcome she can't quite see or understand. . . .

Stop thinking about all this. It's not doing you any good.

She needs to think about the here and the now.

She's on a gravel road. At night. With an owl.

Focus, you dim bitch.

Where will she go?

She has no phone. She has no car. Her first thought is now and always: Louis. Find him, lie in his lap, beg him to take her away somewhere.

But that just draws him in further. Came a time just like this one where she suffered an attack by Harriet Adams, and she ran right into Louis's arms—and that led them to him. Ingersoll took him. Cut out his eye. Almost killed him. Miriam's very presence caused fate to double back on itself, to nearly fulfill the prophecy of his death that she was trying to interrupt in the first place.

She can't call Grosky. Doesn't want to drag Gabby into this.

What, then? Her house is an abattoir. She has a couple bucks on her still. A motel, maybe. Or hitchhike back to Florida. Somewhere to go, to hide, to get her head straight . . .

But then there's Wren. Wren, the reason for all of this. That girl is caught in the glue, same as Miriam is. Harriet was unknowingly hunting Wren, thinking she was Miriam—that scary bitch just got lucky with Uncle Jack. *(Lucky? Or were forces again conspiring against you, Miriam?)* If Wren keeps mucking around, Harriet will find her, too. And then what?

Shit, shit, shit.

She is paralyzed by indecision, destroyed by exhaustion.

Ahead, through the trees, the gravel road on which she walks ends, leading out to another road—this one paved. A few headlights spear the night as cars move past. Miriam just wants to find a pile of leaves to curl up in. Above, the owl remains a comforting presence. Her own special shadow.

Miriam walks out to the intersection, unsure whether to turn left, turn right, or walk into the middle of the road and wait for a truck to flatten her like a blood pancake. It's then that her decision is made for her—

Coming down the road is a police cruiser. And soon as she's in its sight, the red-and-blues come on, and so does the siren.

THIRTY

PO-PO ROLLIN' IN

"Hands up."

Red, blue, red, blue. A carousel of lights, whirling about the black.

The cop stands there. Door open. Him behind it. Gun up. Miriam is pinned by headlights. His service pistol holds firm, its barrel staring her down.

Trembling, she puts her hands up.

He tells her, "Get down on the ground."

And she gets down on the ground.

Because she's tired. She thinks, *I could call the owl.* She could summon the bird, bring it down upon him. Maybe it would claw out his eyes, slash his cheeks, beak-bite the nose clean off his face. But this cop, she doesn't know who he is. He's probably just some dumb country buck, doesn't know anything about her, doesn't know what she can do or why she can do it. He doesn't deserve her.

Though the larger question is:

Does she deserve this?

Corralled and arrested? It does not take long for her to realize the ramifications of what has happened—and what could happen next. She's escaped so many scrapes before, it always felt like she would forever be slipping the leash and running free. But now the rope is tightening. Wren has left a trail. And Wren looks like Miriam now. They tried to catch Wren at the campground, and who did they see running across the paths? Miriam. Who now has a dead ex-FBI agent in her house? Miriam. Who's been running around this country, probably leaving behind inconclusive serial killer evidence all over the place with wanton disregard? One guess, and her name rhymes with *delirium.*

They're going to lock her up.

Maybe for things she did.

Certainly for things she didn't.

Maybe that's okay. Maybe it needs to be over. Suddenly, a long haul in jail sounds almost comforting. What's the saying? Three hots and a cot? *I could be good in prison. I'll be the wild-ass queen of Cell Block Nine. All the bitches will give me their cigarettes and their toilet wine, and I'll tell them how they meet their well-deserved maker and we'll all laugh and give each other tattoos.*

They could form a club. Wait, no, a gang. A proper gang.

She presses her forehead against the asphalt. It's cool. It's calming. She concentrates on her breathing, in and out, in and out. Tinnitus rings in her ear and she focuses on that, too. Behind her comes the scuff of shoes. The cop is coming toward her. He has trepidation in his steps, like he's not sure what he's dealing with.

No need to be scared of me, man. Stick a fork in me, I'm done.

Her mind wanders to Louis killing Samantha. And Wren out there on her own. A surge inside Miriam says, *These are your people, you have to do something, you're obligated and responsible, you can't give up now*. But she drowns that in a tide of exhaustion. Because to hell with all that. She doesn't need to be responsible to anyone but herself. At least in jail she'll get a fucking nap.

She winds her hands behind her back, crosses one wrist over the next.

"I'm ready," she says. Her voice sounds tired. Raw, like her vocal cords have been run over a cheese grater. "I'm okay. I'm cool."

But the cop isn't coming any closer. She hears a buzzing sound—

And then he's on the phone.

"Yeah," he's saying. "It's her. It has to be her."

Who is he talking to? He's not on the radio. Which means he's not talking to the police. *Harriet.* Could it be? Maybe he's not police at all. Or maybe he's on the take—in her pocket. She said she had rebuilt Ingersoll's empire . . .

Miriam suddenly pushes herself up. But she hears the hammer of the gun click into place as he hurries forward, and the gun barrel presses hard into the back of her skull, the pistol's sights digging into the skin and the bone beneath.

Her mind wanders out now to find the owl, but she can't see the bird at all—has it gone hunting? Has it given up on her? The owl is not a carrion bird, and perhaps now that she's dead meat, it cares nothing for her. *Please . . .*

"You're not a cop," she says.

"I was," he answers, digging his gun into the back of her head. "Still got the uniform. Still got the car."

"You're with *her*."

He laughs softly. "Harriet. Yeah. She's got a real thing for you, Miss Black. But good news: she wants you alive. Says she needs something from you."

Then comes the jingle-jangle of handcuffs and the buzzy sound of him opening one cuff, then the next. Metal touches her left wrist, and she feels tears at her eyes. *I'm not going to jail. I'm going back to Harriet.* As he closes the first cuff on her wrist, his thumb grazes her skin—

The vision is fast.

The lights. The horn. The crashing of metal.

"Ten seconds," she says without meaning to.

"What?" the cop asks, pausing.

The ground throbs beneath her.

Lights, new lights, bathe the space. White pushing back the red and blue.

She counts aloud:

"Nine, eight, seven—"

Miriam yanks her hand away, spinning around and whipping the not-cop in the face with the one free cuff—only her one wrist is bound, and so the other becomes a weapon. He cries out, the gun going off, she ducks it—

"Six, five—"

His face is bleeding. His face is alive with rage.

And now, the side of his face is bathed in white light. Miriam's mind flits to the owl's mind, too—the owl sees the light, feels the rumble of rubber on road.

Four, three, two—

Miriam kicks out, catching the not-cop in the stomach. He staggers backward, away from the cruiser, into the middle of the road—

Lights bathe him. Almost erase him.

A little hatchback car plows into him.

The cop doesn't even have the chance to cry out—he's sucked under the front tire, then the back, before the car skids to a halt and he's thrown up back onto the road, a dead and crumpled mess. In the vision she had, she felt all his bones break like old, rotten broomsticks over a firm knee. *Snap, crackle, pop*. He was dead before the hatchback stopped moving.

The hatchback's horn is on permanent honk now. *Bwahhhhh.* Miriam stands, the cuff dangling from one wrist. She tries to shake it off like it's a wasp, but of course that doesn't work and she feels stupid for even trying. She looks up, dizzy and dazed, as the driver of the car steps out. A woman. Heavyset. Hair all mussed up in a tower of panic and chaos. Her jaw is slacked in horror as she sees what she's done. "Oh, no. No, no, no." Tears shine in her eyes.

Miriam says, "He wasn't a cop."

"You . . . Cuffs . . . He was a cop."

"I just said he *wasn't a cop*." But the woman is blinking, hands waving in the air like she's trying to deny that any of this has happened or is happening still. Fuck it. Shock has taken the woman. A line of blood is snaking down from the lady's scalp—she must've hit her head on the steering wheel. No airbag. Looks like an older model Honda. Whatever. "You got a phone?"

"Phone. Phone . . ." The woman says it like she doesn't even know what it is. Maybe she doesn't. Could be she's got a concussion.

One broken cookie . . .

Miriam takes the initiative, heading over to the car—stepping past the pile of death that was the not-cop—and throwing open the passenger-side door.

There. A cell phone sitting in the cup holder. Miriam reaches in and snatches it up. She makes the one call she can make.

Louis answers.

"I need you," she says.

And that's all it takes.

PART FOUR

THE BLACK MARK

THIRTY-ONE
A CABIN IN THE WOODS

Midnight.

A night in early December.

Blue moonlight cuts across the middle of the bed like the blade of a straight razor. Miriam sucks in a sharp gasp of breath, panic suddenly whirring through her veins like the bit on a power drill. It's cold, but she's sweat-slick. She feels beset from all sides—shadows pressing in, hands reaching for her, shapes at the window. Pure evil with many eyes, many hands. For a moment, she has no idea where she is—

And then she looks over. A shape lies next to her—the familiar human topography, a mountain range formed by a man's body. The quilt is wound around Louis's feet in a tangle. The white sheets are pulled up to that space below those two perfect lines that angle downward from his hips to his cock. His chest rises and falls, slow and steady, his breath soft and with the faint whistle of air between half-open lips. He moans a little.

Miriam gets up. She knows the score. When sleep hits the wall and she can't help but awaken, the only recourse is to get her ass up and moving.

A brightness comes in through the window. At first, she thinks it's just the moon, but then she sees it's more than that: it's the moon's light mirrored on a landscape of white. *Snow,* she thinks. Not much yet, but out there in the forest she sees white mounding between and up against the trees. Flakes whisper against the glass as they fall gently, lazily, unperturbed by wind.

Well, fuck all this beauty, she has to pee.

She yawns, staggers naked into the little bathroom. Miriam thinks to leave the lights off in case she wants to cool back down and rejoin Louis in bed, but already she feels alive—her skin tingling with the electric buzz of unswerving consciousness. She turns the lights on, and when she does, she is once more greeted by the shocking image of what has happened to her head.

Her hand runs across her scalp. The hair—so blond it's the color of scarecrow straw, and cut so short she only has a couple inches to mess with. Her fingers slide through it. Some of it is mashed down, the rest rising in fickle peaks. She doesn't look like herself anymore. That's the point, isn't it?

For a while after that night, the night Harriet came back, the night Grosky lost his head, they went from motel to motel, watching TV on whatever piece-of-shit boob tube the room had bolted to the wall. Wasn't long before the news had her scent, which rattled her like a cup of dice.

For a long time, she'd lived her life at the periphery: a woman at the margins, a ghost who didn't seem to have much effect on the world except for one person here, another there. She felt like one of those fish on the bottom of sharks: a shadow unseen, hiding in the belly of much meaner beasts.

But then Grosky showed up and revealed to her the world of Reddit—her as the Angel of Death, nameless and mythic. And then came the night Grosky died, and the news was over it like flies on a horse's ass. MASSACRE IN PENNSYLVANIA. DEPOSED FBI AGENT SLAIN IN BRUTAL MURDER. Her name, splashed across the screen. Then they found the Reddit, too, and then it wasn't just Miriam Black, but it was Miriam Black: Angel of Death. They had her number. They had her look. So, she chopped off her hair, dyed it bone-blond, and that was that.

When they came here to the cabin, Louis made sure the place had no TV. Even though coverage of her died down after a couple weeks—and no leads, thank whatever sick gods govern this world—he didn't want her glued to it.

She found a better place here.

A place of peace. Wild woods. Dark forest. Distant cabin.

It's nice. Like she's no longer a part of the world. Like she's gone back to the margins, back to the periphery . . .

Her bladder reminds her why she came in here, so she sits, she pisses.

Her mind continues to wander. Her natural inclination is to wonder and worry about what comes next, but lately, she's been burying that inclination in the dirt of her own mind. And instead, she gives herself over to the bliss of the moment. Where she is—where *they* are—it feels good. It feels right. And a desperate little voice tells her, *Maybe this can go on forever like this.* This time away. This exile. Maybe this break in the status quo can *become* the status quo. What's the saying?

The new normal.

Not like she ever had anything close to normal, anyway. The moment that crazy lady beat her half to death with a snow shovel—that set her on a path perpendicular to normal, far away from it as fast as possible.

But this, where they are now, it feels something like normal.

It feels something like life. Or *a* life, at least.

Above her head, in the corner of the room, a little house spider spins a web. Fat butt dangling as its tiny legs stitch the silk. "I'm just like you, dude," she tells the arachnid in a low voice. "Just hanging out." Hanging out away from everything. Staying warm. Staying cloistered. Fuck the rest of the world.

Miriam wipes, flushes, and decides she's really truly awake.

She goes and puts on pants, a T-shirt, Louis's big-ass frumpy barn jacket, and she heads outside. The cabin isn't big, it's barely two rooms without the bathroom, so she has to be quiet as she slides through the galley kitchen and to the door outside.

Outside. The air has a bite to it, but it also has that odd winter's warmth—the snow falling feels insulating somehow, like it's a blanket. Like it's a skin on the world covering up all the exposed sinew and muscle left behind when autumn goes and winter strips everything down to the bone.

Of course, it's not really winter yet, is it? The solstice is still a few weeks away. Wait, is it the solstice, or the equinox? Whatever. Fuck it. Miriam cannot summon the energy to care. The word they use, solstice or equinox, it changes nothing. Everything is a placeholder, a proxy.

Miriam draws the cold air into her lungs. She looks down the long gravel drive cutting through the pine. Louis's pickup truck, the bumper since replaced, sits nestled up next to the little dark cabin. The air smells of burning wood from the pellet stove. Snow collects on her eyelashes and she blinks it away. The moonlight fills all the spaces. All is still.

Everything is quiet. No highway. No trains. Nobody yelling. No gunshots, no sirens, no TV noise, no nothing.

Her current fantasy is this: The world has ended and they are the only two left behind. It is a peaceful apocalypse as everything slows to an inevitable death, and they get to be here and ride the pony until it lies down beneath them and comfortably passes away. Then they crawl up inside it like it's a tauntaun with its belly split, and they too go away with the world.

It occurs to her sometimes that thinking of things that way is pretty fucked up. Most people imagine themselves at the center of a living world. And here she is, pretending that the world is dead and she and Louis are the last witnesses to it.

That fantasy bubble is burst every morning when Gordy shows up to bring them the news or their groceries. And in those moments, her mind is like a wild horse that hates its stable—it busts out of the barn and gallops fast through signposts with names burned into them. *Wren. Gabby. Harriet.* Sometimes, she imagines the signposts are gravestones, and it helps her get back to the comfort of her fantasy.

Her breath gets ahead of her like an escaping ghost.

Miriam rubs her hands together.

It's time to hunt.

She goes out into the trees. With the air so still, the only noises around her are those of falling snow and the *munch-a-crunch* of her boots pressing into the new powder. Soon, the cabin is just a spot on the horizon, and when she's far enough away, she lifts her chin and closes her eyes and lets everything out of her head.

In the darkness of her mind, shapes stir. Like little embers burning in the night—stars, sparks, cigarette cherries. Each is a living thing. A bird. Many roost and perch, asleep: titmice, nuthatches, chickadees, cardinals. Hiding in nests, sleeping in tree hollows and dead stumps.

Others are awake. But it is only one she seeks.

There. Slicing the night on both sides, wings spread wide, comes the owl.

The bird lands with barely a flutter of feathers on a nearby evergreen. The branch dips just enough that snow slides off and to the ground with a *flumpf*.

Miriam opens her eyes. She regards the owl. The owl regards her.

"Hello, Bird of Doom." That's what she's taken to calling it. When Louis's friend, Gordy—their patron and sorta-kinda-landlord—saw that they had an owl with them, he blanched before getting excited. Gordy said in the nasal growl that marks his voice:

"My ex-wife used to hate those things. We had a screech owl in a tree outside our bedroom, making its sounds at night.

Sometimes, it'd fly by and scare the panties off her. God, Marcia'd scream like a mouse just ran up her coochie. She said, *They're bad luck, Gordy! They fly by your window, that means you're gonna get sick and you're gonna die. I just know it.* And she'd worry and worry about how it meant she was likely to catch some disease and it'd kill her." He laughed like it was crazy. "She whispered to me one time, *That's a bird of doom, is what it is.* Me, I like owls. Helps me sleep, knowing they're out there. And the fact that they upset Marcia just makes me like them even more."

And so, Bird of Doom it became.

"You ready to scare up some prey?" she asks the owl.

Bird of Doom cocks her head like a confused dog, as if to say, *Of course I want to hunt, you stupid hairless bear.* Miriam gives a clipped nod, pulls the hood over her head, and lopes into the forest. The owl takes wing.

Through the dark woods, they hunt.

THIRTY-TWO

BLOOD AND BREAKFAST

The sun rises and shines through the trees in broad, crepuscular bands—the light catches in the last few flakes of snow falling, and it pools in the spatters of blood on the picnic table sitting out behind the cabin. It glitters and gathers.

Bird of Doom is on the ground nearby. She's mantling—meaning she's got her wings puffed up and pressed to the ground, making a kind of perimeter defense around her like she's afraid some other owl is gonna cheat off her test. In this case, the test is a squirrel. The bird's head dips and stabs underneath its wing shelter, plucking bits of stringy meat into its beak. Snap, snap, swallow.

Miriam has her own squirrel. Gutted and bled and skinned. Her hands are still red. This one's cooked, though: with enough charcoal and lighter fluid, it was easy to get the fire going around four AM. And the cold air kept the squirrel fresh.

She pulls strips of meat off her own kill. This squirrel she killed—not in her own body but while riding the owl. Sometimes, Miriam puts herself inside Bird of Doom and takes over. That part is getting easy now. Hunting isn't second nature to her, not like it is for the bird, but she can borrow the creature's instincts—can feel the animal's pull toward prey. It's a helluva thing, feeling your wings out, your talons down—and pinning some unsuspecting woodland creature to the snowy ground. The hardest part about it is knowing to let go and not just greedily eating. Miriam needs to eat—Miriam's body needs the nourishment, not the mind.

Which is what she's doing now. Taking to the squirrel like she might take to a plate of stacked pancakes. Her teeth along bone, pulling meat.

"I'm not gonna eat yours, long as you don't eat mine," she says to Bird of Doom. The owl looks up, wide-eyed like, *Shut up, pink-skin, I'm trying to eat.*

The back door of the cabin pops open, and here comes Louis—blanket wrapped around him as he blinks sleep out of his eyes. He slides in next to her, gives her a kiss on the cheek, then nods in Bird of Doom's direction.

"Owl," he says. Then, to Miriam: "Another successful hunt, huh?"

Miriam *mmmfs* in agreement, slurping stringy squirrel meat into her mouth like it's a wayward noodle.

"Didn't scare me up one, huh?" he asks.

"Sorry," she says. She holds the carcass at him. It's charred in places where she overcooked it a little. "One last bit of thigh meat, if you want it."

He waves it off. "It's fine. We have eggs. I'll make some."

"Make some for me, too. Squirrel's pretty lean." She wishes they'd gotten a rabbit. Bird of Doom can nab bigger prey, big as a raccoon, possum, or groundhog. But those aren't good eating, Miriam has discovered. At least, not just flung onto a little charcoal grill. Maybe a more nuanced chef knows what to do with raccoon, but right now she's at the most Neanderthal, FIRE GOOD stage of cooking. Which is where squirrels and rabbits shine. For a moment, she lets her mind go—like a bike chain or a transmission slipping, it briefly goes to the owl. Her mouth fills with the taste of blood and meat: raw, fresh, like squirrel sashimi. It gives her a small thrill and then—*shoop*—she's back.

Louis starts to get up. She grabs a fistful of the blanket, pulls him back down. With the taste of blood and meat on her tongue, she kisses him—her lips smashing against his, her teeth against his teeth. His moans meet hers. Miriam pulls away long enough to say, "Thank you."

"I think I should say thank you for that kiss."

"No, I mean—for this, for all of it." If it wasn't for Louis coming to get her that night, who knows where she would've ended up? On Harriet's hook? In the back of an actual cop car on her way to jail? Would've been a manhunt. But Louis came and took her away, and he didn't flinch when a mile down the road, an owl landed on the hood while they were at a stoplight. Miriam asked if the owl could come with them, and without missing a beat, Louis said, *Anything for you.*

And that was it. That was the moment she knew who he was, who she was, and how they needed to be together. Hell or high water. Till the oceans boiled and the sun went dark. They came here after that. He said they needed to hide out, and that he had an old buddy he used to work with at the trucking company, fella named Gordon Stavros. AKA Gordy. Gordy had this very remote hunting cabin near his house in the northeast part of the state, not far from the New York border. It was off the grid. Solar power. Wood heat. Louis cut a deal with him and that was that—since he was now an accessory to all of Miriam's legal and spiritual sins, the both of them took the leap together, ejecting from normal life and going off to hide in the woods.

That was almost two months ago.

And now she doesn't want this to end. She wants this cabin, this forest, her owl, her man, to be forever.

(A little voice pokes at her: *Gabby. You're forgetting about her, aren't you?* And Miriam has to shut that voice out. She has only so much love to give, and Louis has taken the leap—but maybe Gabby can be safe wherever she is. Even as she thinks it, it feels like a lie, like she's denying the truth of both who she is and who *Gabby* is, too.)

Her hand reaches under the blanket, sliding up along the outside of his knee—across the muscles of his thigh—

Louis leans into it, then back into another kiss. "Eggs," he mumbles.

"Sex," she counters.

"Well argued, counselor."

She starts to stand, melting into him. And then she does the porniest thing she can possibly do, which is split her perception for just a moment—now she's in the owl, looking out through Bird of Doom's eyes at her and Louis doing the lust-lizard tango out here in the snow.

But a sound snaps her back to her mind and flash-freezes her blood—

The sound of an engine. A car or truck. She stiffens, pulling away—

Louis puts a gentle, reassuring hand on her shoulder. "Probably just Gordy." From out back of the cabin, though, they can't see. Miriam hustles toward the corner of the cabin and peers out.

It's a truck. A rat-trap Chevy Silverado, mint-green. Poking its way down the gravel drive, through the three or four inches of snow that have gathered.

"It is Gordy," she says, letting out a whistle-breath of relief. Then she sneers. "More like Gordus Interruptus, am I right?"

"We can finish this when he's gone."

"Fine." She sighs.

"I wonder what he's brought us."

"I wonder indeed."

THIRTY-THREE
WHAT GORDY BRINGS

This is Gordy: he's in his midsixties, head like a pumpkin sitting around too long after Halloween. It gives him a funny underbite and pinched eyes and a nose that kind of lies out across his upper lip like a hot dog left on the side of a car. He is not an attractive man—though, according to Louis, Gordy still gets a lot of tail. Women young and old. Unconfirmed how much of that tail is actually from prostitutes he picks up in Scranton. Miriam won't judge. Sex work is work, same as bagging groceries and building bridges. A service to mankind, she figures.

Gordy steps out of his minty truck, a brown paper grocery sack in each hand. Louis hurries inside to get on some pants, and Miriam meets the old trucker and helps him with the bags.

"Bit of the ol' white stuff, eh," Gordy says.

Miriam shrugs. "Looks like the season came early. I always heard winter had a problem with premature ejaculation." Then she winks.

Good news is, Gordy's an old pervert. Not real witty, but he appreciates her wit, and that's all that matters. He bellows with laughter so hard, the laughter resolves into coughing and wheezing. They step inside the cabin and he's still laugh-coughing as he sets the bag down. Gordy wipes his eyes and says, "Oh, oh, that's a good one. Snow's white. Like a man's goo."

"That it is," Miriam says, suddenly finding the joke distasteful now that someone explained it. Especially using the word *goo*.

She starts pulling the groceries out—staples, mostly, bread and eggs and milk—and putting them away as if she were a proper domestic goddess. Gordy says he has a few more things, then heads back out to the truck. Louis shows up, pulling a shirt down over his chest. "He gone already?"

"Getting a few more things."

Louis passes by her to help put stuff away. His hand graces the middle of her back, fingers trailing. A chill grapples its way up her spine, like an electric spark gone up a copper wire. It thrills her. Though in the wake of that touch, she has this feeling like an icicle stabbed clean through her middle. *This can't last forever, Miriam. You're on the clock. Tick-tock, tick-tock.*

That thought: is it her own?

Or is it the Trespasser?

She hasn't seen her demon once since they've come here, which suddenly worries her more than if she hadn't seen that monster at all. The specter's absence is more conspicuous than his presence. *What is the Trespasser planning?* Surely, that demon has not left her to her peace. . . .

Gordy's back in the door now, and he's throwing down a couple newspapers. "Got the usual run. *Times-Tribune, Morning Call*, the *Intell.*" Miriam doesn't want to pick any of them up except to throw them in the pellet stove in the other room. And yet, obligation compels her to disrupt her safe little bubble. Soon as she picks one up, she feels her blood pressure tighten as if there's a pair of pinching fingers closing off the arteries on both sides of her neck.

Thus begins the routine. Miriam sits down at their little nook table, the one that wobbles because two legs are too short (or two are too long), and she begins flipping through the papers page by page, mostly looking at the crime beat.

They haven't found anything about Wren. No unusual

murders. Some *usual* murders, but ones that always had an easy through-line—a big blinking blood-stained arrow pointing to the husband or a burglar or some crazy guy next door.

As she's flipping through, Gordy sidles up to Louis.

Gordy is about as subtle as a firecracker going off in a closed hand. He fishes into his vest pocket and something crinkles as he hastily uncrumples it and passes it to Louis. Since the cabin presently only contains three people, it means he's trying to do it so she doesn't see. But of course she sees. She could have both eyes gone, not just one like Louis, and she'd figure it out.

She decides to play it cool, though. Miriam keeps her eyes mostly on the newspapers in front of her, and then side-eyes Louis for his reaction. He looks troubled. He turns away from Gordy, facing the sink. Head down, shoulders up, a tense hunch to his back. She thinks for a moment, *I could get a bird to read it.* Wouldn't that be a thing? Find some errant blue jay out there, have it perch on the window over the sink, use it to read whatever he's got in his hand . . .

Now you're thinking with birds.

But then, as her eyes drift down to the newspaper, something steals her attention. A small article, not front page but under the crime beat. *Reading, PA police officers dispatched to 429 Conifer St where they found the body of suspected heroin dealer and white supremacist, John "John Boy" Bosworth.* Farther down: *sources say his tongue was removed and shoved down his throat, though whether this was the cause of death remains unknown.*

Her mind hops in the Wayback Machine and goes way, way back. To a motel in North Carolina. Her sitting there on the bed. Del Amico standing near after he just popped her one—the socket around the eye still throbbing.

The time is now 12:43.

"You have epilepsy, Del?"

The question registers, and she knows now that he does. It explains what's about to happen. A moment of calm strikes the man named Del Amico, a kind of serene confusion, and then—

His body tightens.

"And here it is," Miriam says. "The kicker, the game ball, the season-ender."

The seizure hits him like a crashing wave.

Del Amico's body goes rigid, and he drops backward, his head narrowly missing the corner of the motel dresser. He makes a strangled sound. He sits upright on his knees, but then his back arches and his shoulder blades press hard against the matted Berber.

Del Amico. Choked to death on his tongue.

She didn't kill Del. He was one of the ones she simply let die, and then she took his shit and hit the road. Less than an hour later, she met Louis Darling, the man standing ten feet away, reading a piece of paper he's trying to keep secret.

Another white supremacist dead. And dead in a way that echoes Miriam's own life once again.

Or maybe it doesn't mean shit.

Or maybe it's a trap, because Harriet—that impossible monster who shouldn't even be alive right now—is still hunting your dumb ass.

Gordy leans into Louis, and the two of them share some quiet words that she can barely make out. Something about *didn't tell her*.

Her who? Her Miriam?

She stands up suddenly, chair juddering noisily behind her. It startles Gordy, but Louis—it's like he's ready for it. Or like he's still lost in whatever's on that piece of paper. Gordy mutters something about having somewhere to be, and then he's out the door faster than Wile E. Coyote chasing the Road Runner. Isn't long before his mint-colored truck backfires to life and heads back up the road.

Miriam's jaw tightens. "Don't keep secrets from me now, man."

"I'm not. I just . . . It's Samantha."

"What about her?"

"She's, you know, she's looking for me. Pinging a lot of my old buddies, reaching out, seeing if they've seen me."

"And Gordy—"

"Didn't tell her, no."

Whew.

"But you're bugged by it."

"I just . . ." His nostrils flare and he runs his hands up across his face and through his hair. "I just left everything. I left her behind. I ran away."

"We ran away. And we had to." Her jaw tightens. "This was your idea."

"I know," he says, holding up his hands. "I know! I'm not blaming you. I'm not even saying this hasn't been amazing. I'm just saying it's hard and it's . . . it's messed up, is what it is. Samantha . . . she had changed, something wasn't right with her, like she wasn't all there. And that thing with the feather . . ." He sighs. "Even still, what I did to her wasn't right."

"None of this is right," she says sharply, too sharply.

And there it is. It's happening. This carefully constructed illusion, it's starting to fall apart. Like cracks slowly spreading across the glass of a snow globe. *Oh, damn. That's what this is, isn't it? It's our little snow globe. Set away from the world, in a perfect little bubble, with snow gently falling on our cabin.* She can almost hear the glass popping and crackling.

"Well," she says with no small bitterness, "I think our little exile might be over anyway." She scoops up the paper, gives it one good fold, then marches over and slaps it against his barn-door chest. *Whap.*

He takes it, stares down at it. While he does that, she pulls the printed-out email out of his hands—and he doesn't resist.

He reads the paper. She reads the email.

The email is short. *Dear Gordon, my fiancée has been missing now for two months, and I know he's caught up in something. The police said he was a person of interest, but I don't believe that. If you see him, please help me, and tell me.* Blah blah blah. She leaves her phone number behind. And her email address, obviously—

Louis starts to say something, but Miriam's mouth goes dry and she nearly drops the piece of paper. The email address.

*Scarlet-tanager*99 at pil-dot-net.

She blinks. In the dark behind her eyes is a new memory, this one recent enough: her sitting in the Florida house with Grosky. Grosky is showing her the subreddit where they're talking about her, calling her the Angel of Death, and people are discussing her like she's a myth, a piece of folklore, not a real human being. And one of those Reddit handles:

Scarlet-tanager99.

Everything starts to spin. She feels like she needs to press her heels into the floor to hold the world down. Pieces are adding to the puzzle, but they don't make a clear image—in fact, every new piece of information only creates a stranger picture. Why would Samantha use that handle? Scarlet tanager is, what, a bird, right? She's been watching. *Spying.* And she stole Miriam's feather in the vial, too. Is Samantha with Louis just to find Miriam? Who the hell is this woman?

Louis is setting the newspaper down, a look of consternation drawing lines across his brow. "We don't know that this is Wren, Miriam. Question is, if it ends up being her, what do we do about it?"

But Miriam is barely listening. Her mind is elsewhere.

Instead, she blurts out:

"You're going to kill Samantha."

It's like an axe splitting a log, *ka-thunk*. This is the one thing she hasn't told him during their time here. Everything else has been fair game. He knows about her and Gabby. About Jack, about Harriet, about Grosky. She's kept nothing from him except this one, awful, precious thing: a murder he will soon commit.

Part of it is because he's just too damn good. Louis is one of the nicest things in a life that contains almost zero nice things. He's *good people*, and there are very few of those—the ones she does meet, the world seems to chew up and pick from its teeth. But somehow, he remains. And he remains *with her*. Despite all they've seen. Despite all of what may come. Up here in this cabin, in the snow, it's been too damn good, and this one piece of information—*you're going to kill Samantha*—ruins it all. Like bloody phlegm spat on van Gogh's *Starry Night*.

She says those words, she speaks that prophecy, and he just looks confused. "I don't understand."

"On the night of your wedding, you choke Samantha in a tub, and you drown her, and that's how she dies. I saw it."

He laughs, but it's not a happy laugh. It's nervous and dissolves into a small, troubled moan at its end. "That's not me. I'm not a killer."

She thinks but does not say: *Untrue.* He's killed for her before. A sudden spear of panic lances through her: *I made him into this. He kills because this is where I've led him.* She's like a bad disease, or worse, some kind of parasite. *Once Miriam Black is in your marrow, nothing will get me out.*

"I'm sorry." It's all she can say. And it sounds like she's apologizing for just this one thing, when really, she's apologizing for all the things.

"Miriam, I . . . I love her. Or loved her, once."

That makes her flinch. "And yet you kill her."

Now he looks mad. Because she has the temerity to keep insisting on the truth. "Maybe you're just mad. Salty because I found her and she found me and . . . even if it doesn't work out, you're jealous."

"I had someone else too. I had Gabby. Maybe *you're* the jealous one. Or maybe, just maybe, you don't really know your precious bride. That email address of hers? I've seen it before."

Another body blow leaving him confused and reeling. "What?"

She explains it. How Grosky showed her the forum dedicated to her, how that address was there as a user handle.

"That's not possible. Samantha isn't like that. It's just a coincidence."

"Sure. Just like it's a coincidence she stole my feather."

"Maybe . . . maybe that was an accident."

"Louis. Look at me. Look around at all the shit that's gone down since you and I met. How much of it has been coincidence? Or an accident?" She shakes the email page at him. "The universe is operating with sinister goddamn intent. Something or someone has a plan, and I have no idea what it is. But all of this adds up. I just don't know how yet. You said she had changed. That she was . . . different."

"I wouldn't kill her."

"I hope you won't have to. But in the thread of fate I tugged on, it sure looks like you do. And maybe it's because she's not who she says she is."

Anger sparks in his eyes like whole matchbooks going up in flame. "You said no secrets. Right here, you just said it. 'Don't keep secrets from me now.' But you were sitting on this the *whole* time. You knew where this was headed. Where I was headed. All this time and you kept that from me."

"You don't understand." She feels tears threatening to boil over. "I didn't believe it myself. And I didn't want to ruin any of this—"

"I'd say it's good and ruined now, wouldn't you? I came to you. I'm . . . messing around on her to be with you. And maybe she's not who she says she is, and maybe Samantha deserves some comeuppance. Maybe she even deserves my hands around her neck for something she did or will one day do. But I damn sure don't deserve *any* of this. You're a tornado, you know that? You just whirl in and tear shit up, and you throw everything and everyone in the air because tornadoes don't give a shit about anything. They go where they go, drawing a path of chaos across the land like God's finger."

She shrugs. "I told you not to get involved with me."

"Right. Because that's a good excuse. You've been selling that one since the beginning, you're right. And maybe I should've listened. But it doesn't change that you have responsibility, Miriam. You're obligated."

"I know!" she screams—a banshee wail. Hard enough it leaves her throat feeling like she just sucked down a shot of battery acid. "I *know.* Okay? That's why I'm trying to help Wren. Because I set her on a path and I didn't even realize it. I didn't realize it because I was too damn busy thinking about myself. Or not thinking at all. But I want to fix it. I want to make things right. Or at least better." She rubs her eyes. The tears are gone now. Dried up as a wave of desperation wicks away the grief. "So, whatever you think of me, I'm sorry. But whatever's going on with Samantha, with you, with me, right now Wren is out there and she needs our help."

He's silent for a while. Just standing there, arms crossed, the newspaper folded up and held in a crushing grip. Finally, he sighs and says coldly, "Fine. Let's go help her. You got a plan?"

"I didn't," she says. "But now I think I do."

THIRTY-FOUR

THE ENEMY OF THE GOOD

Miriam says goodbye to it. To the cabin, to the forest, to the snow. To these two months seeming to exist outside time and space. She's not one to be overly wistful, and of course she can't go letting the cabin thinking it's all special and shit, so she cuts her meandering mental goodbye short and says out loud:

"You were too good to exist. Fuck you."

She has no idea if they'll ever come back here, but if they do, it'll be sullied. Today was a stain, and no amount of bleach will get it out.

Miriam goes inside, gets the Remington 700 rifle from the closet—the one Gordy keeps in there and told them about. ("In case you want to do some hunting up here," he said.) She slings that over her shoulder, then heads outside.

It takes her a moment to rouse Bird of Doom—the owl has found a dead tree in which to hunker down and sleep. But once she does, she rides it back to her human body. It lands on a fallen maple, snow falling as the branch bows.

"You ready?" she asks the bird. "We got work to do."

It trills and chitters in the affirmative.

She holds out her wrist, and the owl alights upon it.

Time to go find Wren.

THIRTY-FIVE

SERENITY IN REARVIEW

Day to night. Down here, the snow has already started to melt—and with the coming darkness, a lot of that has frozen on the road. It makes traveling slower, but even with that difficulty, Reading isn't far for them. It's a three-hour drive, and by seven PM, they're parked on a side street at the south side of town, not far from 429 Conifer Street, where John Boy Bosworth died, his throat clogged by his own severed, swollen tongue.

Miriam unfolds the map awkwardly over the dash. The owl—who sits in the bitch seat between her and Louis—seems irritated at the rustling paper.

"Look," she says, pointing at the map. "We're here. Bottom of the city. Conifer is a few streets up. Residential." And shittily residential, by the look of it. Little boxy houses stacked next to each other. Chain link fences slick with ice. Lots of streetlights, none of them working. "But this I think is the magic spot, right here." She taps a green area just south of them—close enough to see out the passenger-side window of the truck. It's all thick trees that go up, up, up. "They call this area Neversink Mountain." (Her and Wren drowning in a river, saved by Louis, never to sink. Harriet, unable to be killed. Louis, drowning his bride in a tub.) She shudders. "Wren wouldn't have gone deeper into the city. She would've fled this way. It's got miles of trails. And any development on this mountain is done and gone. It's wild, all of it."

Like Wren.

Like me.

Like Gabby.

Maybe even like Louis.

"You think this'll work?" he asks.

"Yes. No. I don't know." Suddenly frustrated, she says, "It has to."

"Cops might be looking for my truck," Louis says. He's nervous. They didn't speak much on the way down here. She doesn't know what he's thinking. And a part of her doesn't—or can't—care about him and his feelings right now. Her mother's words echo: *It is what it is*.

Miriam nods. "I know. You see a cop, you bolt."

"What happens to you if I do that?"

"I don't know. If that happens, we'll find out."

He sighs. "We're doing this?"

"We're doing this."

"Be careful out there."

She smirks. "I'm not the one who's going to be out there, am I?"

And with that, she looks to the owl. The owl chirrups and barks. Miriam rolls down the truck window, and a blast of December air hits her. She gets her hands around the bulk of the bird and helps it wriggle out of the window, catching a wing-tip up the nose for her trouble.

When Bird of Doom takes flight, she takes flight with her.

THIRTY-SIX

BIRD TV

The owl is light. Her wings are silent. The transition is quick—she swiftly stops thinking of herself as a person with all the person things, with rubbery fingers and gangly getaway sticks and that strange piggish face that human beings have. Gone is her personhood. Once again, she is a bird. Her humanity is like a memory or, stranger still, like something that belongs to someone else. Someone in another lifetime. Someone on television.

Television. That word, that thought, it brings her back. Just a little. Not to her body, but to the margins of it. She again recognizes that faint ember flaring in the dark of her own human consciousness—an awareness of being a person in a bird, and not the bird itself.

And she must remember that she is a person. Because what she wants to accomplish here is not a bird goal but a Miriam goal.

The owl soars over the night. She takes the animal north, the dark streets of this dead city passing underneath her downy belly. There: two cars, black-and-white cruisers with colored lights on top, parked outside a house. Across the door is a slash of yellow tape. The windows are barred.

Why would the cops still be here?

An idle thought: *They're looking for me*.

At Miriam's behest, the owl opens its cloaca and lets fly with a spatter of white waste. It lands on one of the cop cars with a faintly satisfying *splat*.

The owl wheels south once more. She has nothing she can do here. Wren won't be present. And Wren wouldn't have gone into the city—Reading has crime, and that means cops. But the trees, the mountain, the trails . . .

The owl glides, occasionally pumping her wings to stay aloft. Miriam brings the bird low, just over the tops of the trees as the mountain rises beneath.

It's then she reaches out.

The owl has tremendous senses. As a spider can detect vibrations up and down the silken threads of its web, the owl can detect such vibrations in the air. This is how an owl hunts: it feels the air stirred by a songbird, or the nearly unobservable tremor of a mouse's feet tapping across the dirt. Its hearing and sight are nearly unparalleled in the bird world. Perhaps in all the animal world, though Miriam cannot say: she can only ride with birds. Why that is, she can only speculate, but long ago someone told her that birds are psychopomps, shuttling souls from the world of the living to the land of the dead. Bird of Doom certainly doesn't know anything about souls, though. It knows only about flight, and hunger, and fucking. *The best things in life*, Miriam thinks, a distant human thought. *Maybe that's why I can join with birds. We're all too alike.*

There. Down below, something perturbs the air. A bird. Another owl, this one a small screech owl. It chases another bird, this one a small song sparrow breaking from cover over the trees. The screech owl swoops, and Miriam has to move fast: it's like parachuting from one plane to another below it, her mind suddenly untethering from Bird of Doom and lashing the screech owl—

She's in the smaller predator now. It's like pulling up on the reins of a horse—the owl extends its wings and slows its vector of attack. The song sparrow begins to escape. Miriam thinks: *Can't kill the songbird, Mr. Owl. I need it.*

It's not just the sparrow she needs. Nor the owl.

Out there, in the dark of the forest, she feels the little candle-flame flicker of a hundred different birds. A red-tailed hawk. A red-shouldered hawk. Another screech owl. And then the song-birds: dozens of them, from cardinals to woodpeckers to song sparrows, all remaining during the winter because food is reliable, so why bother migrating south?

The thought hit her back in the cabin, when Louis was reading that email by the window. *I could have a bird read it* . . . a bird, like her own personal organic camera. A creature with eyes through which she can see.

Now you're thinking with birds.

She focuses herself.

Here comes the real trick.

Miriam has done this before.

(Though, ahem, not intentionally.)

It's like putting her foot through a mirror, except the mirror is her mind. She shatters it into a hundred different pieces, each her but not her, each a reflection of her. And she takes these fragments and flings them out into the world. Each finds its home in the mind of a different bird: a turkey buzzard, a house finch, a dove, a blackbird, a crow. Miriam feels strained and spread out, each piece of herself connected by the barest filament—

And each filament is thinner and thinner, like a wire stretched too far.

Hold on. Just hold on.

Birds have small minds. But they are not stupid—they are simply efficient. They do not have long, complicated memories, but they do remember. Crows hold grudges. Pigeons can recognize words and numbers. Birds need to remember people and places because that helps them know where they might find food, or where there is danger. They don't go to sleep and forget all of what transpired.

Birds remember.

And Miriam needs that. She needs their memories and their eyes, and into the network of bird brains she thrusts a single image:

Wren. Wren as she looks now. She throws this image out there, pinging their collective minds—

There comes a flash. A glimmer of memory. Not in one bird, but in several—

She starts to lose it. It's hard to hold, like fishing wire slipping fast through her grip. Not just one wire, but a hundred, all receding in different directions. She feels herself hammered thinner and thinner. *Hold on, hold on—*

But hold on to what? What is she holding on to?

What is she looking for?

Who even is she? She feels tossed about in an endless roil, a turbulent vortex. She twists in the dark like a snake protesting its captor's hands. *You're a tornado, you know that*? *You just whirl in and tear everything up that was anchored down.*

That voice. Who said that to her?

The name is almost there, almost on the tip of her consciousness. . . .

L . . .

Lou . . .

And then it's gone. Flensed by that storm. All the birds take flight. A flurry of wings rises in the night. She is with them. She cannot escape them. A piece of herself in each of those birds, the mirror broken, the pieces refusing to come together, and each reflection drifting farther from the next.

INTERLUDE WREN

They call it the Witch's Hat. It's a stone pavilion built—well, Wren doesn't know how long ago, but it wasn't recently. Fifty years ago? A hundred? She doesn't know, doesn't care. It looks well enough like a witch's classic peaked hat, surrounded as it is by dead scrub and ground gone dry in winter. The pavilion sits at the peak of Neversink Mountain and overlooks the Reading skyline. Which isn't worth much of a look.

Right now, the skyline is a series of glittering lights set against the dark. It's cold up here, exposed to the wind, and Wren is really feeling it. She's curled up inside the pavilion in a ratty red sleeping bag she stole from a local Army-Navy store. Wren shivers. From the temperature, yes, but from something deeper, some greater fear that won't let her go.

The .22 revolver she once stole from Stinson's pawn shop is clasped tight against her chest. It's loaded. Her finger isn't on the trigger, and the hammer isn't drawn back, though she's vaguely aware that the gun could go off and, if it did, the bullet would catch her under the chin and go up into her skull. Rattle around like dice in a cup. Scramble her brains like eggs.

Maybe that's fine, she tells herself.

The next thought is:

I'm going to get caught.

She should have gone farther. She's close, too close, to where she killed that sick fuck with his Nazi tats. The cops are going to be looking for her.

Or looking for Miriam.

Miriam. She's still alive.

And then, on cue, a pair of boots clomp up next to her. She can see their shadow and shape more than their detail as she peeks her head out of the puckered sphincter of the closed sleeping bag. The smell of cigarette smoke fills the air, and Miriam kneels down before transitioning into sitting cross-legged in front of her. In the dark, she's more a silhouette, but Wren knows it all too well.

"Hey, psycho," she says, her teeth chattering.

"Hey there, See You Next Tuesday." The sizzle of the cigarette cherry is eerily, impossibly loud. "Comfy?"

"Eat my ass."

"Friendly, too."

"Shut up, liar. You're a liar. Just leave me alone."

Miriam, who isn't real, who she thought was a ghost but now she's not so sure, whistles low. "This is bad, Wren. The world is closing in on you. The walls are falling down. Right this very moment, the cops are looking for you. And so are others. Even me. I'm out there. Hunting you."

"You're not real."

"The real me is real."

"Fuck you with your stupid doublespeak! You lied to me. You said you—you said she was dead."

The shadow offers a perceptible shrug. "She was, in a way." Then this Miriam mutters under her breath: "Bitch is dead to me, anyway."

"I thought you were her. I thought you were her ghost."

"I never said I was. You just assumed that. And you know what they say about those who assume." Miriam chuckles; the laugh is deep and unlike what Wren expects. In there is a crackling sound, like a burning campfire. "Does it matter who I really am? I've been helping you. I've been guiding you."

"You made me into a murderer."

"You made yourself into a murderer. But I made those murders mean something. You see what you see and that's a special gift. You are given a privileged glimpse at the future. Don't piss in the gift horse's mouth, little girl." Miriam's hand runs along the length of the sleeping bag. It's meant to be reassuring, but it just chills Wren all the more. Miriam sighs. "I know, it's upsetting. But you're doing such good work, Wren. The best work. You're saving people. You're changing fate. Doesn't that count for something?"

"I just want to go home."

"You have no home."

"I just want to be normal."

"And I want a fucking pony," Miriam counters with a hiss. "But I don't get a pony and starving kids don't get to eat and the Devil doesn't get a sno-cone and you, my dear Wren, you don't get to be normal. The horse is out of the barn and the barn burned down. Can't put the snakes back in the can, blah blah blah." Miriam sniffs. "Besides, someone needs to do the work. The other me, the real me, well, she's just not that into me right now. Fine. Fuck her. That means it's all you. Congrats."

"Please—"

"Please what?" Those two words, full of venom and disdain. The shadow-shape of Miriam shifts again, and that glowing cherry dips and drops. It winds closer. All around, a new sound arises, the fluttering of wings, the caw and chirp and squawk of birds, and Wren shuts her eyes and unwittingly makes a low and droning moan in the back of her throat to block out all the noise. And then Miriam is there with her, in the sleeping bag, whispering impossibly in her ear: "A conversation for another time. You have a visitor."

And then the pressure is gone. The specter has fled.

Wren gasps, sitting up in her bag. Panting. Sweating. The cold air washes over her slick body and it feels good for a moment—until it feels bad.

Then she realizes:

I'm not alone.

The sound of the feathers rustling, the birds squawking—it's real. All around her are birds, perched on the stone ledges of the pavilion's arched windows. A pair of vultures. A murder of crows. Little songbirds shifting from foot to foot, wings shuddering to adjust. They're not just here, either. They're on the steps out. They're on the dead ground outside. And the sound above her—the *clicky-scratch* of claws on old shingle—tells her they're up there, too.

She swallows hard. Wren grabs for her backpack nearby, pulling the handgun out. She points it from one bird to the next and the next after, drifting gently in a circle, finger creeping toward the trigger.

"Get out of here," she whispers.

But the birds just cock their heads, black eyes shining in the moonlight.

Wren slowly starts to work her way toward the way out of the pavilion—but the birds don't leave. Worse, they gather tighter at that spot.

She points the gun.

"What is this? What do you want?"

And then a massive owl lands. Feathers peak above its eyes, giving it devil horns. The owl doesn't hoot—it squawks. An angry warning. It fluffs its wings up, spreads them out wide.

It happens. Wren's perceptions shift for just a moment—it's like being whisked down a hallway really fast, like the world is rushing past her even though she's standing still. And then, around the owl is drawn a black line, blacker than any shadow, blacker than night. It pulses like a demon's heart. A black handprint sits in the dead center of the bird's chest—

The black mark.

And then it's gone again.

Wren eases back. "Miriam?"

Then: voices. From the forest. Men yelling. Wren looks in that direction, sees spears of light—flashlight beams—cutting through the trees.

Police.

In one movement, all the birds take flight. All but the devil's owl. Its head cocks this way and that. Golden eyes fix on Wren and the beak opens, the bird's tongue out and waggling in the air—

"Fffffollow mmmmeeeee."

Then it squawks and takes flight.

Wren doesn't know what to do. What is happening? Is this real? The men's voices are closer now—but suddenly, they're crying out. She hears branches breaking, birds squawking in a discordant chorus, and then gunfire. Bang, bang, bang. Wren swallows, looks out over the dead ground—

And there is the owl.

Staring at her. No—waiting for her.

Wren runs toward it.

The owl lifts into the air, flying only as high as Wren is tall. From her left, a man yells: "There! We've got her!" And then a gunshot splits the night and she feels something zip through the black just inches from her nose.

They're going to kill me.

A little voice responds with *And maybe I deserve that*.

But despite that thought, Wren pumps her legs and, gun in hand, follows the owl right into the tree line. Crashing through brush. Trying not to slip on ice and mud. Following an owl criss-crossing ahead of her, landing from branch to branch, threading the night.

THIRTY-SEVEN

EXEUNT

Miriam sucks in a breath, then cries out as she awakens. Her hands fly up at her face, and she sees her fingers are talons. Feathers line the tops of her arms as if stitched in there—the skin raw and red, blood trickling down to her elbows. She tries to say something, but her teeth clack together, *snap-snap*. *No, not my teeth. My beak.* A horrible beak pushes from her mouth, her jaw cracking and straining as it urges forward, breaking her teeth, pulling the tendons in her neck—

And then it's gone. Over. All an illusion. A hallucination.

Louis looks at her. "You're back."

She swallows hard, looking around the truck. Miriam puts her hands on the dashboard. She has fingers, not talons. "I'm not becoming a bird," she says.

"That's good. Did you see anything? Did you see Wren?"

The most horrible answer she has comes out of her mouth: "I don't know."

Panic goes through her chest like a sniper's bullet. She really doesn't remember. She remembers being up there in the sky with all the birds, and she remembers breaking herself apart—

And then that's it. It's like falling asleep. One minute your mind is there, the next it's dim, then dark, then you've gone somewhere else entirely. Did she see Wren? In the back of her brain is a hazy dreamlike memory of Wren, and then she shudders as she feels her feet turning to bird talons, and beneath her leathery toes she feels cold stone, and she remembers men yelling, and beams of light crisscrossing the night. She forms her hands into fists and pushes them into her eyes. It hurts. The pain is good, it's clarifying. It anchors her back to herself.

"I heard sirens," Louis says. "A couple cop cars went down past the block—another passed us here. Didn't see us, though."

"Oh. Okay." Her mouth tastes of worms and seeds. Something suddenly touches her mind, like fingertips sliding across the top of her awareness—

And Bird of Doom settles down on the hood of the truck. The owl shrugs her wings and stares down her beak at them.

"Your owl is back," Louis says, gesturing with his chin.

"Yeah, I—"

Outside the truck, someone screams. Then she hears men yelling.

A shape is darting through the tree-lined darkness, headed right toward them. A human shape. A Wren shape. A few hundred yards behind her, flashlight beams illuminate the forest.

Wham. Wren slams into the truck, her fingers splayed and pressed against the glass. Her voice is muffled but the words are clear enough: "Let me in! Let me in, damnit!" Wren hurries to the back of the pickup truck and lifts herself up, ducking down into the truck bed.

"Jesus," Louis says. "Was that—"

Bang. A bullet thuds into the front right side of the truck. More gunshots follow, and the window of a parked car ahead explodes. "Go, go, go!" Miriam cries, and she slides down the seat, trying to stay hidden. Her mind flicks to Bird of Doom: *Fly, dummy!*

The owl does as it is told. It spreads its wings wide and goes up.

Louis backs up hard, crashing into the car behind them—a

Saab from the late nineties. Its headlights pop as he angles the truck, spinning the wheel.

A police cruiser turns the corner behind them, and its lights go on as its siren whoops. Louis plows forward as more bullets punch into his truck. He barrels around the corner, only to see another cruiser come in ahead.

Miriam knows she could do something about this. She could summon the birds again. They could swarm the cars. Fling a couple doves in through the windshield or grille, fill the heating vents and the front seat with blood and feathers. But fear has its hands on her. She doesn't want to lose herself again. It almost happened out in the desert, and it nearly happened again right now. Even if she wanted to, she's not sure she could do it.

Which means that this is on Louis.

But if there's one thing he knows, it's how to drive a truck.

"Hold on," he growls, and he cuts the wheel to the right. The truck leaps the curb and bounds over the sidewalk—

And then it's skirting the tree line. To their left, the street pulls away, and ahead, the slick and icy grass gives way to a different avenue. If Miriam remembers her map, they just left South Street, and ahead by a quarter-mile is Fairview. But they'll only make it there if they don't die first—

The back end of the truck fishtails left and right, the wheels barely gripping the ground. Behind them, the two cop cars try the same maneuver, and Miriam thinks, *We're screwed.* Cops know how to handle their cars. They're taught defensive driving, aren't they? Shit. The night fills with the red-and-blue strobe and the banshee screams of their advancing sirens—

But then the car in the lead loses control. It spins out, its back end suddenly where its front should be. And the second car slams right into it.

As that happens, Louis—knuckles gone bloodless as they wrap tight around the steering wheel—gets control of his truck.

Everything still feels slick and slippery, like the whole world might shoot out from underneath them and launch them into space, but then the vomit-comet ride is over as the truck rockets toward Fairview. The vehicle bangs and shudders as it leaps the curb anew, and then they're back on the road.

She sees signs for 422 ahead, and Louis guns the engine.

PART FIVE

THE ROOST

THIRTY-EIGHT
EXILE, REVISITED

The truck judders over the uneven gravel drive. It's morning, but early enough that the dark is still over the world like a hand pressed across its eyes and its mouth, keeping it silent and blind. Ahead is the cabin.

Their escape from Reading was easier than expected—Louis zigzagging from highway to back road and back to highway again. Nobody stopped them. No red-and-blue lights. No Harriet descending from the dark, eyeless and mad.

A half hour in, he pulled over, and Wren crawled into the cab with them. The owl joined them, too, which made for less than comfortable conditions. The two hours back north were spent in silence. The owl occasionally tilted its head and glared at everyone, its expression both murderous and bewildered.

And now they're back. Back to the forest, the snow, the cabin. Back into exile, back to the snow globe. But Miriam knows that the globe is still cracked, and that everything it contained is leaking out. Drip by bloody drip.

THIRTY-NINE

NO REST FOR THE WICKED

Louis says, "I think we've all had a long night—"

"No." One word, sharp as a stabbing knife. Miriam points to Wren with a single finger gun, drops the hammer, bang. "I want to know."

Wren blinks. Just looking at her is throwing Miriam for a bowel-churning mental loop—she looks like Miriam did when she first started out on the run from her mother, her power, her life. The black knife-slash hair, the dark eyes, the white T-shirt, the denim run ragged. This is a girl on the edge. Miriam knows, because she too was on the edge. *Did I ever leave the edge? Or did I just buy real estate here, right on the razor's line?*

Shit.

The girl's face twists up. A sneer tugs at her lips and defiance shines on her face like lightning. She looks to Miriam, but then she looks to Louis, too. Staring at him hard. Not just at him—through him. Like she's pinning him to the wall with spears. Is she afraid of him? Miriam gives him a nod and he eases backward into the cabin, pressing himself into the corner, where a small chair waits near the bed. He melts into it, lost to shadow.

Wren's swagger and anger fall away. The girl looks tired. Her voice is weary and older than it should be when she answers, "Fine. I can tell you whatever. What do you wanna know, psycho?" Even that word, *psycho*, it's lost its teeth. Just hollow bluster, rote.

"I . . ." Miriam flounders, flopping around in her own uncertainty. "I don't know. Something. Anything. Everything."

"Got a cigarette?"

"I don't smoke anymore."

Wren gives her a look like she's a space alien with a pair of rubber dicks for antennae. "Oooookay." Her fingers fidget, dancing like spider legs. "I thought you were dead. I really did. I was told . . ." The words die in her mouth.

"It was me that told you. Or something that looked like me."

Wren hesitates. "Yeah."

"Said I was dead."

"Uh-huh." The girl licks her lips, nervous.

"The Trespasser."

"What?"

"I have one. In my head. I see it sometimes. I call him the Trespasser. I don't know what it is, but it's a phantom and it's there when I don't want it and not there when I want it. And it's always pushing me. Pushing me toward some new bullshit. Some death. Some twist of fate that I'm supposed to fix. Or break." She hears the desperation in her own voice, and it mirrors Wren's. Maybe not a mirror at all. Maybe it's like looking through a window. "I don't know. I know you have a power, though. Right?"

"It's a curse."

"I know it is." She leans forward, eager. "Tell me about it."

"It's like yours. But different."

"How?"

"I don't see how people are going to die."

"What do you see?"

"I see people who are going to kill."

INTERLUDE

WREN

She sees them a lot. Since her time in the river, in fact. For a while when she was younger, she thought of them as the Silver Lining People, because that's how it looked, right? There they are, plain as day, but around them is this bright, shining line. Like light flashing off a knife. But that kind of ruined the idea of a silver lining for her. A silver lining was supposed to be a good thing, and she knew that these people were bad. Knew it down in her gut. How bad, or what that badness meant, Wren didn't know.

Then she thought it looked almost like liquid metal. Sliding around their margins. Like the metal of a gun, melted. Like mercury.

So, that's how she thinks of them now. Mercury Men. Even when they're women. In a crowd, there's always at least one. Standing out from the rest, popping out like the image in a Magic Eye painting. The Mercury Men look 3-D in a 2-D world. Raised up, embossed, above and beyond the others.

When she sees one, her stomach goes sour. Her chest burns and her heartbeat quickens. At her temples, she feels this pressure, like a pair of thumbs pushing in hard, real hard, like they're trying to pop her head like a zit.

For years, she's been seeing them and she doesn't know why, and now she's sitting outside a truck stop near to midnight, and she sees one get out of his truck. It's dead here mostly, just a couple truckers in and out of the place, but this one stands out. He's got sludgy shoulders, a broad chest, and a wide gut. Hair shorn tight to his scalp, a head the shape of a pencil eraser. Dopey-looking. And yet, there it is—that shining line drawn around him. *Mercury Man*.

"You see him?" comes a voice to her right. Wren is sitting there alone with an empty French fry carton in her hand—one she fished out of a trashcan so she could swab salt out of it with a wet finger—and the voice is instantly familiar. She wheels on it, surprised.

"It's you," Wren says, her voice small and breathless.

"Hey, See You Next Tuesday," Miriam says. Cigarette dangling from her lips. Eyes rimmed with makeup and shadow. She hooks a nearby stool with the toe of her boot and drags it noisily over before sitting down. "Been a while."

"How the—where the—" Wren looks around, bewildered. She's out here in the Middle of Fucking Nowhere, Pennsylvania, and somehow Miriam Black just zeroes in on her like a sniper's bullet? She blinks, thinking this isn't real. But it's real. There she sits. Puffing on her cigarette. Anger bores through Wren like the bit on a power drill. "You abandoned me."

Miriam shrugs. "Pfft. It's what I do, doll."

The Mercury Man crosses the lot and heads toward the truck stop. All the little fast food places in there are closed, but the gas station is open, as are the bathrooms and the vending machines. He steps inside, and Wren lets out the breath she was keeping in her chest. *He's gone*.

She turns to Miriam.

"You were supposed to look out for me."

"I tend to look out for me first. But whatever. I'm here now."

Memories whip through Wren's head. All this time on the road. Hitchhiking. Homeless. Hooking up with whoever she has to hook up with just to survive. She's slept in Porta-Johns, she's had to fight off truckers and bikers and cops who wanted something from her she wasn't willing to give, she's been chased by dogs and stalked by drunken college assholes in pickup trucks. Just this week, she got into a real claws-out fight with Vic, the Oxy dealer she'd been living with up in Scranton for the last couple months. He punched her in the stomach. She slammed a door on his hand, broke his fingers. He punched her in the face, and now the cut over her right eye is crusted over but sometimes still bleeds. Wren stole his wallet on the way out, but turns out he didn't have any cash, the fucker. Everything sucks. And all the while, she's been waiting for someone to come to her, to offer her a hand and say, *Come with me*.

She's been waiting for Miriam.

"You said you'd come back for me."

"I said I'd come check on you in a few years." Miriam shrugs, ditches her cigarette—the bright cherry pinwheels through the dark before it hits a puddle left there by spring rains. "It's been a few years. Ta-fucking-da."

"I thought I'd see you sooner."

"I was busy."

"I was busy too."

Miriam looks at her, eyebrow raised. "No kidding. You look like road trash. You look like me. Except for the being-dead part."

"Wait, what?"

"I'm dead."

"You're an asshole, because you're right here. Alive."

Miriam holds up her hand. "High-five me."

Wren wrinkles her nose but whatever, fine, she does it. She raises her hand and slaps it against Miriam's—

Except it doesn't slap. It goes clean through. Whiff.

Reality feels like it flips upside-down. A sense of disconnectedness runs through her, like all of what she knows and believes is sliding through her hands like a slicked-up rope.

Wren turns and throws up. She doesn't have much food in her, so what comes out is just a spittle-stream of what feels like battery acid. It burns her stomach as her gut cinches in again and again until she's heaving up nothing.

A man's voice asks: "You okay?"

She startles, looking up—

A trucker stands nearby. Not the Mercury Man—this one with a big beard and a bald head. Chapped lips, pockmarked face, but kind eyes. She doesn't see many kind eyes out here, so when she sees them, she remembers.

"I . . . I'm fine."

"Okay." But he's still standing there, unsure.

"Am I alone?"

He gives her a look like she's lost her damn mind. "What?"

Wren is about to say, *Do you see this woman here?* But when she turns, Miriam is already gone.

(The smell of her cigarette remains.)

The man says, "There's a clinic nearby." He must see the look of confusion on her face, so he explains: "North River Street in Wilkes-Barre. Alcohol but methadone, too, if you need that. And I think you might."

He thinks I'm an addict. "Fuck you," she says, suddenly venomous. "I'm fine. Just please go away."

He holds up both hands in surrender. But those kind eyes of his hold true. He slides a twenty-dollar bill under a nearby napkin holder. "God bless," he says, walking backward a few steps before turning around and heading toward a nearby Peterbilt.

Wren stares suspiciously at the twenty.

"Take it," Miriam says, suddenly back. She lights another cigarette with a Bic lighter. *Click, click, sizzle* and *puff*. "You need it."

Wren takes the money but fixes her eyes to Miriam. "You're dead."

“Dead as the American Dream, baby.”

“You’re a ghost.”

“We can go with that, sure.”

“You’re not real.”

Miriam talks around the cigarette, juggling the cancer stick between her lips. “If that’s what helps you sleep at night.”

“Fuck off. Go away. I don’t want you here.”

“A crude exorcism. Usually there’s a young priest and an old priest and some loftier words, but hey, cool. If that’s what you want, I’m outtie like a belly button, bitch.” Miriam kicks the stool backward, standing up. “I’ll see you in a few more years, and maybe then you’ll be willing to hear what I have to tell you.”

Miriam takes a few steps.

“Wait,” Wren says.

A small smile haunts Miriam’s face. “Do I have your attention?”

“What do you need to tell me?”

“Say pretty please.”

“I don’t beg.”

“Of course you don’t. I wouldn’t either. You’re defiant like me.” Miriam turns, wets her lips as the cigarette perches in the softly closed scissor-grip of her fingers and she says, “Here it is. I can tell you what the Silver Lining is about. I can tell you who the Mercury Men are.”

“Tell me.”

“They’re monsters.”

Suddenly, there it is: the pressure at her temples, the snare-drum roll of her pulse, the dry mouth, the high-pitched whine in her ears. She knows what it means: here comes the Mercury Man back out of the truck stop. He’s got a coffee in one hand, a couple candy bars held in the other. He heads back to his truck.

The light around him gleams like chrome.

“I don’t understand.”

Miriam points with her cigarette, the ember drawing searing

circles around the Mercury Man. "That fella there? His name is Robert Bender. Bob. Bobby, Bobbo, Bobbing-for-Apples. Bob is a monster. But you already knew that."

I did, Wren thinks. Or if she didn't know it, she damn sure felt it.

She wants to puke again. Or cry.

But a little part of her feels good, too. Like this is a puzzle piece she's long been missing. An answer to a riddle she didn't know she was asking.

Miriam continues, even as Wren watches Bob juggle his drink and his candy and now his keys as he tries to get into his truck. "Bob is a monster, but not of the supernatural variety. Bob is no vampire, no werewolf, no sexy Frankenstein. Bob is the most mundane kind of monster. He is human. And he is a murderer." Miriam shrugs. "Or at least he will be. He has not killed yet. But he will. Soon."

Across the lot, Bob finally gets his door open and starts to slide his butt into the seat. Wren says, "How do you know?"

"It is my job to know."

"How do I know you're telling me the truth?"

"You don't. You feel it in here—" Miriam reaches out and knocks on Wren's breastbone like it's a door. Wren startles—the touch is physical, unlike the spectral high-five. She feels it echo, *thud, thud, thud*. "But the only way you really know is you find out on your own. Watch him. Follow him."

The truck's headlights come on. Bright spears of bold light.

"Hunt the monster," Miriam says—and Wren looks to her, but she's already gone. Only thing left is a serpent of smoke still in the air, slithering before fading to nothing as Miriam herself has done.

Wren stands up as the truck starts to pull away.

She runs over, stepping in front of the truck, waving her hands.

The brakes squeal. The man leans his head out. “Get out of the way.”

“I need a ride.”

He waits a moment. Like he’s chewing it over.

But then he waves his hand. “All right. Come on. Let’s go.”

That’s how Wren meets Bob Bender, soon-to-be murderer.

FORTY

SWEET CHILD OF MINE

It's 4:15 AM when Miriam says, "So you killed him with a knife. A fillet knife." *Like the one used on Louis.* "You put his eye out with it."

Hesitantly, Wren nods. She's not proud of it. That's good. If she were proud of it, if she wore it like a badge, then she'd be too far gone.

The girl looks to Louis. He remains awake but stays seated and quiet in the dark corner of the cabin. Miriam wants to go to him, crawl into his lap, and have him help her through this. But even though he was the one who fished her and Wren out of that river, he isn't obligated to do this.

Not like Miriam is.

"Where'd you get that knife?" Miriam asks.

"It was there. At his house."

It's here that Louis speaks up. "I thought he was a trucker. How long did you stay with him?"

Wren flashes Louis a cold stare. It's one shot through with fear. She stammers, "I don't know. I just know his house was nearby."

"Not a long-haul trucker," Louis says with a small, soft grunt. Like he understands now. "Must've been a driver for local routes only."

"The knife," Miriam says. "You found it there."

"Not exactly."

“What does that mean?”

“Someone showed it to me.”

“Bender?”

“You.” She rubs her eyes with the heels of her hands. A long, exasperated sigh escapes her lips. “Not you-you. The other you. The ghost you.”

“Trespasser Miriam showed you the knife?”

“Yeah. I was sleeping on his couch. That’s where he let me crash. And the basement door opened up and I saw a face hidden there in the darkness. It was you. Her. It. Whatever. It whispered to me to come downstairs, and I did. And there I found the wall of knives.”

“How many knives?”

“I dunno. Like, dozens. The way some guys might have tools on the wall, Bender had knives. All kinds. Hunting knives, diving knives, machetes, skinning knives, and then the fishing knife. Miriam told me to take that one.”

“So you did. Then you went upstairs and killed him?”

“He found me downstairs. He was . . .” She shudders. “He had on a dirty white T-shirt, but he was fucking naked below that. He had a stun gun in his hand. I knew what was going to happen.”

Miriam’s jaw clenches. She knows too. She’s seen it. She’s been there. It’s not that every man is a monster, but there are enough out there hiding in plain sight, wolves wearing the skin of the sheep, hoping to take a bite out of Little Bo Peep. “What happened?”

“I killed him.”

“Why in the eye?”

“You—she—told me to. Guided my hand and everything.”

“Is it like that every time?”

“More or less. I see one of the Mercury Men. She’s there. She pushes me.”

“Ever try not to listen? Not to do what Trespasser Miriam wants?”

Wren swallows. “Yeah.”

“And?”

“I always end up there anyway.”

Miriam thinks to keep probing, to keep asking about all of it—every murder, every weapon, every last drop of blood spilled. But it’s becoming increasingly obvious that Wren is just a pawn in a game Miriam doesn’t yet understand. Is Wren’s Trespasser the same as Miriam’s? Are they different? Do their agendas connect or clash?

Wren’s a puppet. Is Miriam a puppet, too?

“I think it’s time for bed,” Miriam says.

“Agreed,” Louis says, his voice dry and growly. “You two take the bed, I’ll crash out on the chair.”

Wren says nothing to that, no thank you, no anything. She tears her stare away from him and looks to Miriam. “She’s mad at you, you know.”

“She who?”

“She you. Your Trespasser. Your doppelganger specter. First, she told me you were dead. She said you were shot and you wandered out into the desert and died out there.”

A chill spider-walks its way up Miriam’s spine. Because that is, for the most part, exactly what the fuck happened. She did get shot. She did end up in the desert. But she didn’t die there. *Or did I?* Dead or no, how does Wren know? How did this Trespasser know? Is this Trespasser truly different, or do she and Wren share the same haunted head?

“But when I found out she wasn’t you,” Wren says in a low register, “she got mad. Fucking spitting pissed. She said you abandoned her. You wanted out of your job and that’s where I came in. That if you weren’t going to do it, then I’d be the one to fill your boots.”

"How did that make you feel?"

Wren sneers. "You're not my fucking therapist."

"Fair point, but don't be pissed at me."

Now her voice is getting louder: "Why shouldn't I be? It's like I told that thing in my head: you abandoned me. You fucked off on your next adventure, and you left me holding an armload of heavy-ass emotional baggage. You ever think about me? Out there with all this in my head?"

"Fuck you," Miriam says, suddenly seething. "I'm not your mother. I figured your life was a whole lot better without me in it."

"How'd that turn out, you figure?"

"Eat shit, you little brat. Your little pre-crime killing spree has left the cops coming after my ass. I could turn and point them toward you, you know. Or even better, throw you to a different set of much nastier, much more rabid wolves: the criminals you keep killing. There's one nasty little bulldog out there who wants to chew me apart for what you're doing. So, don't come laying this at my door like I'm the one obligated." All this comes pouring out of her mouth, but even as she's saying it, she's not sure she believes it. Debt hangs around her neck like a dead bird. She did abandon Wren. She just let her go like a paper boat in the ocean.

Fuck fuck fuck.

Wren's about to lay in deeper, but Louis steps in, separates them. "Hey. It's late. We're all tired. Let's just hit the hay, see what tomorrow brings."

That is a question that suddenly haunts Miriam. The question of tomorrow is a scary one. She didn't think about any of this. They've gone and gotten Wren—what happens now?

But the big dude is right. Now isn't the time.

That is Future Miriam's problem.

Present Miriam is worn out like a decades-old pair of panties—elastic blown out, moth-eaten, left on the floor to be forgotten.

And with that, they each go to their corner. Nobody changes into pajamas. Miriam barely has the presence of mind to kick off her boots. Sleep hits them quickly, a vicious duck-duck-goose game dropping each of them into their own dreamscapes and nightmarelands.

FORTY-ONE

THE LAST SMOKE

Wuzza.

Wooza.

Snnnrrgh.

Blink, blink.

Voices intrude—hot pins popping the slumber bubble in which Miriam has found herself. Last night, she did not go to sleep so much as she was shoved into sleep's burlap sack and stolen away to the Comatose Kingdom. Climbing back out of that lovely, lightless realm is hard, like escaping a slick-walled pit. When she does, the voices reach a fever pitch and then her heart jumps as she hears a truck door slam.

She smacks her lips together, tasting the copper tang of dry spit in her mouth as she hauls herself up to the window the same way someone might dangle from a steep cliff—fingers on the ledge, barely pulling her chin up over it.

Outside, she sees Gordy in his truck. He's got his window down and he looks pissed. Louis stands there, arms crossed, looking half defensive and half apologetic. Then Gordy rolls up his window and the tires spin gravel as he hauls ass out of there.

Miriam spies Wren at the edge of the drive, near the trees. She's got her ragged coat—a grape-purple winter jacket that's been patched to hell and back—pulled tight around her.

She's smoking a cigarette.

Just looking at her is like looking at her old self, and it brings a new tidal wave of desire crashing down on her. For just a moment, Miriam imagines herself frolicking giddily in a sun-warmed tobacco field as she plucks cancer stick after cancer stick from each bush she passes. One in the gap between each finger, all lit, all in her mouth—she plays each handful of cigarettes like a carcinogenic harmonica. The imaginary relief floods her, and then vacates her immediately because it's fucking imaginary. When it does, it leaves only hate in its wake.

How dare that little brat smoke. I didn't give her that cigarette.

Miriam doesn't bother putting on a jacket, and she only barely stuffs her feet into her Doc Martens—the left heel lives outside the boot even as she heads through the door. She stalks through the remaining snow with an uneven gait, heading right to Wren.

She gets there and with a quick slap swats the cigarette out of her mouth. It hits snow with a *tsssss*.

"Bitch!" Wren says. "That was my last smoke."

"Good. Smoking is bad for you." It sounds completely bonkers coming out of her mouth. It's like wearing someone else's wedding dress. *Those were not my words. I sound like someone's mother. Ugh fuck shit ugh.*

"I got lucky and found it in my pocket and you fucked it up."

"I fuck everything up. Get used to it."

"No kidding."

"Yeah! No kidding."

The two of them stare at each other, their breath huffing out in plumes. Louis walks up, boots crunching.

"You two done?" he asks.

Their only answer is mopey silence.

Miriam still smells the cigarette smoke in the air. It's been a while since she's had a good proper nic fit, and this one's like a dug-in tick. Makes all parts of her feel queasy, uneven, stretched thin. *One cigarette would fix anything. And a shot of bourbon. And a cup of coffee. And touching someone and seeing how they die by heart attack, car crash, the whirring tines of an out-of-control farm combine, autoerotic asphyxiation . . . nnngh.* Finally, Miriam shakes it off and says, "What was Gordy's deal? He looked peeved."

"He saw her." Louis gestures to Wren.

"So?"

"We came in last night late, he saw our headlights, and so he came to check on us this morning—and now he sees her. You and me picking up some teen girl. Who of course just stood off to the side, smoking and looking pissed off at us."

Wren shrugs. "Whatever."

"You told him she was, like, my sister or some shit, right?" Miriam asks.

"I didn't really say anything."

Damnit. Miriam rolls her eyes. "You have to get better at lying to rubes, dude. Gordy's gonna think this is pretty weird. We're hiding out up here and bringing some teen girl to our little cabin compound? We look like a couple of perverts, like she's our little sex slave."

"Ew," Wren says. "That's not what you want from me, is it?"

"Shut up, no."

Louis says, "It'll be fine. Gordy just didn't know she'd be part of the deal. He's a friend. He's not going to call the cops or anything."

"You sure?"

"I'm sure."

"Fine." But Miriam's not so certain. She feels like forces are aligning against her, and she can't see their measure.

She needs to clear her head.

"You," she says, pointing to Wren. "Come on."

"Where are we going?"

"Hunting."

FORTY-TWO
THE HUNT

Above them, the owl crosses from tree to tree, tightening the morning sky in a zigzag stitch. The snow has gone from the trees, leaving them looking like skeletal hands thrust up out of Hell, stretched toward a Heaven that sits forever out of reach.

Beneath, Miriam and Wren walk.

"You and Louis," Wren says.

"Me and Louis what?"

"You guys been together the whole time, huh?"

Their feet crunch on snow. "No. I . . . We left each other for a time. I was with someone else. A woman named Gabby."

"Bi is all the rage now."

"I don't do it because it's all the rage; I do it because I do it."

"Where's the chick now?"

Miriam sighs. "She's . . . off living her life. I hope. I dunno." A sudden arrow cuts through her middle—an intense desire to see Gabby again manifests inside her like an old injury torn asunder, a hemorrhage of sorts. The blood of love and longing fills her up and seems to weigh her down. "We parted ways because I'm no good for her." *Even though she's perfect for me.*

"But Louis, you're good for him?"

"I'm . . . not, no, but he's here anyway."

They walk for a while. Wren seems on the edge of saying something else, when a shadow passes over them, a shadow deeper than the night. It's the owl. It's Bird of Doom.

"What's the deal with the fuckin' owl?" Wren asks.

"Who? Bird of Doom? I control her." But it feels crass to put it that way. Like it's a disservice to the bird. Miriam suddenly draws that line in herself: *I don't care about disrespecting people, but I care about disrespecting birds. Huh.* She tries to course-correct: "No. Okay. It's not control. Not exactly. I ride her. My mind in hers. I'd like to do it better. I'd like to be able to . . . share both bodies. Me and the bird's. But I can't do it." *Not yet*, a little voice says.

"Ooooookay."

"And it's not just the owl. I can do it with other birds."

"I know. I saw."

"Saw what?"

Wren tells her about the birds that came to her on top of the mountain. Songbirds, ravens, owls, hawks. Miriam feels her pulse quicken; panic crawls through her like ants through their tunnels. *I don't remember that*. That terrifies her more than anything. That she was out there, broken into pieces, each splinter of her stuck in the mind of a bird. *One broken cookie* . . .

At least, even unaware, she got the job done.

Yay me, she thinks drearily.

"I didn't know you could do that," Wren says. "Any of it."

"When I met you, I didn't know either. I first learned I could do it there, at the Caldecotts' estate. I found myself looking at myself from inside the body of a raven." *And it subsequently tore out the tongue of one of the Mockingbird killers.* Some nights, she can still recall, instinctively, the raw, ripping feeling of the tongue being unmoored from its roots inside the man's mouth.

"Why birds?"

"Fuck if I know." She sighs. "I'm told that birds are soul-carriers. Psychopomps."

"Well, you are a psycho."

"God, you're a jerk."

"*You're* a jerk."

"Takes one to know one."

Wren gives her the finger. Miriam gives it back.

They keep walking. Ahead, a fallen tree sits broken over a massive flat boulder—a rock Miriam thinks of as an altar, as it looks almost sacrificial.

Above, the owl lands on a branch. Something drifts across Bird of Doom's awareness, and so too does it reach Miriam—a vibration in the air, a scuttle of little feet on snow, a dark shape darting. Fifty yards out, a chipmunk.

Not now, Miriam thinks. *We'll find bigger prey*.

"Lemme ask you something," she says to Wren.

"Ugh, fine."

"Does it bother you?"

"What?"

"Killing people."

"I dunno." Her voice is cold and flat when she says it. "Sometimes, it fucks with me. Other times, I don't feel it all."

"I never really feel it."

"And that doesn't bother you?"

Wren stops walking. She stares at her feet. "It does. Because it's almost like it's not me. It's like I'm . . ." Her hands circle like she's trying to pull words and ideas out of the air. "Like I'm the knife. When I killed Bob Bender, I held the knife, right? But it's like something else was holding me."

"Like you're a tool."

"Yeah. A tool."

"I know that feeling."

"That's the part I don't like. It's not the killing. I mean, I don't like that part, but that part feels like it's happening to someone else. Like it's in a movie I'm watching. The part I feel is the part where I lose myself to it. I don't feel like it's me, and I know it. I'm, like, aware of it."

It's never been exactly that for Miriam. She's always felt in control. Hearing Wren talk, she almost wishes she wasn't in control, because how perfect would it be to have someone else to blame for her actions? Then again, it seems to be bothering the girl. And why wouldn't it? Miriam's always felt like she's had her hands around fate's throat. Wren, though, feels more a cog: a gear turning in a machine too large to understand. *Maybe I don't understand it either*.

"You ever think you're wrong?" Miriam asks.

"'Bout what?"

"Oh, I dunno, the *fucking killing people* thing?"

Now Wren's posture changes. "Do you ever feel wrong?"

"I have. And do. But at least I actually see what's coming."

"What's that supposed to mean?"

"It means that when I touch the victim, I see how they're going to die. I see if their heart explodes or if an ice cream truck runs over their head—that really happened, by the way; guy named Zack, midtwenties, he was high on meth and wanted ice cream and then fell down as the ice cream truck drove away. Died from diabetic complications in the hospital. Whatever. I see what happens *before* it happens. I see if they're sick, if they fall down, I see if they're murdered. I live it with them. *Through* them. I sometimes see the face of the killer. You don't see anything. You don't get a beacon, a warning. You just . . . act."

"I see the outline. I see the Silver Lining."

"You see a hint of what's coming. That they're a killer—"

"A murderer."

"Do you know that?"

"What?"

"Do you know they are murderers and not, say, a drunk driver? Or a cop who has to kill in the line of duty? Or a soldier?"

Wren's face twists up as she yells: "I know what they are! I know *who* they are. Even if I don't know the specifics, I know."

"Do you investigate? Bob Bender, okay. Pantsless with a stun gun—safe to say you were right. Mark Daley, I found his secret photo stash."

"What stash?" Wren's eyes narrow. Miriam tells her. The basement. The box. The photos. "See? Killer."

"But you didn't *know* that. How about the others? The dealers and drug-runners, fine, safe bet. What about Danny Stinson? Or Harley Jacobs? Or Sims, Wayland Sims? Were they really going to be killers?"

"I . . ." Wren backpedals a few steps, feeling her pockets, no doubt for cigarettes that aren't there. "Stinson was a scumbag. An old thief. Ran a pawn shop and I think he'd killed people before. Sims picked me up when I was hitchhiking and I saw the Silver Lining, and he . . . he was going to kill me; he took me back to his trailer down near Maker's Bell and he had me in his garage and came at me with a hammer—"

Miriam remembers what Grosky told her: Wren dispatched him with a barbecue fork. Just as Miriam killed the gunman in the store at the Jersey Shore.

"Jacobs, I don't know. I don't know about her. She had the glow. She was a drunk. Shitty marriage. I saw her at a bar and I had a gun, a gun I took from Stinson's pawn shop, and . . ."

Miriam knows. She shot her.

It's hitting the girl now. Maybe she was protected from it before. Or maybe that was just an act. Either way, her shoulders shake. Her eyes glisten as she cops a faraway stare, looking off at nothing—and maybe seeing everything.

This is a moment of crisis. The waves are coming in fast and heavy. Her seawall is starting to crack.

Miriam knows she could let it go. And it would stay cracked but together. Or she could try to mend it—making soft, reassuring sounds while gently applying a generous swaddling of emotional duct tape.

Or she could do the other thing.

And Miriam, she's good at doing the other thing.

She keeps at it: "Maybe that woman, Harley Jacobs, could be she was going to kill her husband. Maybe her husband came home every day, would beat her ass because dinner wasn't ready, or because she wouldn't get down on her knees and suck him off, or just because she looked at him funny. That's murder, her killing him for that. But it's the kind of murder that's different from other kinds. It's the kind I can get behind. The kind I'd help her commit if I had half a chance. But your Silver Lining, maybe it wouldn't show you that. Maybe your Trespasser is a liar, like mine is. Maybe you are a tool—a gun in a very bad hand."

And it shatters. Wren gasps, a gulping, wracking sob. She drops to her knees and buries her hand in her face. Then she falls farther, like a star collapsing in on itself: head down against her knees, arms folded up behind her head. She's small now, like a piece of furniture, and she just sits there, shaking and weeping.

Miriam feels the owl's impatience. A new target has entered play, and Miriam lets Bird of Doom go and find her prey. Wren stays collapsed like that while the owl goes off. Wren shakes and cries. Miriam lets her.

Soon, Wren's wracking sobs have dissolved to a slow, simmering grief. As she stands, Miriam shows her a dead rabbit—intact except for a few talon holes. The owl brought it while the girl was on the cold ground, crying. Miriam says to Wren, "Come on. Let's go eat some breakfast."

FORTY-THREE

THE CURIOUS SILENCE BEFORE TOTAL DISASTER

For two days, it feels like the snow globe is patching itself back together. A new snow falls on the first night—just flurries, but enough to light the dark with the white of softly falling stars. Louis chops wood. Miriam and Wren hunt a little, but mostly, they just talk. They talk about their lives before all of this went down. They talk about their bad mothers. About how Miriam got to reconcile with hers, and how Wren never found that chance. They talk about life on the road. How bad it is. But sometimes, how good it can be, too—the freedom, the open road, the endless unrolling possibilities. They talk about their powers, too. Miriam says she doesn't know if she's using hers for good or for evil anymore, and if she's just a pawn in someone's game or if everyone else is a pawn in her game. She explains too that her head's been cracked around so many times, there is at least a 17 percent chance that all of this is just a collective hallucination anyway, so fuck it.

The best thing that comes out of it is that Wren says she's going to do better. She's going to think more about what she does and what her power is, and if she even wants to use it. Miriam says she'll work with her. They can work together. And here blooms a curious, improbable feeling that somehow, in the middle of this snow globe (freshly repaired with duct tape and clean water), maybe what they'll have is something a little bit like family. A twisted, fucked-up version, maybe. But a version just the same.

Then comes the midnight that begins the third day.

And that's when it all goes wrong.

FORTY-FOUR

THE DRIVER AND THE PASSENGER

Midnight.

Headlights spear the dark at the top of the long road leading to the cabin. They gaze ahead like demon's eyes, and slowly, surely, the demon crawls forward down the gravel, leaving tracks in the dusting of fresh snow.

The demon, like many demons, travels in an unassuming form: it's a forest green Ford Focus, a couple years old. It's in good shape but for a dent in the door.

As it gains speed, the tires spin a little when they hit a frozen puddle. Then it hops the slick pothole and lurches forward, quarter-mile after quarter-mile until the cabin is in sight. The trees lining the road and surrounding the cabin stand like the spear-tips of shadowy sentinels standing guard in the night. The forest seems to swallow everything whole.

The car pins the cabin with its headlights. It eases up, still rumbling for a couple minutes before the driver turns the key, cuts the engine.

The door opens.

And the driver gets out.

The passenger, though, remains hidden.

FORTY-FIVE

THE BOON OF A SLEEPLESS NIGHT

Miriam is not sleeping.

She's had a good run of it. Last few nights, she's managed some deep Zs. But ever since kicking cigarettes, booze, and now coffee, it's like her body's chemicals are a kite in a strong wind. Sometimes she's in free fall, plunging toward the earth and sticking fast in the mud as fatigue draws her down. Other times it's like, hey brain, hello brain, what the fuck, brain, no, no, sure, let's lie here and just think and think and think about things like hey yeah let's go over every mistake and every moment of trauma and abuse and terror and let's wad them all together and force them to fight inside my head like coked-up squirrels. And when that happens, the kite takes flight in an erratic wind. Up, down, around and around. Battered by the elements. Buoyed into the storm.

So, she's awake. Louis is on the chair. Wren is next to her, snoring. Because of course she snores. The girl snores worse than Grosky.

Grosky. There we go—add another name to the frenzy of thoughts feasting on her sleep. More chum churning the water. His severed head floating up out of the mists of memory, tied to a string like a hovering balloon.

Regrets, I have a few.

Then: light through the window. Headlights brighten the

room. The others stay asleep, but Miriam, she's up. She was already right on the edge of fight-or-flight mode, and now she's deep in it. Someone's here, and she wants to know who it is. Because whoever it is, it's not good. It's not Gordy. It's not the ice cream man. It's someone bad. Someone with ill intent.

She grabs the Remington 700 rifle. Slings it over her shoulder.

On the way to the door, she bats at Louis's hand. She hisses at him to get up. He snorts but doesn't wake. Fine. She can handle this.

The lights cut out. Darkness returns.

The sound of a car door opening and closing reaches her.

Miriam gets by the door. She hears keys jingling. Footsteps, too. Coming closer: the soft cough of boots on loose, snowy stone. Gently, Miriam eases back the bolt of the rifle, then urges it forward again—a bullet rattles into its cradle, is put into play. *I'm ready*.

Closer, closer.

Miriam draws a deep breath, and—

Wham. She throws open the door. Rifle up. It's got a scope and that won't help here, so she keeps her left eye open. Her thumb flicks forward the safety. Her index finger snakes toward the trigger.

"Don't move," she says to the shadow standing there.

"I . . ."

A woman's voice. Trembling in fear.

It's not Harriet.

It's not a cop.

Not even Gabby.

Who the . . .

"It's me," the woman says. "Samantha. Do you remember me?"

A chill, one unrelated to the weather, one deeper than winter's bite, ripples through Miriam's body. She keeps the rifle up. "I remember you."

"I . . . Please . . . put that gun down."

"Not a Popsicle's chance in hell, honey."

"Miriam. I'm just here for Louis."

Panic throttles her. Because this doesn't make any sense. Samantha? Just showing up, unbidden, on a gnarly winter's night? "First, explain how you even found this place. In fact, I've got a whole bucket of questions that need answering before I'll let you set foot in this cabin."

"Gordon. Gordy. He answered my email two days ago."

Shit. Of course. He saw them with Wren up here and—to his credit, he didn't call the cops. But he did send out for Samantha. Right now, she wants to kick that old bastard in the teeth, even though what he did was fair as cookies.

"So, you thought what? You'd come up here and . . ."

"I don't really know. I was hoping just to see him, Louis, I mean. Just to find out what was going on and why he ran away. Please. Put the gun down."

She's pleading now. Hands up and out. Palms forward.

But Miriam doesn't trust her. Something's up. This bitch has been creeping at her margins. A scarlet tanager up in the trees, trying to hide the flash of her red feathers.

And she's about to lay into her, too. But then a voice—

"Miriam," Louis says. "What's going on?" A half-beat later: "Samantha? Is that you?" Instantly, his trust is a wide-open door. He puts a steadying hand on the top of the rifle's scope, trying to ease it downward. "Put the gun down, Miriam."

"Fuck that," Miriam says, yanking the gun away. She takes a few steps in a half-circle away from him and away from Samantha, keeping her gun trained the whole time. "Louis, use your head. This doesn't seem strange to you?"

"Please, Louis," Samantha says. "I've missed you. I'm just here to talk."

"Miriam," he says, "I'm sure it's—"

"It's *not fine*," she barks. "Think about it. How'd she find us? How'd she get up here? Something's off."

"Gordy told me," Samantha answers. "Louis, it was Gordon."

"Gordy. Of course." He nods, like it makes sense. Maybe it does. Maybe this is all perfectly aboveboard. So, why does Miriam's blood feel like ice water?

"Louis," Miriam says. "I think we have questions."

"We do. But we can do it inside. Like civilized people. Put the gun down and we can all go inside and work this out."

Her skin prickles. It's cold out here but she feels like she's burning up. *Don't trust her,* she thinks. Something's not right. *Just shoot her*. But that's not right either. Miriam's a killer. But she's not a murderer.

There's a difference, isn't there?

Like the difference between being a bird who kills to eat and a cat who kills to play with its prey. One wants to survive. The other wants to revel in death.

Which one am I, again? Which one is Wren?

She keeps the gun pointed and says, "I'm not putting it down. But go on. You two go ahead. I'll follow in. But hooker, I swear: you flip your pretty hair the wrong way and I'll put a bullet through your lung."

To that, Samantha says nothing. Nor does Louis.

Together, they march inside.

Everyone but the passenger.

FORTY-SIX

NO ONE EXPECTS THE SPANISH INQUISITION

They sit Samantha in the recliner in the corner. Already, Wren is awake. Her hair sticks up at odd angles, like the broken feathers of a car-struck crow. "What the fuck is going on? Who is she? Why are you holding a fucking rifle?"

Miriam gives the hastiest, shittiest explanation she can muster: "This is Louis's fiancée. She shouldn't be here."

Louis shoots Miriam a look. He's on the fence. She can see that. He still loves Samantha—or, at least, loves some idea of her. But he also knows she's not telling them the whole truth. Worse, he's with Miriam. He's already cheated. Louis has gone over the barrel in that waterfall and there's no way back up. Life doesn't have a rewind button, and he's too good a guy to even try.

But just the same, the war is playing out on his face. In his one good eye is a battle of loyalty. He believes Miriam. But does he trust her? Will he side with her when all is said and done? She hopes so. She needs him to.

"Samantha," he says. The war in his heart makes his chest rise and fall like a surging tide. "You lied to me. I think you've been lying to me. I don't understand what's going on. You need to help me understand it."

"Louis, I love you," Samantha stammers. "I just—"

"Please." That one word, dropped like an axe splitting a log. "You don't get to play that game with me right now. You don't start there. You start with the truth. Anything less than that . . . and I don't know."

Miriam thinks, *We can't just let her go. We do that, she goes and brings the police.* Not that they can just put a bullet through her head, either. Which means keeping Samantha here until . . . until what? Until when?

All these are Future Miriam problems. Present Miriam has a different set of concerns. And she's thankful Louis seems to share them. She eases the gun down, pointing it to the floor. Maybe Louis will be her big gun. Maybe he's *always* been her big gun.

Wren, though, seems uncomfortable. She's cagey. Staying to the edge of the room, staring. "I don't like him grilling her like that," she says. "Something's wrong. I don't like any of this."

"Wren, now's not the time. Shut up," Miriam says. Because anything that's not Samantha spilling her guts is a distraction.

"The feather in the glass," Louis says. He looks sad as he lays it out. "And your screen name. Scarlet-tanager99? Same email and name attached to a forum where people are talking about Miriam. And then I think back to how eager you were to meet her. And how much you talked about her, almost like you knew Miriam already, even though there was no way you could have—"

Samantha stammers, "She seemed important to you, so I—I just wanted to know m-more—"

"That's not it," he says. "That's not all of it."

"I worried she was dangerous—"

"Enough!" he barks, filling the space with his booming voice. It startles even Miriam. It's not often he gets angry, pushed to this point. She's gotten him to this place before: lied to him, same way Samantha has.

Wren moves in from the edge of the room. Her jaw is set. She's staring daggers at him. "Miriam, I don't like him like this. Tell him to quit." Then, to Louis: "Don't you hurt her, dude. Don't you dare."

Miriam fires off a glare in Wren's direction. "Wren—shut up. He's not going to hurt her. For once, this doesn't fucking involve you."

But Louis ignores the both of them. He is like a storm—a great anvil-headed cloud, dark and looming, as he steps forward, planting his hands on the arms of the chair and crushing Samantha with his shadow. Miriam's mind flashes suddenly to him doing the same to her in a tub: his bulk dwarfing her, his hands around her neck. Miriam's muscles tighten.

"Louis," Miriam cautions.

Through clamped teeth, he says, "Tell the truth, Sam. Now." The threat is clear. Miriam doesn't believe he'll do anything. He's not that guy.

But then again—

Hands around her throat—

Screaming as he pushes her under the water—

Samantha's eyes brim with tears and those tears run in shining rivulets down her cheeks. Her lip quivers as she says two words: "You're right."

Miriam gulps. "Right about what?"

"You're right. I . . ." Samantha turns to Miriam. "It's about you. It's always been about you. I . . . I'm sorry, Louis. I've been looking for her. I was there. In Florida. I don't know what's happening to me. I was at a tiki bar in the Keys—"

It's like her heart stops.

Synapses fire. Connections thread together. *Pine Key. A tiki bar. Miriam is there drinking some epic tiki drink called an Ancient Mariner and in comes Ashley Gaynes. . . .* Gaynes, gone mad, had been hunting her. He found her, as she suspected he would. But her extraction was not easy. Ashley pulled a pistol and shot every last person in the place. They all died. The bartender. The old salts in the corner. The two girls drinking Windex-colored booze out of a fishbowl.

“No,” Miriam says. “Everyone died at that bar. I saw them die.”

“I didn’t. I—I was in the bathroom.”

This is a lie. It has to be. “Don’t fuck with me, Samantha.”

“I was there with a couple girlfriends. We’d been down in Key West, but it was too busy down there, so we came up a ways and found that bar. And the three of us ordered a big drink, some sweet drink with blue curacao in a bowl—”

Two girls drinking Windex-colored booze out of a fishbowl.

Was there ever a third girl? A third chair? She can’t remember. All she remembers from that day are moments punctuating the horror: Ashley stepping to the bar, making a joke, threatening, then a pistol dancing to his hand and *bang, bang, bang*. All before he put the gun under her chin and dragged her out of there.

But Samantha knows. She has that one detail—the ladies with the shitty 2000 Flushes girl drink. You can’t just pluck that out of nowhere.

But it still doesn’t explain.

“Why me?” Miriam asks. “Why find me?”

Samantha tells her.

INTERLUDE

SAMANTHA

They kept wheeling bodies out of the bar. All strangers. I sat there at two AM and I couldn't stop sweating and shaking. The policemen had given me a blanket and it was like, you know how you sleep at night and you're hot one minute and cold the next? I kept taking the blanket off, then putting it back on. I felt like I had a fever. Shivering and my teeth chattering. And then they wheeled out my two friends, Becky and Martina, and I just lost it. I remember the police asking me questions. I don't remember much of what I said.

Somehow, I ended up back in my hotel room in Coral Gables. I have memories of the police driving me, but then, my car was also there and so maybe I drove. I honestly don't know. The next couple days passed by in bits and just . . . images. I barely remember what happened. Sometimes, I'd find myself standing in front of the mirror. Staring. In midsentence, saying things . . . like I was practicing a speech. Like I was practicing my own voice.

I know I turned on the TV at one point and they said the man in the bar was a mass murderer, or maybe a serial killer, and his name was Ashley Gaynes and they found his body on a boat. Or part of his body. The news said there was a survivor, too. A woman. And I knew I'd seen a woman—when I was there in the bathroom, I peered out in time to see that man with the gun pulling you outside. Pale woman. Dark hair fringed with scarlet. Was that her, I thought? The same woman they found on the boat?

They never named her.

But *someone* named you.

I still don't understand it to this day. I was there on the bed in the hotel watching TV, and I had room service around me, and then I heard it from the corner of the room—I heard a name. Whispered to me.

It was your name.

Miriam Black.

And I . . . I looked, and I saw someone there in the corner. Someone who shouldn't be there. It was just a big shadow, like someone who was there but not there at the same time. I couldn't move. I couldn't breathe. The shadow lifted a finger to its lips and shushed me. I saw that the shadow had no eyes, just two black X shapes across each socket. It told me that if I wanted to understand what happened, I had to find you.

After that, you were like a . . . hole inside my mind, and everything ran toward it like water toward a train. I kept reliving the event in fits and starts. Replaying it all over and over again. And I kept thinking about that name, Miriam Black, Miriam Black, Miriam Black, whispered to me but not in my ears. It was inside me. Like a living thing. It ran toward that hole, that drain, and it fell in and stoppered it all up. And I went online and I looked you up. I don't even remember doing it. I just remember being there, one day, your name already typed into the search bar. I hadn't showered. I hadn't eaten. I . . . couldn't stop myself.

You had no real presence online. No Facebook. No Instagram. No social media at all. You were just these little blips. These footnotes in news stories. News stories about serial killers or other people dying. Your name floated in the last paragraph here, the middle of a buried story there.

It was like falling down a rabbit hole. I found this subreddit where people were talking about someone who was this angel of mercy, this woman who went around saving people like some kind of superhero, but not. An anti-superhero. The Angel of Death didn't save people from getting hit by cars or from disease. She saved those about to be killed. She killed the killers.

Nothing really connected to the stories where you were involved. But there were always close sightings. In Miami, Philadelphia, Charlotte. And I thought, this is it. This is *you*. Miriam Black was the Angel of Death.

I started dreaming about you. I was home then, back out on the West Coast, and I couldn't shake you. I wanted to find you. I wanted to know what you saw that day. What happened to you? Why did my friends have to die? Why couldn't you save them? I wanted to find you. I needed to find you.

But I didn't know where to begin.

That's when my dreams brought me another name.

The shadow with Xs for eyes said your name, Louis.

Louis Darling.

I found you. You were easy enough to find. You left a truck behind after the Mockingbird murders, and all I had to do was call the trucking company, and they told me you had gone to work for someone else and . . . Three or four calls later, I found out where you were, where you were living, and I got a job there. At the company. Just part-time, working the dispatch.

But that put me in touch with him. With you, Louis.

I fell in love with you. I started to feel more . . . normal, more like myself. I had more time back to myself. I stopped losing hours and minutes. I felt good again. Clean, safe, like I had stopped going crazy, like I was going back the other direction. But still, I couldn't help that one thing. That name. *Your* name. Miriam Black. Crawling through my head like so many worms. Then came the day Louis told me about you—not much, just

who you were, but he said your name. And it was like everything went dark again. Like I was being pulled backward. I saw that shape, that big shadow, and I felt rough, hard hands behind me, urging me forward. Pushing me where I didn't want to go.

I heard myself tell Louis I wanted to meet you. And he said that was strange, but I kept pushing and pushing, just like I was being pushed and pushed. I felt parts of myself lost, gone, stolen away. And I rationalized it. I said, it was just trauma. I told myself this was normal. PTSD from the shooting. And I convinced myself that this was fine, I wanted to meet you because of closure, and that everything was fine. Then I met you. And it was like an electric shock.

Next thing I knew, I woke up in the hotel room. I had a memory, more like a dream than a thing that happened, of stealing that feather from you. Sneaking into your secret places. Searching through your things. Your name perched on the end of my lips, never spoken but always there.

I kept thinking, too, I knew you. Somehow, I knew you. Not just from that day down in the Keys, but from much longer. Like I understood you. I thought maybe one day we would be friends, the best of friends, which—I know, I know, that's absurd, and I don't even think it was my thought. I also remember thinking I knew it was dangerous. I knew *you* were dangerous, Miriam. But that only gave me more of a thrill. It felt like I knew a secret nobody else knew. I'd taunt the people on the forums about knowing who you were. I took the bird name because I knew you liked birds. I stole that feather from you. I looked at it every night before bed. I never took it out of its glass. I just held it. For one minute, maybe five, whatever I could get away with. I thought of you. I thought of that day in the bar. I would sometimes cry, or sometimes laugh, and then I'd put it away again.

Then Louis left me and I lost myself again. Sometimes, I'd lose hours. Other times, whole days. I don't remember writing

Gordon, but I did. I don't remember renting this car. I only remember parts of the drive through the dark, through the snow. Even now, I have pieces missing. I don't even know if I'm really here or if this is really a dream. Please. Tell me. Am I really here?

I'm sorry. I'm so sorry, Louis. So sorry, Miriam.

Please forgive me.

Please believe me.

Please help me.

FORTY-SEVEN

A QUESTION, UNANSWERED

Her guts churn like she's on a carousel going too fast. Round and round, the colors whipping past, the madness of calliope music in the background. Miriam's not sure what to do or what to say. She doesn't give a thimbleful of rat piss about Samantha's obsession with her. Trauma dug its claws into that woman on that day, and those leave holes that never heal. Holes that things can crawl into.

Holes that the *Trespasser* seems to have crawled into.

That's the fucked part. The X eyes, the big shadow—that's her demon, that's the Trespasser. And that twisted fucking specter did not merely whisper in her ear. He slipped into her mind like a parasite. *Has he been in my mind, too?* She has always felt in control. But Wren . . .

Wren hasn't. Wren said it herself: *It's almost like it's not me. It's like I'm the knife. When I killed Bob Bender, I held the knife . . .*

But it's like something else *was holding* me.

Forces are aligning. And she doesn't understand why, or what they are, and she's damn sure there's more to come. Is Miriam a gear in a larger, crueler machine, or is she the target, like the whole goddamn contraption is designed to come crashing down on her head at any moment? She feels sickened by it, by all the unanswered questions, by the overwhelming fear she's

at the center of this strange and shadowy storm. And that the Trespasser is behind it all.

Miriam flicks her gaze to Louis. He looks lost in his own head. Unmoored. She's seen that look before. (She's *caused* that look before.) He turns away from Samantha. He paces a short space in the crowded room.

Miriam sets down the rifle.

"Whaddya wanna know?" she asks in as calm a voice as she can muster.

"What?" Samantha asks.

"I'm saying, whatever you want to know, I'll tell you. You've got some kind of boner for me—well, here I am. You have holes that need filling—that sounds pornier than I mean it, sorry—then, hey, ask. This is your shot." *Maybe*, Miriam thinks, *if I help give her clarity and closure, that'll shut the Trespasser out*. Shine the biggest, brightest light and make the roaches scatter.

"Miriam, don't give her the satisfaction," Louis growls.

Wren sneers but stays quiet.

"It's fine," Miriam says. She thinks but does not say to him: *There's something bigger going on here, something we need to figure out.* "I'm fine. Go on, Samantha."

"I . . ." She sucks in a delicate, dainty breath. Like she's not sure how to proceed, like anything more dramatic will pop this bubble. She stands up, her hands clasped together, massaging one another nervously. "I wanted to—"

It happens so fast, Miriam only parses it after she's got the blood all over her face and chest. From outside, a barking chatter as bullets chew through the wood of the cabin, stitching a pattern that leads to the window. The glass shatters, and next thing Miriam knows, Samantha is in her arms, blood gently pumping from a hole in the side of her neck. Samantha's mouth works soundlessly. Louis grabs them both, pulls them to the bed and then over the edge of it. Wren ducks down with them.

It's then that Miriam's mind catches up to the reality of their situation.

Someone is shooting at us.

She puts her shoulder underneath the box spring and mattress, and with Louis's help lifts it up high. It won't stop bullets, but it'll slow them down a little.

Another salvo of automatic-weapon fire perforates the cabin.

Miriam, breathing fast, checks her people: Wren's all right. Samantha's not. Already, Louis has a strip of bedsheet that he's winding around her neck; blood already soaks the white cloth. Samantha's eyelids flutter. But she's still alive. Louis has her blood on him—

No. That's his blood. A tear in the sleeve of his shirt shows a black-blooded furrow in the meat of his bicep. Fresh red flows.

"You're hurt," Miriam says.

Louis looks down. "Oh. I'm all right." Then he looks at her, eyes pleading. Whatever control he had over this situation is flagging. Why wouldn't it be? "What do we do? Who is—"

Another chatter of bullets chewing into the wood. More glass breaks. A painting behind them leaps off the wall like a frog stung in the ass by a wasp. Wren screams, hands clapped over her ears.

"Who is doing this?" Louis asks.

INTERLUDE

HARRIET

Then:

Harriet stood, eyeless and broken, outside the monster's house. She could not see the bone that jutted out of her arm, but she could feel it. She could also smell the greasy, coppery stink of her own blood, freshly drawn. Her knee was out of joint, too, from where the bitch kicked it.

She quieted herself and listened as Miriam fled into the forest. Her senses were stronger now, since coming back. Each sharp as a thumbtack. Even in the air she could taste Miriam's fear: the brine of sweat and cowardice that made her run instead of fight.

Already inside her, things were beginning to shift. Bone grinding against bone. The boil of white blood cells. Internal organs tumbling together like so many stones. To any other, these injuries would be grievous. And to her, they were too. But only temporarily. Already, the edges of her eye sockets had begun to itch, signaling the healing. Already, her arm had begun to feel dead, like a sack of ground sausage hanging from her shoulder in its casing. The bone spearing from her skin would dry out and break off like a half-rotten stick. The skin would heal over. The bones would mend aggressively and with great pain.

But pain was now a distant concern. Harriet felt pain the way one might feel the poking and prodding of surgical equipment while under anesthesia. It was there, yes. She detected its presence, was vaguely aware of its sting.

But she could no longer muster the ability to care.

The leg would mend first. Then a race to see whether her eyes came back next, or whether the use of her arm would be returned.

After that, she would hunt Miriam. She would find her, kill her, and eat her heart and take her power because she has been assured by the voices that this is how things work. The circle of life. The tangle of death. The transmission of power, and the evolution of nature to supernature. Eat the meat of another and consume its life, gain its energy. Eat Miriam's heart and gain her power: the power to see the weave and weft of death. The interplay between light and dark, fate and free will, liberty versus destiny.

But how to find Miriam, exactly? Now that she'd fled again?

What was it that the little kitten said?

You could've just Googled me, you stupid fucking bitch.

Perhaps that was where to begin.

It took time, of course. But already, the news media did half her job for her: tying Miriam to some online Internet-only urban mythology, some figure called the Angel of Death. Harriet did as Miriam once suggested, using the Internet to drum up answers. Searching for it took her to a forum discussing the Angel of Death legend, and took her similarly to a woman under the handle *scarlet-tanager*99 claiming to know exactly who the Angel of Death was.

Harriet created an account.

And then she sent this woman a private message on the forum.

I WANT TO MEET THE ANGEL OF DEATH.

I CAN PAY CONSIDERABLE MONEY TO YOU IF YOU CAN FACILIATE THIS FOR ME.

And then she waited.

And waited.

She considered an alternative route: after all, she knew Russians from her days working with Ingersoll. The mob was changing these days, flush with hackers—most of them working the so-called carder market, meaning they stole and sold credit card numbers in bulk on the deep web. Others performed ransomware: hacking control of anything from a single thermostat in a wealthy man's house, to stealing all the data and function from an entire hospital network and then demanding payment to return control to the host. It would be easy enough to put a bid out to hack the scarlet-tanager99 account.

But then, fortuitousness.

Weeks later, a response hit her inbox.

And so began her communication with scarlet-tanager99.

The woman did not identify herself. Not immediately.

But she did say that she knew the identity of the Angel of Death. That the news was correct. And that soon, she would know where she was.

The woman was unguarded. She shared information freely.

Including her name: Samantha Ardent.

It became clear that this woman was obsessed with Miriam. That she was experiencing trauma and psychological issues resulting from a shatterpoint moment—this Miss Ardent was present for the shooting in the Keys, whereupon Ashley Gaynes shot up a tiki bar and abducted Miriam. (Idly, Harriet thought back to that time in Ingersoll's car when they sawed off Ashley's foot. Those were good days, working for Ingersoll, and she missed them terribly.)

It also seemed quite possible that the woman had suffered, or was presently undergoing, a psychological break. And that break meant leverage. Any fissure, however small, gave Harriet room in which to move, in which to *intrude*—like how a small tendril can, over time, wind its way through the crack in a wall and grow in that space, slowly but surely breaking down what seemed to be sure to stand.

Even still, Harriet grew frustrated. This was taking too long. This broken—and still breaking—woman was not giving her anything of value. It seemed a dead end. Fun, in its way, to help chip away at the woman's mind, but it gave her little more than an illicit thrill. She still had no Miriam.

And then came the day in December.

A message from Samantha led with the subject:

I know where she is.

Harriet wrote back:

TELL ME.

And then Harriet formed a plan. She asked to meet with the woman, and meet they did, in a small Pennsylvania diner. Harriet had black coffee and nothing more. The woman, Samantha, picked nervously at a piece of huckleberry pie—though, toward the end, something interesting happened. Samantha, who looked timid and indeed quite broken, suddenly . . . changed. Her demeanor shifted. Her eyes flashed with newfound confidence and a brash, flinty carelessness. And in an instant, she demolished the pie like she had been starving, like she'd never before gotten to taste pie and this was her one chance to have that flavor in her mouth, that satisfying lump in her stomach. She didn't even wipe her mouth at first, just grinning out across the table, mouth smeared with berry guts. Predatory. Feral, in a way. Harriet understood her in that moment. And also recognized that not only was the woman undergoing some fundamental shift—a genuine psychotic break in her personality—but something potentially deeper, stranger, altogether *unnatural*.

Samantha said then, "I'll take you to her. Miriam needs a push."

Harriet nodded and, though gratitude is not something she easily can stomach these days, forced out a thank-you.

And then, like that—*snap*—Samantha returned. She wiped her mouth hurriedly. She pushed away the pie and burped quietly into her fist before having to run to the bathroom. Harriet smelled the sour mash of puke-stink on her later.

And together, they got in Samantha's rented Ford Focus.

Together, they traveled to Miriam.

Harriet sat in the passenger side for most of the trip—and then, upon finding the drive, she clambered into the backseat, throwing a blanket over herself. Little did Samantha know, while the woman was in the bathroom, Harriet popped the trunk and put in there a pair of friends: the Uzi (technically a Mini Uzi carbine, modified from semiautomatic to fully automatic) and the machete. The machete is a brutal affair, imprecise in the wrong hands. But she is surgical with it. And oh, how the blade is sharp.

It will do well to chop Miriam Black to bits and to cut out her heart.

And just in case, she has a lockback hunting knife in the back pocket of her corduroy pants. For the finer cuts.

(And she has a .380 SIG Sauer strapped to her ankle.)

(So, make that four friends.)

Harriet waited as Samantha parked, and now here she sits. It is time. She throws off the blanket. She reaches into the front seat and pops the trunk latch. Then Harriet leaves the vehicle and rescues her friends from the trunk.

She checks the submachine gun and jacks the action. Her arm still feels a little loosey-goosey, like a transmission nearly slipping out of gear. Soon it'll be fine again. The question that has yet to be properly answered is: is she functionally immortal? She feels more alive than she ever has. Will her body stave off disease? Does she age? Is aging just a disease or a natural, necessary entropy?

(*Can't kill me,* she thinks. *I always come back.*)

This is a question that won't be answered for a long time.

And it has no bearing on the situation at hand, which is:

Harriet has found Miriam Black.

She intends to kill her, cut out her heart, and eat it.

Harriet stands, Uzi in hand, machete in a sheath at her side. Ahead of her is a window, and in that window she sees shapes moving by the light of the cabin's interior. It's enough of a target. The Uzi needn't be precise. It isn't here to kill them. It's just here to announce her presence.

So, announce her presence she does.

FORTY-EIGHT

FIGHT OR FLIGHT

It's when the bullets stop that Miriam knows they're in trouble.

If this is Harriet, then she's not done. And she's not going to stop.

Louis is talking to her. Wren is too. Samantha is bleeding. But she can't hack any of that right now. She needs eyes. So, she finds them.

Her own eyes close.

And Bird of Doom's open.

The owl stirs in the dark. Wings up and out, she descends with Miriam riding inside her mind. The bird swoops low through the trees, the glow of the cabin not far. There, in the driveway, sits the car. Near it, a boxy submachine gun.

But no Harriet.

A moment of panic stuns Miriam—

Then she remembers:

I'm in a bird, motherfucker.

Every heat signature, every vibration, it calls to the bird. Bird of Doom can hear the dull heartbeat and ragged breath of Harriet Adams, and it swoops to the far side of the cabin. The woman is there, stalking toward the back of the building with her machete in hand.

Miriam pulls herself back to her body and finds the discussion between Louis and Wren has turned heated. They're arguing about what to do, where to go, how to get help for Samantha.

But Miriam can't care about any of that.

Harriet will be here soon.

Thirty seconds. Maybe less.

Harriet wants Miriam. That is the bet Miriam is going to take. It has to be true. That monster wouldn't come all this way for second prize. Louis, Wren, Samantha: they're all incidental. Once upon a time, Harriet might have used those people against Miriam. But this is a changed Harriet. The Harriet from before was cold and calculating. This one is too, but with the singular mind of a starving animal—it sees meat, it goes for the meat.

And I'm the meat.

"Stay here," Miriam hisses. To Wren: "You still have the gun? The .22?"

Hesitantly, Wren nods. "It's across the room. In my jacket."

"Good. Keep it close. I'm going out."

Louis catches her arm. "Like hell you are."

"Stay here. Watch them. Keep them safe."

"Miriam," Wren says. Panic is electric in her eyes. "There's something I have to tell you—"

"Not now. Later."

"It's important."

"*Later*, I said."

And with that, Miriam is up. She spies the Remington rifle on the floor, by the chair where Samantha caught a bullet. She hooks the strap with a toe, tugs it toward her, scooping it up before springing to the back door.

It starts to open just as she reaches it—

Miriam crashes through it like a train. Harriet staggers backward, legs pedaling even as she keeps her footing. The machete is in her hand, blade hissing as it cuts the open air.

For a second, Miriam sees Harriet's face. Her eyes are bold and white. Her arm is unbroken. Her leg, unbent. Fear is thrust through Miriam in a saline rush: this is worse than Ashley Gaynes. Ashley had the ability to always know what attack was coming. Harriet doesn't need to know. Because Harriet can't be killed. She returned to life. Her eyes grew back. The bone jutting from her arm is gone, and that arm is good as new.

"Miriam," Harriet growls, saying the name like an insult. She comes on hard, the machete coming right toward Miriam.

Miriam holds up the rifle, and the blade clangs against the scope. She returns the attack, whipping the butt of the stock right toward Harriet's mean, bulldog mug.

But the woman easily ducks it, leaning back as the gun butt catches only empty air. This is where Miriam knows—she can't do this here. This fight, it can't happen at the cabin. The others will come. They'll try to help.

And they'll die.

So, the plan is the plan, it is what it is—

Miriam shoves Harriet.

Then she runs.

FORTY-NINE

THE FOREST OF THE DEAD

Miriam ducks her head, charging fast into the trees, trying not to slip on the snow and ice, the fallen leaves and pine needles.

Bullets carve through the air. Branches pop off around her. *Harriet has another gun. Shit.*

Miriam has her own gun—the rifle in her hand. But she's not proficient with it. And it's not made for running and gunning.

Harriet is hunting her. But Miriam needs it to be the other way around. She needs to be luring her into a trap. As a bullet *thwacks* into the trunk of a tree ahead, casting up pale splinters, Miriam takes a hard right. She leaps over a fallen log, moves past the flat rock where she sometimes sits to clean Bird of Doom's kill—a rock red with frozen blood. She slides over it, then zigzags north again.

She knows there's a dead creek bed ahead. Hasn't been water flowing there for a long time, according to Gordy. It's not deep, but it's overgrown with a snarl of dead briar—and she finds as narrow a gap as she can and darts through it, the thorns ripping into her as she does. She drops down as soon as she's into the creek bed, bringing the rifle up and urging the barrel through the briar.

Miriam squints through the scope. It's fogged up and she can't see a damn thing. She has to quick-pull her sleeve up over her thumb and give it a swipe.

Once more, she peers through it.

Looking through a scope is nothing like it is in the movies. There's no clear image, no perfect circle with the target pinched in the crux of the crosshairs. It's blurry. The circle moves through a sea of blackness. It's hard to get your bearings and even figure out what you're looking at. Worse, every little twitch you make, every breath you take, the image goes wifty again.

She sees nothing. No one.

She turns her ear to the forest: the sounds that greet her are ones all around, like the creak of old trees swaying in the wind, the faint rustle of brush, the distant settling of the ground in winter. But nothing that sounds like a footstep. Nothing that sounds like her pursuer: no gunshots, no labored breathing, not a damn thing.

Seconds pass. They gather into minutes. Miriam shivers. She tries desperately not to move the rifle, because every time she does, the dry thorn-scrub is disturbed—and when disturbed, it crackles.

Just the same, she has to look, has to keep trying to find her hunter.

Bird of Doom pings her radar—the owl is up there in the trees. Above her by thirty feet. She thinks to use the owl's senses, but she's afraid to leave her own behind—

There.

Miriam moves the scope gently right, and as soon as she does, she sees Harriet fifty yards away—and the woman is doing the same thing she's doing. Crouching down, in her case by the trunk of a paper birch tree. There's a glint of moonlight in a blue-steel barrel—

Harriet is pointing a pistol right at her.

Shit.

Miriam pulls the trigger.

So does Harriet.

The rifle kicks in Miriam's hands, the butt of it giving her a hard punch to the shoulder. It rocks her back and as she goes, she feels something chew a furrow along her ribcage, just under her left armpit—it feels like a searing line of lava and she cries out, tumbling onto her ass, her head crashing into a pillow of tangled thornbush. It grabs her hair, and she has to wrench away from it.

Gasping, she works to army-crawl her way out the other side, but her left arm isn't working so good now. Pain lights up her left side, and that arm is starting to go numb.

Move, you fucking asshole, move. She whimpers and grits her teeth, pulling herself free of the briar and back out into the forest proper. The brush cracks and crackles as she uses the rifle as leverage to help herself stand. The air stinks of eggy, expended powder. Her side is wet. Already, the pain in her side is succumbing to the numbness in her arm. *Shit, shit, shit.*

Footsteps come hard-charging through the forest.

Harriet.

Miriam wheels with the rifle, but she's slow and clumsy—Harriet's on her like a cloud of flies. The woman's hand comes up underneath the rifle, grabbing the stock and pushing up hard. The scope smashes into Miriam's nose. Blood erupts and her eyes water. She lets go of the gun, stumbling backward. Harriet shoves the rifle aside. The machete is up and out in her one hand, the pistol in the other. Both shine in the moonlight.

The ground is slick. Miriam steps on a patch of icy leaves—

The machete cuts through the air where she was. Because now she's falling, her heel skidding out, her tailbone cracking hard against the earth.

And still she can barely see. She tastes blood. Her face feels like it's full of concrete. Her side and arm feel like they don't even belong to her anymore.

Harriet advances. Through her watery gaze, Miriam sees

now that the other woman is bleeding. A gore-rimmed ditch has been dug out of her collarbone, like someone used an ice cream scoop on her. *She hit me with her shot, and I hit her with mine*. Only problem is: Harriet doesn't care. Miriam's not even sure she feels the pain.

I'm dead.

Above, the air current moves as Harriet advances and a black shadow swoops down fast. Claws out. Wings wide. Bird of Doom is here to save the day. Miriam feels a swell of pride, because she's not there—she's not inside the animal's mind, she's not controlling her. The owl is doing this on her own.

But Harriet must sense the stirred wind, and she moves fast—faster than is reasonable. The woman holds up her forearm to protect her face. The owl's talons dig in, and the small pistol drops from Harriet's hand. But the machete in the other swings in a tight arc like a windshield wiper.

It cuts the bird down in a rain of feathers and a spray of blood.

Bird of Doom hits the ground with a thud. Pain and terror bloom together in Miriam's mind, a white nuclear flash as she feels what the bird feels.

Run. You've already lost. Go, go, go!

Miriam scrambles on the ground, finding the rifle in front of her. She clumsily catches the strap, hugging the rifle to her, and bolts into the trees.

INTERLUDE

MIRIAM, THERE'S SOMETHING I HAVE TO TELL YOU

The .22 revolver feels cold in Wren's grip.

Miriam left them behind and now she feels naked, alone, and scared. Louis is there, hunched over Samantha behind the propped-up mattress.

The mercury shine slides along his margins. Sometimes, it looks dull enough Wren can forget that he's one of them, that he's a killer or will be one soon—but now it's got the dark gleam of black ice.

Above her head, a plume of smoke blows.

Miriam clucks her tongue, leaning against the wall. "See what I see?"

Wren doesn't answer. She doesn't want Louis or anyone to hear her talking to a phantom, to a ghost, to whatever this thing is. Instead she says, in willful denial of its presence, "Is she okay?"

Louis looks over to her, his face ashen. "She's alive. The bleeding isn't stopped but it's slowed. I dunno."

"We could drive her out of here."

"We could." But he stays there. He doesn't get up.

The silver lining around him shimmers like a living thing.

"Fine," Not-Miriam says. "Ignore me." She puffs on the cigarette, which only makes Wren want one. Not-Miriam drums her fingers on the wall. "But he's killing her right now. And if he doesn't kill her here, he'll kill her somewhere. That's her fate. To die by his hand. He believes her to be a betrayer and so he'll kill her. And you're killing her too."

Shut up, shut up, shut up.

"I won't shut up," Not-Miriam says. "You ever know me to be the shut-up type of gal? Yeah, me neither. What's the saying? Well-behaved women rarely make history? That means something here, little girl. You want to watch her die, then sit here on your hands, doing nothing. But you want to save her, well." The gun in Wren's hand seems to tingle. Like a little electric charge has gone through it. "You want it bad enough, you can do it."

Miriam, please come back. . . .

I don't know how long I can hold out.

FIFTY

DEAD ENDS

She runs and runs, until she can run no more.

Miriam staggers into a clearing. Flurries begin to fall anew. An idle thought crosses her mind: *It's almost Christmas*. She nearly laughs.

Behind her, the dot-dot-dot of blood. Her fingers find the injury under her arm. She's had worse, but the bullet did more than just graze her. Even with her skinny-ass bony-ass body, there's a hank of flesh under the armpit leading to the shoulder blade, and the bullet punched through that. And the hit to her face isn't much help, either. Everything in her sinuses feels gummed up and crusted, as if someone shoved a pack of cotton balls and pebbles up there. She keeps wanting to sneeze, but her body—blessedly—won't let her.

She staggers forward.

And stops.

She can't do it. Can't go on. She's gone on so long now—it's not just tonight, not just running from Harriet. It's all the running she's done. A life forever in flight. Everything has been the escape. Jesus fuck, she's tired.

Behind her, Harriet's words echo across the clearing. "No more running?"

"I guess not."

Miriam slowly, miserably turns. The rifle is in her right hand, tucked up under her arm, the barrel pointed to the ground. Her left arm is shit. Her fingers feel fat, like blood sausages waggling.

There stands Harriet a hundred feet away. Her chest is streaked with her own blood. She never reclaimed her pistol. All she has is the machete. She holds it up and points it toward Miriam. Snowflakes land on it and melt.

"You are like a blister under my tongue," Harriet says.

"One of my many gifts," Miriam slurs.

"I can't stop feeling for it. Can't stop poking and picking at it. It's always there. *You're* always there. I close my eyes, and there you are. I would like to say that it's nothing personal, but this is all very, very personal."

"Get in line. Everyone's got a picture of me in their locket."

Harriet smiles. Miriam isn't sure she's ever seen the woman do that before. It's somehow even more terrifying.

"I'm going to come for you now," Harriet says. "And then I'm going to eat your precious heart. One animal eating the power of another."

"You can try."

"You can't stop me."

"I can try."

Harriet gives the machete a twirl. And then she stalks forward, that vicious grin leading the way. Ninety feet. Eighty. Seventy. Miriam struggles with the rifle, hauling it up with one hand and wincing as she points the barrel in Harriet's direction and—

Bang.

Behind Harriet, the crackle of brush as the bullet goes wide. Miriam nearly drops the gun, the kick is so bad, and she's got nothing stabilizing it.

Harriet keeps coming. Halfway now.

Miriam backpedals, lifting her meatsack left arm and using it as a blunt shelf on which to prop the rifle. She clumsily works her right hand, snapping back the bolt and launching another round into the chamber. Her finger fumbles to find the trigger—

Forty feet.

Thirty.

Bang.

The demon's stink of the discharged bullet fills her nose even as Harriet takes the round clean through the left thigh. It hits her with a palpable sound, the rough *thwap* of an arrow going through a side of beef.

She keeps coming. Unfazed. Unfaltering.

Miriam mewls in fear, trying to hold on to the rifle and swing it up onto her arm—hand slipping on the bolt, nearly tripping over her own feet, bolt back, then forward, the bullet in the chamber, Harriet marching closer and closer, twenty feet, ten, almost on her—

An awareness hits her. A presence.

A living thing. An owl.

Bird of Doom.

Not dead. Out there on the ground. An image hits her, a gift from the strange creature in the form of a memory:

A gang of crows harassing Bird of Doom. Gathering on branches, mobbing the bird from every direction. The owl can sense them from above and from the sides, but has a hard time tracking the too-fast birds coming up from underneath. And the crows figure that out. They take shots at the owl one by one, flying down and then back up again, hitting the owl in the chest and knocking it off its precious balance, one after the other, coming from below—

Below.

I'm not a predator. I'm a scavenger.

Harriet lunges—

Miriam drops hard—

Her finger tugs the trigger—

Boom. A cannon's roar.

Harriet's head jerks upward. A blooming flower of blood erupts from the top of her skull. Her head shakes and judders.

The machete tumbles into the snow. *Kfft*.

Harriet tumbles on top of it. Heels kicking out. Just like the last time. Just like when Miriam put a bullet through the side of her head.

For a time, Miriam chooses to remain there. Sitting in the snow. Her ears ringing from the gunfire. She tries to find Bird of Doom, but there's nothing there. No presence. No light, no life.

"Sorry," Miriam mumbles into the snow, which has started to come down harder. Not a blizzard. Just a still and steady snowfall. Cold, but warm in its way, too.

She groans as she stands.

And that's when Harriet groans, too.

The woman's back arches suddenly. Her hands splay out, clutching the ground beneath the snow. "Nnnnggh," she says, teeth clenched even as blood bubbles between them. Her eyes go big as moons as she starts to stand, words coming out of her mouth in an infernal growl: "Can't kill me. Always come back. Can't kill me! Always come back!"

For a moment, Miriam watches. She hopes and prays it's just a spasm—one last gasp before death. Lots of people get it before they kick off. They die once, then gasp, or lurch, or babble—

(*Carpet noodle,* Miriam thinks.)

And then they die again.

But Harriet is half-sitting up like an infant just learning to support itself, the blood streaking her stone-colored face, pouring down over her chin even as she gargles words past the crimson gush. *"Can't . . . kill me. Always come back!"*

It's clear that Harriet is right.

She's going to keep coming back again and again.

But then Miriam remembers what Harriet said.

And that's when she knows how to finish it.

INTERLUDE

HARRIET

Harriet comes in and out of darkness. She remembers her blade cutting across the void. She remembers Miriam dropping down, the gun barrel pointed skyward. She remembers feeling her teeth smash into one another, biting through her tongue, her brain and all her thoughts ejecting out the top of her head into the air even as snow began to fall harder.

She knows she's not dead.

She knows she can't die.

Can't kill me.

Always come back.

Already, her skull plates are jostling together like tectonic mantles. Even now, her brain is rebuilding itself within her. She will be whole soon. She will continue her hunt. Forever and ever until the hunt is done, the prey is down, the heart has been taken.

The heart.

Something jostles within her.

Her eyes jolt open. Darkness remains, but she sees the bold white of snow above. The skeleton fingers of dead winter trees.

And then her face looms into view. Smiling.

"Hi," Miriam says. She waves with a waggle of her fingers. Those fingers are dripping with red. In the other hand, Harriet's own machete dances. "You might be wondering: Why is she still here? What does she think she's accomplishing?" Miriam sucks air between her teeth. "Well, I had me a hunch. And it's based on something you said, actually, so thanks for the inspiration. What was it you said? Oh, you said: *then I'm going to eat your heart. One animal eating the other*. No. Wait. The *power* of the other. Right? So, wouldn't that be something? If maybe I just reached in here—sorry, I'm not a surgeon, this is pretty messy business because wow who knew there was that many ribs or that much blood!—what if I reached in and grabbed this big meaty red hunk of beef—"

Harriet's body shakes. She feels Miriam's fingers deep within her chest. Rooting around like worms in earth. The worms moor around the center of her being, *her heart*. "Nnnnnnn," she says, trying to say *no*.

"What if I just ripped it out—"

And she does. Harriet feels her heart tear free from its home in her chest. It makes a sloppy, wrenching sound—the sound of someone pulling weeds from muddy ground. Miriam holds the heart up. It beats in her hand, *lub-dub, lub-dub, lub-dub*. Arteries dangle like torn wires.

"And then, what if I took a big ol' nasty bite—"

Miriam smiles, opening her mouth and:

Chomp. Teeth into the muscle. Sinking deep.

It's like being hit by lightning. All of Harriet's body seizes in a paroxysm of pain and electricity. Miriam, her face ghoulish and scarlet, her mouth smeared with heartsblood, takes another bite. And another. She has to work at it. Teeth grinding up the meat of the organ. With each chomp, another lightning strike. And before the last, only a flappy bit of ventricle left, she says some of the same words Harriet said to her once, back in a shack out in the Jersey Pine Barrens: "There we go. A docile little girl."

"Ppppnnnnhgggh."

"Carpet noodle, cunt."

The scavenger finishes her meal.

FIFTY-ONE

THE CROW

Harriet is dead. Her chest is a cratered cavity. The heart sits in Miriam's belly, heavy as a stone. She *urps* into her hand. Snow falls on the corpse, and the skin on the body begins to blister and turn black. Then it vacuum-seals to the bones of the little blunt woman, *shoomp*. The bones stiffen and crack, the cavity in her chest coughing up a cloud of ash like a tired volcano.

That's how the body remains.

Miriam picks up the rifle and staggers back through the woods to the cabin.

INTERLUDE

ELEANOR'S PROMISE (A REMINDER)

Miriam shivers against the cold. Out beyond the trellis she sees the gray nothing of pounding rain. The smudge of distant trees. Above her head, water filters down through the old vines and the trellis top, forming puddles at her feet.

"I want to see Wren."

She moves toward the greenhouse. Eleanor Caldecott touches her arm. "It's through her that I saw you, Miriam. You are a part of her life. You are just one more piece of her wreckage. Because of her, a piece of you will one day go missing." Eleanor's voice grows quiet. "We're not so different, you and I."

FIFTY-TWO

A PIECE GOES MISSING

The cabin door creaks open.

Miriam steps in, a whorl of snow following behind.

Chaos has taken hold here. The mattress remains on its side, springs jutting. Samantha lies in Louis's lap, her face empty of life. He sits cross-legged on the floor, against the end of the overturned bed. "Louis," Miriam says.

He doesn't answer.

She takes a step forward, and it's just vibration enough—

His head slumps forward. It's now she sees the red hole in the side of his temple. A lone fly, defiant of winter's chill, takes flight.

Miriam stands there shaking. She is not certain how long she stands like this, and whether it can be measured in seconds or minutes or long threads of infinity stretched out on a lathe. She gingerly takes another step forward, her lips pursing and quivering. A voice inside her tells her to stop, just turn around and go, because outside this cabin is the real world and inside it is some kind of nightmare unfolding, some Trespasser-made artifice meant to torment her, to inspire her to some action she has yet to understand.

Gently, she kneels by Louis.

His lips are cold. The skin on his face is tight.

The bullet hole exiting his other temple is small. Like from a low-caliber weapon.

Miriam eases Samantha aside. The woman's body is stiff, and moving it is difficult. Then she sets her rifle next to the body and curls up into him. She props his arm up around her. She stays there for a time. Tears crawl down her cheeks. She stares at nothing. Louis is cold, not warm. He does not return the embrace when she holds his barrel chest tight and pulls him closer. Louis is dead.

At some point, she crawls away from him and weeps on the floor. The house of cards that is Miriam, that has improbably stood for all this time, collapses. She craves oblivion. She wants to break herself to pieces and throw herself to all the birds in all the world, one molecule of her mind in each, her humanity and her memory of being human gone, cast away, forever forgotten.

A floorboard creaks.

"You did this," Miriam says.

"Uh-huh," says Wren. She's been in the bathroom this whole time.

Slowly, Miriam stands. She feels dead inside. Like there's nothing left. As she rises, she brings the rifle with her.

Wren has the pistol in her hand.

"*Why.*"

Wren's been crying too. "I told you I had something to tell you. I saw Louis. He was one of them, one of the Mercury Men."

"He has killed before. He has killed *for you* before. He helped tear down the rotten Caldecott tree, the one in which you were ensnared."

"I . . . I know, but it's not like that, it's not like I can control this. You were gone but then—" Now the girl is crying once more. "But then you were here again, and I knew it wasn't you, but still, you kept telling me things, like how he was going to kill Samantha, how he was going to just let her die and how if I wanted to take her to a hospital, I had to do something. I had to take care of him—"

Wearily, Miriam seethes: "And how did that work out for you? Did you save Samantha? Is she here with us now?"

"No. I was too late."

"You were too late. That's ironic, isn't it? Too late."

"I told you it's not like I'm in control, exactly—"

"You were too late. I told you not to trust how sure you were. I *told* you not to listen to the Trespasser. I love very little in this world, you fucking little cunt, and Louis was one of those precious things I loved. And now you took him away."

Miriam points the rifle.

"Miriam. Please. I . . ."

Miriam opens and closes the bolt, loading another bullet. She wets her lips. She still tastes Harriet's heartsblood on and around her mouth.

"The line from the Bible," she growls. "Thine eye shall not pity, but life shall go for life. Eye for eye. Tooth for tooth. Hand for hand and foot for foot. My mother used to say that. She'd say that to remind me that the world worked that way—it demanded grim balance, and I've always been an agent of that. I take one life so that another may go. I balance those scales. Now you took a life. A very big, very beautiful life. I don't meet many nice people, but he was one of them. Killing you won't even begin to balance the scales."

Wren drops the gun. "I know."

Miriam's finger coils around the trigger. "I should have let you drown in the river. Eleanor Caldecott was right about you. She told me, she said you were a bad little girl. That I was part of your wreckage. That you would rob me of something, some important piece. And here we are. Prophecy fulfilled."

"I know. I fucking know. I know, I know, I know . . ." Her words dissolve into a babbling brook of spit-slick mess. The sound that comes out of her is not a word but the sound of a beaten, cornered animal.

Miriam's thumb moves to the safety.

And then it turns the safety on.

She throws the rifle to the ground.

Wren seems jarred by it. "No, no, no. You kill me. You need to kill me. You need to—I did this, I did this wrong bad thing and—"

"Shut up."

And Wren shuts up. Her face pale and awestruck.

"I can't do it. I can't kill any more people. I don't have my owl. I don't have my Louis. You need to *go*. Take the car. Drive far the fuck away. Live a life of reparation and repentance. And if you ever cross paths with me, you dire little beast, I will cut out your heart and eat it."

They stand there for a while. Silently regarding one another.

Then Lauren Martin goes to Samantha's corpse and fishes the keys out of her pocket before darting out the door. Soon, the engine starts. And the car drives away. Wren has fled the nest.

Now Miriam has to flee too.

PART SIX

THE NEST

FIFTY-THREE
A PIECE RETURNS

The handcuffs are loose. She expected them to be tight. She's still bloody. She walked into the station this way, streaked with frozen blood and shivering. The cops put a blanket around her. They took her statement. (Which was, through chattered teeth, *I don't know, fuck you, I guess I killed a lot of people*. She named a bunch, including some of Wren's.) It's like they don't know what to make of her. There's only three cops even here. All of them are now wearing latex gloves in case this blood is diseased. And maybe it is. Who knows?

Who cares?

She sits there at the desk, the handcuffs binding her wrists at the front. The cop pecks and pokes at a computer, occasionally staring at her with worried eyes. This cop's got a big broad right-angle nose and a boot-brush mustache. The other two cops she thinks of as Fatfront and Fishbowl. Fatfront is a short, big dude whose dick and balls form a kind of deflated-basketball bulge at his crotch. Fishbowl is a woman. Her name, Miriam knows—Sarah Weber. She knows it because Officer Sarah tells her. Weber has the eyes of a goldfish—specifically, the eyes of a goldfish warped and magnified by the curved glass of a shelf-resting fishbowl, or, in this case, a pair of too-big eyeglasses. Those two whisper. She hears the words *mental breakdown* and *cracker factory*. They think she's nuts. Fine. They can send her wherever. Jail. The cuckoo parade. Guantanamo. They can throw her ass in a shallow grave somewhere. She just wants the rest.

She knows how all three of them die, of course. It does not excite her. Bootbrush dies from stomach cancer in twenty-three years. Fishbowl is on a train when it derails, crashing into another train, and she dies in the wreckage. Fatfront chokes on a meatball at a restaurant and nobody helps him.

Bootbrush says to her, "I guess we ought to get you cleaned up and in a cell until we can figure this all out." He really just thinks she's crazy.

"Don't you want this blood as evidence? It's not mine."

So, they do that first. But this isn't a crack forensic team. They take a picture of her sitting there. Then one of them comes over and scrapes some of the blood off into a plastic baggy that they pull not from some high-tech forensics lab but from a galley kitchen adjacent to the main room of the station.

Then shower-time. It's Fishbowl who takes her back into the showers. Soon as she's disrobed, Fishbowl gasps. "That blood is yours," she says.

"Huh?"

Miriam looks.

Oh. Right. The injury. She lifts her arm and the injury reopens, making paint-peeling sounds as the scabs split. She cries out, wincing. They tell her she's going to have to go to the hospital. While she washes herself (handcuffs still on), they'll call an ambulance and *ugh*, Miriam just wants it all over. She just wants to lie down. She just wants to die. *Like Louis. Like Bird of Doom. Like everyone I meet because we all die and this is how it is, so why fucking bother*.

The soap is a pink color so unnatural, it must be extraterrestrial in origin. It smells like motor oil. She scrubs it everywhere, including into her scabbed-up nose and into the crusty wound under her arm. It burns. It hurts so bad with her probing fingers, she wants to pass out, and she almost does. The pain feels right.

And then as she's stepping out—

Touching no one or nothing but herself—

Reaching for a towel—

INTERLUDE

THE VISION

From nothing comes something. From the void comes light. From death comes life. The entity sees the aperture, a fontanelle from which it will escape. It does not understand this in a complex way, only in a primitive, primeval, instinctual way. That way is out. This was home, but now it is not. Out is all the entity has, even though it wants desperately to remain here. *This* place is safe. *This* place is shelter. To leave it is to be exposed. The light out there is bright and then it is eclipsed—something grabs ahold of the entity, and the fingers are sharp, and then there is blood, and a twisting sound. The entity wants to scream but it cannot: its throat is filling, its body is cinching tight. Pink to blue to black. Choking. The light, crushed. Life, extinguishing bit by bit, crude hands holding it down, slippery and inept, its head buried in soft tissue as the loop around its neck tightens—

FIFTY-FOUR
EMBER AND SPARK

Miriam gasps and falls to her knees. Fishbowl gasps, too, surprised by this, and rushes over to help her up. But Miriam's legs have gone to noodles. She can barely stand. The cop brings her a chair. "The ambulance will be here soon," Fishbowl tells her. Miriam nods.

Her eyes shine with tears.

The vision. It hit her like a wave.

(Like a red snow shovel to the back.)

It was a death vision.

But she didn't touch anyone.

She already saw how these three Keystone Cops die.

Which means—

"I need a phone call," she bleats.

"What?" Fishbowl asks.

"I get a phone call, and I want it. Now." She summons something resembling respectfulness. *"Please."*

"Sure, sure, hold on." Fishbowl goes and gets a cordless phone and hands it over to Miriam. Miriam tries to bring spit to her mouth so she can talk, and with trembling fingers she taps out the phone number. *Ring, ring, ring.*

A bleary Gabby answers.

"Hnnnh," she says. "Whozit."

"Gabby."

A moment of quiet. "Miriam."

"I need your help."

"Why? Where are you? What's wrong?"

Miriam blinks, and tears push themselves out of her eyes and down her cheeks and onto the phone. "Gabby, I'm pregnant. Louis is dead, and I am pregnant with his baby." And it's this last part that she can barely say: "And the baby is going to die. I need your help. Please come get me. Please."

"I'm coming," Gabby says.

Miriam hangs up the phone and holds it to her forehead like an object of prayer. The future suddenly looms both bright and dark, and she does not know on what side of it she will land.

ACKNOWLEDGMENTS

I wrote this book before, during, and just after the 2016 election took place. That should give you a pretty solid sense of exactly how broken my brain was when I wrote this book, but I like to imagine that the *seething anxiety* and *creeping insomnia* added a certain, oh, I dunno, *feral edge* to it. Just the same, thanks go to Stacie Decker, Joe Monti, and Richard Shealy for helping tame the book in the wild places where such taming was needed.

Thanks to Adam S. Doyle for the astonishing cover artwork.

Thanks to Kevin Hearne for always being a huge advocate of Miriam and this series.

And thanks, as always, to the readers, for staying with this series.

Coming up next, the last of the bunch: *Vultures* circles in 2019.